I0618932

WALKING WITH THE SCORPION

Book One of the Guardian Trilogy

WALKING WITH THE SCORPION

Book One of the Guardian Trilogy

JESSICA NEWTON

J. Kenkade
PUBLISHING®

Bryant, Arkansas

J. Kenkade Publishing
5920 Highway 5 N. Ste. 7
Bryant, AR 72022
www.jkenkadepublishing.com
Social Media: @jkenkadepublishing

J. Kenkade Publishing is a registered trademark.

Printed in the United States of America
ISBN 978-1-955186-31-5

PROLOGUE

"Alnilam, why are you doing this?" cries the deep voice of Orion. The warrior thrust his arms forward, only to be held back by golden chains. Trapped against Malai, the oldest tree in the orchard, Orion's stare bore into the three women standing in front of him. Alnilam, the eldest of the three, just a few years born after Orion, stepped forward until she was inches from her brother. "Whatever has darkened your heart, sister? I am sure we can fix this together."

Alnilam shakes her head, "Don't you see, brother?" She looks into his eyes, holding out her hand while a small parchment appears. "This is your fault. It always has been. Acting like you are better, stronger, than us." She glances around, her eyes falling on the twelve Guardians surrounding them, each trapped in a sphere of energy. "For so long, we have stood in the shadow of your greatness, your power binding us to this place. We are not able to roam free, to be our own."

"You were created as I was, sister! To serve and protect the skies and space. To keep balance in this Solar." The energy around Orion could almost be seen, his golden tanned body slightly glowing.

"Alnilam," the youngest sister says urgently in almost a whisper. Her eyes glance up, seeing the planets getting closer to alignment.

Alnilam nods her head at her younger sister and brings her attention back to Orion, "You're wrong. We were not created equal. How could we be, when you were the one who gave us life? We will be free, brother. We do not need your help. Only your power." She steps back, standing back next to her sisters.

Orion tries once again to break free of the chains holding him, but whatever magic his sisters had used was too powerful, even for him. It must have been the spheres. Alnilam knew that siphoning the power from Orion's Guardians would cause his own power to make up for that loss. He could feel their life force now. All of them, growing weaker. The planets were aligning. With *that* spell, they could use his life force to blow apart the solar system, causing chaos in their realm and be free to go wherever they choose throughout the universe. He could not allow that. There was only one thing he could do.

With Alnilam and the other two distracted with their spell, Orion calms himself, letting out a deep breath. With absolute concentration, he could start to feel his soul stir within him. Very faintly, he could hear the sound of his name being called. He knew that voice, but he could not waste time acknowledging it.

"Orion! NO!" was the last thing he hears before his soul suddenly exploded from his body. The ball of light shoots through the sky, disappearing in order to find a new hiding place. The last thing anyone sees is Orion's body slowly turning to stone.

CHAPTER ONE

I sink into the blue, plastic chair across from the principal's office, holding my bag in front of my chest. I can faintly hear the big man talking to my father. Every second the conversation continues causing my insides to twist around like someone is ringing out a wet rag. The kid sitting next to me keeps biting his fingernails, driving me to curl my toes because murder is not legal in any way. I glance over to see who it is. Of course. Daniel Mendez. Ugh. He is one of those kids who does not think anything he does is the wrong choice. Sitting here, biting his fingernails, and probably eating them. Why do guys have to be so stupid?

Daniel turns to me as if he just noticed my presence. I stare down at the tiled floor, screaming at him in my head to *not* talk to me. I got away with it for the last ten minutes. A few more would be nice. "Whatcha in for?" he asks in a lame attempt at a southern accent.

I shake my head, "Nothing." He seems to realize that I

am not going to converse with him. He shrugs, going back to biting his nails.

The door opens and the round face of our principal pokes out. His beard covers almost his whole face, while the hair on the top of his head does not compare. He could probably blind someone. "Faye." His calling of my name is basically a command, calling like a dog. I stand and follow him into the office, hearing the soft click of the door behind me. The room is small and stuffy, as he never opens the window directly behind him. I opt to stand instead of sitting in the metal chair. I know what kind of butts sit in that chair. I am not about to join them. "Faye, this is the fifth time you have been caught skipping your biology class this month. Is there something wrong with the class? There must be something you don't like about it since you seem to *only* miss that class."

I shake my head, "Nothing is wrong with the class. I just figure I should skip ahead to the failing part since we both know science is not my area of expertise."

My sarcasm is lost on the man. "Faye, this is unacceptable. If we don't see a change, we *will* have to fail you and you will end up having to retake the class again next year. You can't graduate without a certain amount of credits for certain courses. You know this. This is your third year at this high school. I've notified your father. I suggest you start getting your act together and continue with your class. It is forty minutes of your day. I'm sure there are worse things than learning about cells."

"Yes, sir," I say to placate him. He waves his hand in dismissal and I head out of the office before I have to listen to him anymore. Lucky for me, I am not going back to classes.

Unlike everyone else filing into the hallways to go to another part of the building, I weave my way through to find the exit.

In middle school, I had a teacher who told me that she skipped ahead of everyone else. It was a lot of work, but it was possible for anyone. I was good at school, even at that time. She told me that by my junior year of high school I could be ahead in my classes, and by the time I'm a senior, I could be where no one could catch me. We talked extensively about the whole thing, and that is how I ended up where I am now. Now, I spend the last two hours of my day at the university. My English 101 class makes up for the rest of the English courses I will need in high school. It gives me two hours of freedom outside of high school. Once that is over with, I spend a couple of hours in the college library until Ann kicks me out. She's a sweet older lady, but she has babies to take care of at home. Seven of them to be exact. I could say the name of her cats in my sleep, she talks about them so much.

Heading out of the school, I make my way to my little, blue, Mini Coop. I call her BlueJay and she is currently missing a door handle on the back, driver's side. BlueJay was a gift from my father in lieu of my sixteenth birthday. One of the better days we have had together. Over the summer, I had a full field of freedom that I enjoyed to its fullest. I'm also glad I got it before starting school. Riding the bus with everyone else was a little short of torture. High school boys are disgusting and most of them have yet to hear the term 'body odor.' Worse yet, I'm not sure any of them know what a stick of deodorant looks like. So, yes, I may have cried a lot when Dad got me BlueJay. She isn't the best vehicle on Earth, but I love her.

BlueJay and I drive the thirty minutes or so to the

university. I connect the AUX cord to my phone and blast some Panic! At the Disco with the windows down. There was something nice about not having to go to school in the same city you live in. My little town of Hamilton had nothing but a post office and a cemetery. I have to go to high school ten minutes outside city limits and then the college is thirty minutes outside of my high school. It means I have half a day, sometimes more, away from home.

It is hard to live in a town where everyone knows your story. All the kids who live in that town also go to the same high school. I have learned how to keep others' attention off myself and hide in a corner. It's worked so far.

Mostly.

About halfway through the drive I start to slow and then come to a stop on the side of the road. This spot is a ritual in my daily commute back and forth. During the summer, there are large stalks of corn I have to weave my way through, but since harvest, it is bare. The farmers around here should be getting ready to start growing crops again for the upcoming summer season. From the side of the road, I walk a little bit until I can see the ground start to become just dirt.

In the middle of the cornfields, there is a large crater. I say large, but it's probably the size of a kid's swimming pool. It's not very deep either. When I was younger, my mother would bring me here and tell me stories about a star that fell here. It was why nothing ever grew because the magic of the star still pulsed within the ground. I still believe that story, although the magic of this place isn't the same. Standing on the edge of the crater, I feel a certain kind of calm. I stand on the edge of the hole, looking down at it until I manage to get my feet to move away from it. I will have more time later to stop by, but for now, I need to get to class.

As I pull into the university, I still marvel at the fact that I go here. The university is huge, and I am so glad I only have to find one class. I pass the indoor football field and stop for a moment to watch practice. It's not as though I like watching guys sweat over one another, it's purely for entertainment purposes.

As I am standing there though, one of the guys notices my presence and does a friendly half-wave. It takes me a second to register and my hand is already up in the air waving back. Like a child, I promptly turn and walk away. The last thing I need is to become friends with college kids. I hear a lot of talk about how young I am, even though a lot of them are only a couple of years older than me. It's like the mentality of the seniors to freshmen. Just because they are a couple of years older, they already believe that they are on top of the world. Should I be feeling that way since I am already taking college classes?

Nah. I can't deal with superiority complexes.

I manage to get myself to the classroom before any more encounters, climbing the steps to the back. I slide into my seat and wait for the professor to start. I feel my phone vibrate and open it up to see a text from my dad.

Fend for yourself tonight. Be home in the AM.

I close my phone. My lips twitch in the corner. It has been a while since I have had a night to myself at home. It also means I can talk to him about the call from school tomorrow after he has had some sleep. That thought keeps me focused on my work throughout the hour or so. As the professor finishes up, I start rewriting my notes in a more cohesive way that I can understand and use to study. I do what I can until the rest of the students filter out, and I follow not long after. Halfway through the halls, I find the elevator down. Sometimes I'm lazy like that.

"Woah, wait up!"

My hand shoots out to hold the door open, my insides cringing as I watch a monster of a college kid step inside the door. For a split second, I almost think about running out of the elevator. Being in an enclosed space with one of these guys is intimidating. Especially when I see him in his football attire. Gross. "You going down?"

"What?" I stammer.

The brown-haired, brown-eyed jockey gives me a grin, "You going to the ground floor or going up?"

"Oh, uh, ground floor." Oh, my God. Kill me now.

"Cool," he pushes the little button that has the number one on it. I feel my opening to leave this encounter close as I watch the elevator doors do the same. "You were watching us practice earlier, right? Are you thinking about trying it out?"

I couldn't help but smile at the tease. "No, I don't think so. I can't catch a ball to save my life. Small hands." To make a point, I hold them up and wiggle my fingers. I don't think my five foot three, one hundred and fifteen-pound stature could hold up to the two-hundred-pound guys who pummel each other for pigskin.

The guy laughs and my stomach does a weird little flip. "Good point. Maybe not a player. How about a cheerleader then? A cute little thing like you would look great on the sidelines." He winks before the elevator door opens and he stands aside, holding his hands out to allow me to walk past him.

"Again, coordination? I'm sure I would hurt someone more than you guys do on the regular. Or myself. I've never been very good at doing anything that resembles dancing. Two left feet and all that."

"I've never believed anyone has two left feet. Everyone just needs someone to teach them how to use the feet they have," he chuckles. "Anyway, I have some classes to get to. Catch ya later, Lefty." He does a half-wave and jogs off to his next class.

I stand there, dumbfound, as I watch him disappear around the corner. *What…. Just happened?*

He was tall and broad \-shouldered. His brown eyes were bright like honey and his brown hair was long, sitting in a shaggy wave on his head. Somehow, he made it look like he did not just wake up and crawl out of bed. His jaw was covered in some stubble, and the guy oozed charisma.

"No. No, no, *no*," I whisper to myself as I put my hands up to my cheeks, feeling the heat on my fingers as I make my way out of the building. The cool air hits my face and it seems to fizzle out the growing fire. "He was being *friendly*, Faye. Sometimes, people do that," I reason with myself. Man, I have read way too many fantasy books. The moment the guy walked into the elevator I had already played out fifty different scenarios in my head, all pretty close to cliche moments in books I have read, about how he could have the slightest interest in me. "I'm such a child," I groan.

I suddenly feel incredibly stupid for such thoughts and make my way to BlueJay, my heart full of shame. "What is wrong with me?" I knew what was wrong. The simple fact was, that for the first time, someone I don't know seemed like they liked me. Not in a romantic way, but still showed me the first bit of what could be friendship from someone who did not know me or my family situation.

It was nice.

Of course, my stupid brain instantly takes me to an unrealistic scenario. Besides, the guy could be twice my age! I slam BlueJay's door and instantly apologize for mistreating her. It is not her fault her owner is one of the many misguided youths of today. I start my car and head out of the parking lot, weaving my way through until I hit the main road. Now, I almost wish I had decided to stay and swim. Oh well. There is something else I can do before I head home for the night.

I drive until I see the start of the familiar cornfield, one that is void of the familiar crop now that harvesting is over for the year. I slow and turn into the little, gravel shoulder where I know no one will hit BlueJay. Stepping out, I make sure both my keys and phone are in my pockets before making my way across the field to where the crater is. Stepping into the hole, I stand there and close my eyes, smiling as the ever-familiar feeling sweeps over me. It is hard to describe how wonderful this feeling is. I slowly sit down and wrap my arms around my knees. Resting my cheek against my knee, I dig my fingers into the ground, wriggling them around in the dirt. "What is it about you that doesn't allow anything to grow?"

I yelp as something stings my finger. I pull my finger away and see the slightest bit of blood welling up on my finger. I glance down and dig in the dirt a bit until I see the culprit. I wipe away the dirt and pull out a shard of glass. "Nice," I grumble as I place it in my palm, turning it over. As I clean more of the dirt off, I notice that it doesn't seem like glass at all. It is clearer and the dirt just falls away from the surface. I hold it up to the sky and it reflects slightly different colors as the sun seeps through it. "No way." Did I just find a piece of a diamond? I use my jacket and rub it until the dirt vanishes, allowing me to see the shape. "Someone must be pissed that this broke," as it looks to be in the shape of a heart, or half of one, at least. It looks to be expensive. My first thought is to leave it there so that whoever has the other half will find it.

But looking at it more, I find myself unable to put it back. Maybe I'm feeling something personal or just being greedy, but I can't bring myself to leave it there. So, I place it in my jacket pocket, careful to put it in a way so that it won't stab me again, and I head back to my car. The little bit of time here is all I needed to forget about the elevator guy. I head home for the night to work on homework and get ready for the upcoming tests I have. "TGIF," I say happily to BlueJay and put her in gear as I drive the rest of the way home.

Sure enough, when I get there, my father's truck is missing from the driveway. Our little home sits on the other side of the post office, giving us some room from nosey neighbors. We have plenty of them who walk in front of the house all the time, getting their morning jog or their afternoon walk with their dog. Speaking of...

"Hi, Faye! How was school, darling?" A familiar voice chimes in from behind me as I climb out of the car.

I turn and see Martha Ranshaw. I inwardly cringe, "Fine. It was fine, Mrs. Ranshaw. How's Max?" Her husband, Max

Ranshaw, worked in the cemetery as the day caretaker. He is a nice old man, not nearly as curious as his wife.

Martha shrugs, "At home watching his football. You know how men are with their sports. I have another hour before his stomach gets the better of him and he comes to find me. You have a good night, darling." She waves and continues on her way. I smile politely and wave, watching her walk away, before sighing and heading inside. This is how most interactions are with my neighbors. They are all nice. Too nice. They all ask how my day is, how things are going at school, and just the usual small talk. No one talks about my father, and I don't mention him.

No one wants to talk about the town drunk.

My father was not always like this. He did not always go from job to job, working at one place until they got tired of him and then right on to the next. He did not always spend the nights at the bars and come stumbling up the front porch, sometimes getting only that far. I wonder, sometimes, if we have more alcohol in the house than we have anything else.

When my father was younger, he got into a lot of trouble. His parents did not show him much affection, and I think they may have even abused him. As he grew older, he skipped school, hung with the wrong crowd, and just overall did not have a good life. Eventually, he wound up in rehab, because it was either that or jail. While he opted for rehab, that is when he met my mother. She was one of the volunteers who helped at the rehab center and took a particular interest in my father. Long story short, they worked with each other almost every day. About a year after my father stayed clean, with a little help, she decided to let him take her out. Their relationship took sail from there and about six years later, I popped out. My earliest memories of my parents together are wonderful. My mother stayed home full time with me while my father worked.

Everything was great until a couple of months after my tenth birthday. My mom found out that she had lung cancer. It was unreal, especially because my mother never smoked in her life. Hell, she hardly drank outside of holidays with the family. The doctors could not tell us what had caused it. But once we found out, everything seemed to spiral downward from there. For two years my mother saw multiple doctors, went on what seemed like a hundred different medications, and all for it to be worth nothing in the end. We sat there with my mother in the hospital, watching the machines slowly tell us what we already knew. My mother was dying and there was nothing we could do. For days, my father would leave me with her so that I could spend time with her while he would go back between working and trying to find a cure for something with no known cure. I had never seen him so desperate before.

Sometime during the night, while I had been sleeping, the staff had come in because my mother took a turn for the worse. I guess my father had come and taken me to another room, holding me while I slept soundly away. When I woke, my father's tear-streaked face told me everything I needed to know.

My mother was gone.

Days blurred together after that. My father receded back into himself. He started drinking again, which eventually turned into what it was now. We had to sell the house I had grown up in for the little shack we live in now. I mean, it's not awful, but it could be better. Everything could be better. I think that in some ways, my father blames me for my mother's death. It's not true, but it's an outlet for him, one that I ignore but allow. If it keeps him working and on his feet then what else can I do?

I grab a bottle of water from the fridge and take it with me to my room, dropping my bag on the floor as I fall onto my bed. As I stare at the ceiling, my mind suddenly wanders back to the encounter at school with the elevator guy. He was cute, I'll give him that, but there was no way I could even entertain the thought of being with a college guy. Especially because he could easily be ten years older than me.

"There is something wrong with me," I murmur as I stand to go take a shower.

Once I'm done, I put all thoughts of tall, good-looking men out of my mind as I start my homework for school and begin the preparations for my essay for English 101. Looking up at my clock sometime later, I realize that it's been a couple of hours and I stretch my arms over my head, feeling my shoulders pop.

A sudden howl causes me to jump, my knee slamming against the underside of my desk. I curse and get up to walk over to the window. It was dark outside, the downside of it getting later in the year. The view from my window does not provide much, as half of it is the post office and I can't see anything out in the fields to the other side. Weird. We don't have wolves in Iowa. Perhaps a big coyote? "I guess weirder things have happened before," I say, unconvinced. I hear it again, the sound raising goosebumps on my arms. I hug myself and reach up, pulling the blackout curtain down over the window. I went over to where I had dropped my jacket earlier and pulled out the little piece of diamond I found earlier that day. I smile and I place it on the corner of my desk

That night, I dream of a wolf's howls and brown eyes.

CHAPTER TWO

I wake up to the sound of the front door slamming open and I sit up, rubbing my face. I glance at the clock, seeing the little red seven. It's earlier than I thought he would be home. I swing my feet over the bed and make my way to the bathroom. I splash water on my face, the coolness helping me wake up more. I head into the kitchen where my father is starting the coffee pot. He looks tired, but surprisingly clean, which means he didn't sleep in his truck again. "Hey, Dad," I say with a smile.

He pours some coffee into a mug and turns back to me, not returning my smile, "School?"

I should have known he would not waste time. I tried to come up with something clever but got nothing, "Dad, it's the teacher. He's such a creep!"

He rolls his eyes and walks toward the living room, "That's bullshit."

"It's true. He stares at the girls too much and stands over

our desks. I swear he's smelled me before," I shudder thinking about it.

Dad plops down in his recliner, "High school girls are always making a big deal out of nothing." I walk over and sit on the arm of the other recliner, "Besides, school is expensive. You're lucky you're receiving government help. If you keep skipping your classes, do you think they are going to keep paying for you to go there? Especially your college class. Use your head, Faye."

"I'm sorry," I mumble. We sit there in silence before I stand off the chair. "I'm going to head to the college to get some study material."

"Stop by the store on the way back, will ya? We are almost out of coffee," he lifts the current cup he has in his hand. "You can grab something for dinner tonight while you're at it. I'll be out tonight."

"Are you going to be home in the morning?"

He shrugs and sips his coffee. I stare at him for a second too long before he raises an eyebrow at me, "Got a problem?"

I shake my head, "Nope." I head back into the bedroom to change, brush my head of curled, brown, hair and teeth in the bathroom, and grab my bag to head out of the house. I faintly hear my dad calling out about coffee before hopping into my Coop.

My dad usually comes home sullen and quiet. I knew he was going to ask me about school, but I did not expect the conversation to be as tame as it was. It was the first time in a long time I've had such a light conversation with him, as short as it was. It made my heart flutter in a funny kind of way, but it was a familiar flutter. The kind of feeling I had when my parents were together and my family felt whole. I won't get my hopes up, though.

The half-hour drive to the university takes no time at all and I make my way through the long halls to find the library. Ann notices me and gives me a smile before focusing her attention back on the student in front of her. I wander further within the rows of books until I find my usual table empty. I dump the contents of my bag onto the round, wooden table. It's seated toward the back where there is not a whole lot of foot traffic. I can get a lot of work done without the constant chattering of voices around me. There is still a steady hum, but it isn't so distracting. In fact, I don't think I could do anything in complete silence, which is what I have when I am at home. It gives me too much time to think and there are a lot of things I would rather not think about.

Here I am, listening occasionally to the fun college story and getting all my work done for high school. My teachers like to give me extra work because not only do they know I will get it done, but it gives me a chance to get things done early in the week to focus on my English 101 class.

"Hey there, Lefty." I glance up and my stomach does that funny little flip again. Standing in front of me is the tall, brown-haired elevator guy. I feel like I should learn his name so I don't keep calling him the elevator guy.

I really shouldn't learn his name.

"Hitting the books, I see. What are you working on?" He drops his bag on the table and pulls out a chair.

Oh, my God. Did he just sit down? Does that mean I'm not getting rid of him? "Um, just some work for school."

"Biology? Hmm, I don't think I've seen that textbook before. What class is it?"

Ugh. "That's because it's not for any class here. It's for my high school class."

He didn't even blink, "Cool. It must be for Mr. Cooper's class."

That surprises me and I stop moving my pencil, fully looking up at him. "You had him? Wait, how did you know it is his class?"

"Because there is only one science teacher who uses that book and only one high school near the university. I'm sure you don't travel more than an hour or two between schools."

"Right," I mumble. "So, you liked his classes?"

"Yeah. He's a cool guy. If you take the Advanced Anatomy and Physiology class next year, you can have him again. Cooper makes that class super easy."

"Thanks, I'll try to remember that." I thought my voice sounded final, but apparently, he did not take the hint. Instead, he gives me a grin. Oh, man. I am never going to get my work done at this rate.

"So, how did you manage to sneak into the library without Ann noticing? The woman is a menace about her library. I know plenty of other high school kids who have tried to pass her by."

"That's because I go here, and Ann is a sweetheart. Don't bad mouth her," I tell him, glancing back down at my work.

"You go here? For real? You must be smart as hell."

My stomach flips. "Not really. Just worked my ass off. By next year, I will only be spending four classes at the high school and the rest of the time doing classes here."

When he doesn't answer, I look back up at him. He just sits there, studying me. Those brown eyes were so richly brown that I feel like I could stare at them forever. That's when I notice the little specks of gold in them. Then, he gives me that crooked grin again, "That's cool. So, I guess I'll be seeing more of you here. I'm Theo, by the way." He holds out his hand and I give him mine. He squeezes slightly, shaking them up and down slowly.

"Faye," I say.

Something crosses his face that passes too fast for me to recognize, but his smile remains, "Nice to meet you, Faye. Well, I will let you get back to it. If you need any help, just hunt me down around the field. That's where I spend most of my time."

He stands and gives me a small wave before trotting off, saying something to Ann that I can't hear. I stare after him for a full minute or so before sighing, "Freaking college."

I try not to think about Theo and his interesting eyes as I spend my time doing my work for school and then beginning the research for my paper. Almost three hours pass before I realize how much time has gone by, so I pack up my things, along with the extra material to use over the rest of the weekend. Even though Dad said he might not be home tonight, he will still want that coffee in the morning.

As I head out to the parking lot, I spot someone standing near my car. My feet stop as I stare at the man whose skin looks like it's been kissed by the sun. Long, golden hair hangs down his back and suddenly it feels as though someone pulls their air from my lungs. My head starts pounding, black spots spreading across my vision. I press my hands against my temple, falling to my knees as a high-pitched scream pierces my ears. I grind my teeth together so hard that it feels like my jaw is going to lock up on itself. The smell of sunflowers overwhelms me at the same time a faint voice echoes in my head. My name, being said over and over again. *Find them...* the voice whispers loudly.

Then, everything just stops.

"What..." The word falls out of my mouth as I glance up. The black spots are gone, and the headache stops. The high-pitched scream is a small whistle in my ears that fades. I sit back on my heels and glance around. No one seems to have seen my episode.

"Where did–" I look over to where the man was standing by my car, but he is gone. I stand, the strange scenario seared in my mind as I head to my car. My hands shake as I turn over the ignition and roll the windows down to let the cool air blow through BlueJay as I head to the store and back home.

Once I am home, I put the coffee in the cupboard and find a note on the fridge from Dad, *Won't be home.* The note was short and to the point, like normal. I shrug and decide to head down to the pub to grab something to eat. Since Dad isn't going to be home tonight, he is most likely out of town. No chance of running into him. "Plus, Luke is working," I grin to myself.

The red-headed bartender lives a couple of blocks from me, but I never have time to see him except at times like this when Dad won't be home for the night, and I need to grab something for dinner. I change into my black jeans and a hot pink tank top with a tribal wolf design on the front. I made it last year in our home economics class. I'm actually pretty proud of it and surprised that it turned out so well. I only wear it on special occasions so that it doesn't get ruined by being washed too much.

Putting on just the slightest bit of makeup, I head out, locking the door behind me. It's a good thing I grabbed my jacket, the chill feels like little needles poking my face as the wind blows. It is still early in the year, so the weather is still trying to decide if it wants to start warming up or not. It only takes me a second to decide to head back inside and grab my car keys, driving the three minutes to the pub instead of walking. I don't care what anyone says: walking in the cold sucks.

Pulling into the back of the pub and heading inside, I notice most of the usuals sitting around the bar. Martin's Pub isn't on any kind of map, but when people find it, it tends to become an instant hit. Martin is an older gentleman, who has run this pub since he was about twenty-five. His parents helped him get started, but he built it up from there on his own. Then three years later, he got married to Lisa. Two years after that, they had a pair of twins, Raymond and Rachel. They help out every now and then when visiting, but Rachel is attending a university in Colorado and Raymond is in the Navy, currently on a naval ship. Last I heard, he was in Guam for some time.

I found my usual seat by the bar. Normally, minors wouldn't be allowed in a pub, but I have known Martin and Lisa since I was a baby. One of the perks of being in a small town. And their grandson Luke helps out with the bar every now and then. His mom is a volunteer at the church while Raymond is away. Even though he is underage, he still knows his way around. He just isn't allowed to work with anything other than soft drinks and occasionally the beer if they are too busy. Right now, he is wiping down the bar, smiling when he notices me sitting there. "Hey, Faye. What are you up to?"

I shrug, "You know I only come here to see you, Lucas."

He laughs, "I'm flattered. You want the usual?"

"Yes, please."

"Give me a minute and I'll have it ready for you," he says.

"You're the best!"

"I know," he calls while heading toward the back where the kitchen is.

I can't help but to smile and turn in my seat, looking out at the rest of the pub. It is not exceptionally big, but it does hold a significant amount of people inside. Tonight is karaoke night and there is an older gentleman and what could only be his wife doing a sweet, yet terrible rendition of "Love Shack." It is cute, though, because they could care less about the people around them. I hear the familiar sound of Styrofoam behind me, and I turn to see Lucas coming out with a steaming plate in his hands. When he sets it down in front of me, I practically start to drool right then and there. Martin's signature nachos are sensational and hit every good spot in my stomach.

"You planning on staying long?" Luke asks.

"For a little bit. I have an essay due for my college class, so I can't spend too much time out, but Dad is gone for the night so I figured I could use a dinner buddy."

My parents were longtime friends with Martin and his wife, so when my mom passed away, it was hard on all of us. Martin and Lisa have always taken the time to take care of me when my dad wasn't around to do it himself. I owe a lot to them, and to Luke, for being so kind to me. Everyone knows my dad is the town drunk, but Luke is one of the only people who don't pity me for it. "Of course. You know you're always more than welcome to hang out for as long as you'd like." We sit and talk about how things were running with the pub and our college courses. Luke graduated high school in the springtime and started his own semester at the same college as I attend. It is a bit disappointing because our classes don't align with the same time frame.

Eventually, I glance over at the clock and realize that a good couple of hours have gone by. The pub was still busy, and I hesitated before saying, "I guess I should be heading home. I have to finish that essay."

"You sure? There are plenty more old people singing even older songs coming up." Luke says with a grin, referring to the karaoke that has been blasting all night.

I smile, "I'm sure. Maybe next time?"

"Sure thing." I grab my wallet to pay for the meal, but his hand comes down on mine as he shakes his head, "Don't worry about the bill. I'll have the old man cover it."

I laugh and tuck my wallet away, "Thanks, Lucas. I'll see you later."

It sucks to leave, but he understands where I'm coming from. He knows the deadlines, once they were set, have to be followed if one did not want to fall behind. I had about a month left before the semester ended.

Someone asked me one time if I ever saw myself being together with Luke. His red hair and freckles pulled people in, but it's those dimples that really hooked them. He is cute, caring, and funny. Altogether, he would be a catch for whatever girl caught his eye. But I also remember the chubby, awkward phase he went through. Of course, who could forget the time he ate a worm out of the ground? I guess I would rather keep a good friend around than a boyfriend with the potential of becoming a terrible romantic relationship. So, I will keep myself in the friend zone and move on.

Besides, I think Luke is already seeing a girl from college.

I get in BlueJay and make the short trip home. I make sure my car is locked up and then do the same for the front door I'm once inside. Now that no one can break into my house without a struggle, that gives me time to hop out the window and run to the Sheriff's shack down the road.

I grab my bag, spilling everything out onto my desk. I sort through my books, find the ones I got from the library, open a blank notebook, and start jotting down notes to begin the outline of my paper. A few minutes in, I find myself in a good rhythm. After about an hour or so, I find myself with a huge chunk of work done.

"*Faye...*"

I jump at the soft voice and spin in my chair. No one is there, but the goosebumps on my arms, legs, and every other part of my body tell me that there was something wrong. I lean a bit in my chair to look down the hall of my house, but I do not see anyone; not even a sign that someone could be there.

"*Faye.... It is time, Faye.*"

I stand so fast that my chair tips over behind me. I can't tell where the voice is coming from. From inside my own head? I don't think so. I glance around, looking for anything that can be considered a weapon. The only thing I manage

23

to find is a snow globe that my mother bought me when I was little. I hate the thought of using it like this, but I'm sure Mom would understand that I broke it over someone's head in order to save my life.

I slowly walk down the hallway, turning into my bathroom first. Luckily for me, the shower curtain is already open, so I don't need to worry about looking behind it. And unless the criminal is a toddler, no one can fit in my cabinets. I turn away from the bathroom and head down the hall and into the kitchen.

No one was in sight.

In the living room, I stand and listen for any kind of noise that could signal a stranger in the house. I don't hear anything. No wood creaking, no rustle of clothing: nothing.

My shoulders sag in relief. "Faye, you're officially going crazy. You need a vacation. Stress is bad for the mind and body," I turn to head back to my room and come face to face with the same man I had seen standing next to my car. A scream gets caught in my throat, sounding more like a gurgle.

"Faye. It is time for you to wake them up. It is time for you to wake me *up."*

His mouth doesn't move, but I hear the words in my mind. My hands start shaking so hard that the snow globe falls from my hands and onto the floor. Later, I will wonder how it did not break on me, but now, all my focus is on this man standing in front of me. My eyes sting with tears as my heart hammers in my chest, like it is trying to free itself from the confines of my chest. "Who are you? What do you want?" I choke out the words.

A small smile forms on the man's lips, but it is a sad smile.

The smile disappears as we both hear a howl shatter through the silence between us. *"Wake up, Faye. Before it is too late."*

The urgency in the words matches the desperation in his eyes. Suddenly, he just fades from where he is standing, leaving me alone once again. The pain in my chest dissipates as well. I kneel down to pick up the snow globe and walk on unsteady legs back into my room. I have no idea what is happening, but I think I may need to speak with my therapist. This cannot be normal, can it? Dad will kill me for contacting her again, but I am not going to let some weird visions distract me from my work.

Most people would write this off as stress, not enough sleep, or any number of things that tells them that they do not need to see someone, or talk to someone.

Not me.

I learned early on that any time something bad happens, or something unexplained, it is always better to talk to someone about it. When I was younger, that would be my parents. I told them everything that was going on in my small mind. After my mother passed and my father became, well, what he is, I had no one to talk to. I was depressed for a while until one of my teachers mentioned to me and my father about seeing an expert.

A fancy way of saying I should see a therapist.

Unlike a lot of people who get strangely offended by being told this, I did my research that night on who I would want to see. I settled for Dr. Cordelia Rommen. She was forty-eight years old and has two different PhDs in psychology, along with a couple of other certificates. She has been married for fifteen years and has five children. Two from a first relationship and two from her husband. But they have a fifth one together. It's really sweet, the way she talks about them. I grab my cell phone and glance at the time, hoping she is still at work or has a minute.

Hi, Dr. Rommen. It's Faye. I was hoping we could have a session tomorrow if you have an opening? Something weird is going on and I'm not sure what to make of it. If not, that's totally cool. We can always do it sometime after school during the week.

She normally only works for four hours on Sunday and it is usually booked. So I am surprised when I get a text back from her.

I'm glad you messaged me when you did! I actually had a client cancel for tomorrow. See you at 10am?

Yes! Thank you so much!

You're welcome, dear.

I grin and stretch my arms over my head. It was now dark outside and I head into the living room to put on a movie. The night goes by without any more strange incidents. I end up climbing into bed with a feeling of calm. That night, though, I dream of bright blue eyes, and wolf's howls.

CHAPTER THREE

*A*s I sit in front of Dr. Rommen's office, I'm immersed in a book that I picked up from the library yesterday.

"Faye, she is ready to see you now," the receptionist's voice calls over to me. I put my book back in my bag and swing it over my shoulder. Normally, I would be chatting with the receptionist, but the usual one isn't sitting there this morning.

I slip into the office and Dr. Rommen glances up from her notepad to give me a warm smile. "Faye! It's nice to see you."

I smile back and sit in the oversized chair across from her. She told me one time that she aims for comfort in her office, and who doesn't like an oversized chair to sit in? "Hey, Doctor. Where is Rachel?"

"Oh, she's out on maternity leave. Do you want to see pictures?"

"Yes!" I can't help it. Babies are cute as hell. Doctor Rommen pulls out her cellphone and we proceed to gush over baby pictures for a good five minutes. I knew Rachel was expecting, but I thought she had another couple of weeks before the baby would be here. Apparently, she had a thing called preeclampsia and they had to take the baby out early. From the looks of it though, both Rachel and baby Reagan are doing great.

"She's so cute," I say. "I will have to remember to send her a card this week."

"I'm sure she would love that," she says as she puts her phone back in her pocket. "Now that we have that out of our system, let us get to the reason you're here on this fine, freezing, Sunday morning. You said something weird is going on. Care to elaborate on that?"

I nod, "Yeah. It's just… I've been seeing someone." As her eyebrow raises, I shake my head, "Not like that! God, my dad would kill me and then go kill him. But no, it's more like I think I'm seeing someone. Someone who isn't actually there."

"You believe you're hallucinating?"

"Yes," I nod again.

"Faye, how long has this been going on?"

"Not long, I promise. It just happened yesterday. First in the parking lot at the university and again later that night in my house."

She clicks her pen, "Tell me everything."

So I do.

I tell her about the first incident, which I guess actually started with the random wolf howl Friday night. She lets me know that there has been an increase in coyote activity in the area, which would explain the howls. There is a difference between a wolf howl and a coyote. Did I know the difference? No, so we chalk it up to that. That is the nice thing about Dr.

Rommen. She takes everything I say and does not discredit anything. Then, she will help me separate the things that seem to be smaller than the bigger issues. But to her, nothing I say is considered small. Especially because she knows I only come to her when I have some real issues going on.

I think part of it is that I do not understand why people lie to their doctors. Whether it is a therapist, dentist, medical, or anyone. If a patient does not tell the truth, then how are they going to get better? I understand a little though. Some issues come with a lot of shame and embarrassment that people do not want to relive.

I walk her through what happened yesterday. I tell her about the strange man, the smell of sunflowers, the voice inside my head, and how the same thing happened at home except without the splitting headache. In fact, I guess it happened at home also, but I was too shocked to notice it at the time.

"Well, obviously there was a change in environment but was there anything else you can think of that was different between when you saw him at school and while you were at home?"

"No, nothing that I can think of," I shake my head and shrug. I was alone both times and like the doctor said, the only difference was the place I was standing at the time.

"Interesting. How have things been with your father?"

"Actually, not bad."

"Oh?" She says, mildly surprised. Of course, the last time we brought up this conversation, I ended up a crying mess with a tissue mountain on the desk.

"Yeah. I mean, he has still been going out until late or the next morning, but things haven't been so bad. He hasn't come home drunk in a while. This morning we had a conversation about school, but he didn't blow up on me like I expected. He just seemed...tired. Like, really worn out." Thinking back on it, my father had never looked so mentally exhausted before.

"Maybe he is starting to realize that he cannot continue living the lifestyle he is while taking care of his daughter. For your sake, I am hoping he is starting to prioritize you." Dr. Rommen has always helped me cope with what felt like losing both of my parents at once. What was really nice though was that she did not treat me like a child. What was said in this office never left. She would give reports to my father if he ever requested them, but they just stated that the session had gone well. He never asked for specifics so we never gave him any.

"Maybe, but I am not going to push for anything. It will just be nice if most mornings could be like this one."

"You're right. Faye, do you feel as though there are some big changes coming?"

"Big changes?"

She nods, "Between your father's attitude and maybe even with things at school?"

The first thing that pops into my head is a pair of gorgeous brown eyes and a crooked grin that makes the butterflies in my stomach go wild. "Perhaps. It's been subtle with my dad. I haven't noticed anything big happening with him. As far as school goes, I guess it's been kind of the same. I have a project essay in college before I have to start studying for finals for everything. So I guess I'm nervous about all of that."

"And I am sure that finals manage to make your face look like a boiled lobster?"

Damn.

I sigh, "No, they don't. There is a guy from college that I've talked to a couple of times." I laugh as her brow goes up, "It is nothing! He saw me watching the team practice the other day and then we talked a couple of times. He is a college guy though. Total jock. Not my type."

I notice that she isn't writing anything down as she places her chin in her hand, "I'm sure. Faye, I hate to say it, but I think you are more attracted to this man more than you are saying. How old is he, anyway?"

I shrug, "I'm not sure." I see the concern start to form on her face. "Seriously, I'm not into him. Yes, he is cute and funny, but not knowing his age is exactly why I'm not entertaining any thoughts of possibly dating him."

"Well, it is not as though I can stop you from doing the things you want or with who. Just...be careful about college guys. Finding the ones who don't just want in your pants are rare.

"Enough about the college guy. What I really want to hear more about is this mysterious figure you seem to be seeing and hearing. Are you sure you haven't seen this man before? Maybe in a movie or read about someone like him in a book?"

"No. No one like him. But, there is also something oddly familiar about him," which is something I did not realize until I said it out loud. Both times I have seen him though, there has been a strange connection between us. A familiarity that I am too scared to explore.

We discuss the situation a little more and before I know it, the time has flown by. Dr. Rommen looks at her watch,

"Faye, I want to talk with you a little more on this whole thing. Would you be available on Saturday?"

"I mean, I'm available. But my Dad-"

She holds up her hand, "Don't worry. My Saturday is very slow and I am even closing up shop early. Come in for half an hour, about three in the afternoon." I'm about to open my mouth again when she shakes her head, "And no, your father will not know about this. I am not going to charge you for the visit. Sounds good?"

"Yes, that works. I appreciate this, Doc."

"It's not a problem, Faye. You know I'm always here to talk if you need me."

"I know. Thanks again."

"See you Saturday," she says with a smile as I walk out the door.

I walk out past the reception desk without looking that way and walk out of the building. I slide into BlueJay and just sit there. The conversation we had did not shed much light on what was happening to me. I know Dr. Rommen always did her best to get to the root of her patient's afflictions, but I'm not sure this is something she could help with. Or maybe she can. I guess I won't know until I go visit her again.

I have no idea how much time passes before I finally pull out of the parking space and head home. The drive to and from the office is slow, as the traffic is almost nonexistent on a Sunday. Everyone is either in church or at a brunch after church.

I am almost home when I notice fog rolling in from the fields around me. "That's weird," I say as I slow my car down, pulling off to the side of the road. In a matter of seconds, my entire view is nothing but fog, so much that I can't see the other side of the street. I open my car door and reach for my phone, frowning as it says no signal. "What the hell?" I close the door and lean against my car. I have three choices; I can either wait for the fog to thin out, which I would prefer not to do. It would be another forty minutes if I were to walk, which is the second option. I don't mind walking, and it is still early so there is not a lot of traffic. That would mean leaving my car behind and I refuse to do that. Besides, if something were to happen to BlueJay, my dad might actually murder me.

The last option is to drive through this. The thought makes my head hurt, but there is no traffic and I am sure this fog isn't ten miles long. It beats leaving my car here as well. All I have to hope is that there isn't some moron on the road going eighty and then slamming into me, or that I won't hit a deer. The more I think about it, the more I think that maybe sitting here and waiting for it to clear wouldn't be so bad.

Before I can make up my mind, a sudden howl pierces through the silence. It causes me to jump and drop my phone. I spin around, looking out into the open field. Not that I can see anything anyway. I bend down to grab my phone and when I look up, I freeze.

In the fog in front of my car, there are two distinct golden orbs staring at me. They look like animal eyes. The sound of a snarl causes my stomach to drop. I have no idea what this thing is, but it looks big. I slowly stand, not breaking eye contact. I remember a conversation with my father one time, talking about when animals attack. Never break eye contact. It shows weakness and will make a wild animal attack. As I am thinking about what I can possibly do to get out of this situation, the eyes slowly start to move toward me. As it does, I start to notice the outline of the animal.

This is not good.

Standing in front of me, over me really, is a giant wolf. Its eyes are golden like the sun with little specks of brown scattered throughout them. Its fur is a rich brown and its teeth are more than sharp.

Like, *really* sharp.

I start to reach for the handle of my car and the wolf snaps at me without moving closer. "Well, what the hell am I supposed to do with you?" My voice comes out as a whisper. Almost like it could understand me, the wolf cocks his head to the side and I swear it smiles at me. Goosebumps rise on my arms and at that moment something stirs within me. A loud voice in my head telling me that I was in serious danger. As if I couldn't figure that one out by myself.

Without another moment of hesitation, I dive for my car. At the same time, the wolf lunges at me. Somehow, I manage to get my car door open, but not without sacrificing some of my shirt as the wolf's fangs catch on the cloth. I slam the door shut behind me and move to the other side of the car. The wolf doesn't miss a second as it slams into the car, causing the whole thing to rock. My head slams against the glass and I bring my foot down on the lock button, listening to the little click all around.

I brace myself as the car shakes, the wolf using its claws and teeth to tear into my car. I look around for anything I can possibly use in case it manages to get inside. I remember the hunting knife I keep under the back seats and throw myself into the back, right as the driver's side window shatters. I scream as its mouth almost clamps down over my foot. The door is ripped from its hinges and the wolf rips into the car. I grit my teeth, my hands shaking so much that I can't reach under to grab the knife. I can smell the wolf's breath as its jaws snap at me, clawing my car apart to try and get to me.

One of its claws reaches in between the seats, catching my arm. I cry out in pain and I tug it back against my chest, holding my hand over the gash. I can feel the blood in between my fingers, the warmth making me dizzy. Tears sting my eyes as I watch the wolf get closer and closer to me. Am I really going to die?

Suddenly, everything goes quiet. It's like someone hit pause on the world. The wolf's movement slowed to almost a stop.

"*Faye.*"

I gasp and glance around, recognizing the voice that has been haunting me for the last couple of days. I don't see anyone.

"*Faye. You need to calm your body and mind. His form may frighten you, but I assure you, he is flesh and blood like you. He has weaknesses as much as he has strengths. Stop and think. You can do this. You have to.*"

The voice left a warm presence in my chest. I close my eyes and take a deep breath. I snap my eyes open and the world resumes. I flinch as the wolf inches closer to me, but now I'm determined. I don't know where the voice came from. It felt familiar though. "I am not going to get eaten by some fleabag!"

I reach into the back pocket of the passenger seat, gripping my hand around a bottle of perfume I got a year or so ago.

I pull it out as the wolf lunges again and I slam the perfume bottle against the wolf's snout. Lucky for me, it was a fragile bottle and it shattered in my hand. I wince as it cuts me but the wolf gets the worst of it as the smell overwhelms its senses, causing it to yelp and pull out of the car.

It gives me a chance to reach underneath the seat and grip the hunting knife I have hidden. As the wolf plunges back into the car after me, I thrust the knife out, stabbing the wolf in his snout. It rears back, howling. I listen to it snarl outside of the car, and then nothing. My knuckles are turning white, but I do not move. Not until I'm convinced that the wolf isn't lurking outside my car. The adrenaline starts wearing off and the tears I had been holding back fall freely down my cheeks. My hands start shaking again and the knife falls from them, thumping onto the floorboards. I sit up, whimpering as I see the state of BlueJay. I scramble for my phone, amazed that it still works, but my finger hesitates over my dad's number. I have no idea if he is at home. Instead, I scroll down until I find the number I'm looking for and hit the little green call button.

"H-hi, Lucas? Does Martin still have that tow truck behind the pub?"

CHAPTER FOUR

*A*n hour later, Luke pulls up beside my car, jumping out of his own. Running up to me as I sit on the hood of my car, he nearly slips on the pavement, "Holy shit, Faye! What the hell happened?" Noticing my arm covered in blood, he grabs my hand, turns it over, and sees the gash on my arm, "We need to get you to the hospital."

"Wait." I pull my arm back, "It's okay. It's fine. It's not as bad as it looks. It stopped bleeding, for the most part, I just need to wash and dress it."

"Faye, you and your car look like you've just been in and out of a derby. You didn't win either," he pulls his t-shirt over his head. Too bad he is wearing a tank underneath the shirt but I still got an appreciative view of his arms and shoulders. Luke doesn't show it much, but the guy is pretty well built. He tears it in half and wraps it around my arm. He is gentle about it but makes sure that it is tight.

"You're gonna ruin your shirt," I mumble.

"I think I can live without it. I think I have a dozen of

these. Gramps gets a new shipment of shirts for the pub every couple of months." He pats my arm and then glances behind me at my car. "Be real though, Faye. Tell me what happened. Did someone run you off the side of the road or something?"

I shake my head, "No, nothing like that. You would not believe me if I told you. If it wasn't for the fact that my car is totaled and my arm hurts like a bitch, I wouldn't believe me either."

"I've heard a lot of crazy stories before. I'm sure it cannot be that bad."

I raise a brow at him and he mirrors my look, causing me to roll my eyes, "Okay, fine. I....I was attacked by a giant... wolf." The last word comes out as a whisper and I cringe upon hearing it said out loud.

Luke sits there and stares at me, "What?"

"Please don't make me say it again."

"Faye, I don't think we even have wolves here. Are you sure it wasn't another car?"

I throw my hands up, "I don't know Luke! Could a car destroy the inside of my car like a pack of rabid animals?"

"Okay, okay," Luke, sensing my rising frustration, puts his hands on my shoulders. "Okay, look. Let's get your car hooked up and take it to my grandparent's place. They have a big garage we can put it in and take a look at it. Luckily for you, it seems to be mostly cosmetic damage. The engine doesn't look touched, but we will know for sure once we get under the hood. Go ahead and climb into the truck while I get it hooked up. You look like you may pass out."

I nod and let him pull me off the hood and onto shaky

legs. I watch him for just a moment before hauling myself up into the truck.

I have to tell him about a hundred times over again that I'm okay. My head starts pounding with a headache. By the time we get to his grandparent's house, it is starting to get dark. I drag my feet through the front door while Luke gets my car in the garage.

"Martin is going to have a field day when he gets home and sees the wreck in his garage," I tell Luke as he walks into the living room with a glass of water and some aspirin. I take it gratefully and he sits next to me on the couch. "Are you sure he isn't going to be too mad?"

He shakes his head, "It is fine, Faye. He has nothing in there at the moment. I'm more concerned about your father and what he will say."

The thought of telling my father made me sick. "Yeah. I'm not so sure I'm ready to tell him. Although, he has been in a decent mood the last couple of days."

"Your old man finally got himself laid?" The hint of sarcasm isn't lost on me.

I snort, "I doubt it. I'm not sure what happened, but I don't think there is a woman in this county or any of the surrounding ones who want anything to do with my father. Trust me." I sigh and put my forehead in my hands, "What am I going to do? Even without my father committing murder, I still have no way of getting to school and back. I have tests tomorrow morning and I cannot be late."

Luke wrinkles his nose for a second and then pulls out his phone. "Hey, Cameron. You still got that old hooptie you're trying to sell? Yeah, that one. Mind if I borrow it for a while?"

I glance up from my hands and he holds up a finger, "Nah I'm not trying to buy the damn thing. I just need it for a couple of days. Tell you what. You let me borrow it, and I'll have the old man fix the water pump on it. Yes. Yes. Dude, yes or no? Awesome. Thanks, man. Yeah, if you could drop it off at my gramp's place before the end of the night. Thanks." He takes his phone away from his ear and grins, "There. Now you have transportation."

"Luke, I-"

"No. We are not going to have that whole conversation where you'll keep insisting that you can't borrow the car and I'll keep insisting that you can. I already got the car, it is already on its way here, and I'm not touching the damn thing. So, you're stuck. End of story."

"Okay, I get it," I hold up my hands, thinking I could just cry. "Just one question?"

"Hm?"

"What kind of car are we talking about here?"

Luke laughs, "It is not some piece of crap if that is what you're thinking. It's a 1994 Nissan Maxima." I wrinkle my nose. "Trust me, it's been worked on for a long time. Cameron is just trying to get it sold so he can put a down payment on a new Mustang. What a loser, right?"

"Yes, but he is a loser who happens to have an extra vehicle that will get me back and forth from school."

"True."

"Seriously, Luke. Thank you," I glance over at my arm, looking under the shirt. "I think I finally stopped bleeding."

"Here, let me take a look." He takes the time to remove the shirt, the fabric sticking to my skin. We both make a face, but as it comes off, I notice the bleeding has stopped. "Okay. Let me grab you some clothes and you can hop in the shower. Get this cleaned off and then we can see the extent of the damage. And while you are in there, I'm going to find us some snacks."

"Great, I'm starving." I head toward the bathroom and shed my bloody clothes. I turn on the faucet, wiggling my fingers under the water until I feel it turn warm, then hot. I step in under the spray, tensing for a second, waiting for the burning sensation that usually comes with scratches and other wounds. It doesn't come. I look down to the spot where the wolf had scratched me, but there is still too much blood for me to tell the state of it. My fingers shake as I pump some of the soap onto my hands and rub at the spot, noting that not only does it not hurt, but I don't even feel where the wound would have been. Once the blood is clear, I look again.

Nothing is there. The whole wound is gone, not even a scar that should have been. "What the..."

A knock on the door pulls me from my amazement as it cracks open, "Faye? You good?"

"Yeah, I'm fine."

"I'm leaving some clothes on the counter. They might be a little big, but you shouldn't swim in them."

"Thanks." I hear the door click close again and I sigh. This is going to make a fun story for Dr. Rommen. I take my time, enjoying some peace under the water. I finish up before Luke can start wondering if I keeled over in the shower and got out. I change into what I can only assume is his mother's attire. I put on a pink, floral blouse and high-waist blue jeans. He even left me some socks which I slip on my feet.

As I walk out of the bathroom, I am blasted with the smell of garlic and other spices. Still patting my hair dry, I make my way into the kitchen, "That smells awesome. Spaghetti?"

"You bet. I figured I would make something easy."

"What happened to snacks?" I ask, sliding onto one of the kitchen stools for the island.

He looks up from what he is doing, and in an all-serious tone, says, "This is a snack." I laugh and roll my eyes. He jerks his head toward my arm, "You sure you don't need a hospital?"

I nod, "Yeah, it stopped bleeding."

Lights suddenly shine through the windows of the living room and a moment later, the doors slam open. "Luke!"

I whip my head around to Luke and he smiles sheepishly, "He would have found out anyway."

Martin comes around the corner, his eyes wide, "Faye! You wanna tell me why your car looks like it was on the underside of a monster truck?"

"Hi Martin," I say and grunt as he wraps me in a tight hug. For an old man, he still has a lot of muscle on him. "I, um, it is kind of hard to explain about the car." He lets go of me and stares at me, "Actually, I am kind of hoping you can help me with it without telling you much about it."

"You can't expect me to just have you show up on my doorstep with your car torn to hell and not ask you about what happened to it."

"Gramps—" Luke starts, but Martin holds his hand up.

"Does your dad know what happened?"

I shake my head. Martin sighs and rubs his hand on the back of his neck, "I don't like it. I don't like it one bit." He drops his hand and shrugs, "But, I have to hope that you will trust me enough to tell me what happened before I get this thing fixed. You already got her a replacement?" He asks Luke, who nods. "All right. Well, what are we going to tell Stephen?"

"I'm not sure yet. Whatever I tell him, he is going to be mad."

"Well, is he supposed to be home tonight?" I shake my head again. "Well, it gives us some time to figure out what to do."

"Morning isn't all that far away."

"Well, we can figure it out later. For now, let's get some food in that stomach of yours. I know after an ordeal like that you could use it. Luke, is the food ready?"

"Yes, sir," Luke says as he grabs some plates out of the cabinet. He dishes some to everyone and I sit at the table, grateful for the calm. We don't bring up the conversation about my car or what happened for the rest of the time we sat there. It was all conversation about the pub, my schooling, Luke's schooling, and easy topics. I felt myself relax more and more, laughing with the conversation.

For as long as I can remember, Luke has been family. Even though his parents are not around as much as his grandparents, I can even be comfortable around them. It's a familiarity that I miss in my own home.

A pounding on the door stops our words and Luke hops up, "That's probably Cameron. Hang on."

"Your chariot awaits," Martin smiles.

"Thanks again, Martin."

"Anytime."

"Hey, woah, hang on!" We hear Luke yell and a thud.

"Move, kid. I know she's here." Another shout causes the hairs on the back of my neck to stand on end. "Faye!" My dad comes around the corner, his face red and contorted in anger. "What happened to the damn car?"

"Dad. H-how did you find out?"

Martin comes to my side, "Stephen, wait. There is a good explanation for all of this."

"Stay out of this," my dad growls. I glance down and see his hands flexing. It is something I have seen many times.

I turn to Martin and put a hand on his shoulder, "It's fine Martin."

"Let's go." Dad does not leave room for argument as he turns on his heels and heads out of the house.

"Faye, you don't have to go," Luke tells me, coming to my side.

"It's fine. It will only be worse if I don't go home. I can't move the car anyway. Is there any way—"

"I'll have Cameron drop the car off at your place."

"Thanks, Luke. You're the best." I smile and trail behind my dad, who is already waiting in the truck. I climb inside and silence hangs between us. The smell of alcohol on him is strong tonight. I want to ask him why he changed his mind about coming home tonight, but looking over at his face, I keep my mouth shut.

We drive ten minutes home and my dad gets out of the car right away, heading inside while I wait in the truck for a minute. I want to give him time to cool off, but waiting here starts wearing on my nerves, so I slide out of the truck.

Inside, I notice my dad pacing in the kitchen. I close the door behind me and don't say anything. I knew no matter what I said, I would be in the wrong. Instead, I stand there, just watching him, like a lion stalking its prey. I have seen my dad angry while he had been drinking many times, but this is the first time he has been truly angry because of something I have done. It is not as though it was my fault, but he doesn't know that. I'm sure that if someone hit me while I was parked, it would still be my fault.

He stops pacing and turns to me, putting his arms across his chest, "Where is the car now?"

"Martin's garage."

"Why the hell am I waiting hours to find out you destroyed the damn thing?"

"I was going to tell you, Dad, I swear. It all just happened so fast. Then I had to get it towed and out of the road and in the middle of everything, I didn't realize how much time had passed."

"That still doesn't tell me what fucking happened, dammit!" He shouts and I flinch slightly. "Do you know how much that kind of damage costs? Do you know how much it is going to cost me to find a replacement for you? Do you even think about these things? It looked like you had a damn rager! Or a pack of wild animals tore into it! Did you leave it in the middle of the woods?"

"No, Dad! Nothing like that. It was-" I stop and close my mouth.

"It was? It was what, Faye?" I don't say anything. "*Tell me!*"

"A wolf! A giant wolf attacked me in the middle of the road!" I shout back, then quickly shut my mouth.

My dad's eyes went wide. He turns toward the cabinets

and grabs a whiskey glass, pouring himself some and swallowing it in one gulp.

Suddenly, he spins and hurls the glass against the wall. I jump back as he faces me again, "Why are you lying to me?" His voice is quieter than it had been earlier. I felt my stomach churn and I felt something I haven't felt from my father in a long time.

Fear.

"I'm.....I'm not."

"Giant wolves? You expect me to believe that?"

"No! I mean..." I take a step back as he towers over me.

"What happened to the damn car?"

I whimper, "I don't-"

I couldn't even prepare myself. One moment I am staring at my father and the next, I'm holding myself up against the door. My face stings and there is a metallic taste in my mouth. I put my hand against my face and I slowly turn sideways to look at my father. Before he could say or do anything else, my hand reaches the door handle and I bolt.

I hear him shout my name, but I keep running. I knew he couldn't run after me, not after hurting his knee a couple of years ago. Tears blur my vision and I continue on toward the fields behind our house. I can't tell how far I have gone, my surroundings are too dark for me to see. My foot snags, sending me skidding on the ground. I roll over on my back, breathing heavily. My face is wet from crying.

My dad has always drank and has gotten mad before, but he has never hit me. It has never gone that far and I have no idea what to think of it. I did know that if I told anyone about this, they would haul me off to a group home and my dad would go to jail. Even Dr. Rommen has told me before that if he put his hands on me, she would have no choice but to call child services. I lay there and cry for a while without moving until I feel myself calm down enough to finally sit up.

Wiping my face, I glance around, not recognizing where I am. This is further than I normally go in the field. "Great."

I stand and wipe the back of my pants off. I put my hands on my hips, glancing around to try and figure out what to do now. I can't go back to my house. I don't know what my dad is doing or if he is even at home still, but I can't go back there. Not yet. Maybe Martin's?

Starting the journey back into town, the crackling of leaves and dead grass causes me to stop. It could have just been me, right? I take another step forward and that's when I hear the low growling. The hair on the back of my neck stands up and goosebumps rise on my arms. Steeling myself, I slowly glance over my shoulder into a pair of big, golden eyes.

"Oh hell."

CHAPTER FIVE

*M*y legs burn and my lungs feel like they are going to collapse in my chest. I have a bad stitch in my side that seems to be expanding the more I run. The adrenaline is the only thing keeping me from the teeth of the wolf pounding after me. How? How did it find me? Where did it come from? The only thing I can think of is that it was already out here and it picked up on my scent.

I read one time that wolves can smell further than dogs. This one being twice the size, I am sure that it can smell for miles.

I hear the wolf behind me and then, suddenly, nothing. I hesitate and my feet catch on each other, causing me to pitch forward into the dirt. I see a blur of fur above me, a snarl in my ear. A scream lodges in my throat as it turns and snaps at me, hitting the ground. I manage to get out of the way, rolling in the other direction. I stand when the wolf does too, shaking its body. We stand there, facing each other. Its teeth are pulled back in a snarl.

My heart pounds in my chest and sweat runs down the back of my neck. We stand there for what feels like ages. I'm afraid to move. Even a twitch of my finger could send this thing springing at me. At this point, I have nowhere to run. Even if I get a ten-second head start, its long strides will bring it on me in moments. I can only stand here for so long. I am already tired from running from my dad, and now I'm exhausted after running from this wolf.

I think it is time for us to stop playing this game of cat and mouse, don't you think?

I recoil, recognizing the deep, cocky voice. I am afraid to turn my back on the wolf, but I can't help myself. My eyes slowly scan around me, but I don't see any other body for the voice.

Disorienting, isn't it? Trust me, I know what that is like. Getting hit with that perfume bottle was a smart thing on your part, wasn't it?

My whole body starts to shake, "T-Theo…" As soon as I say the name out loud, the wolf grins at me. It screamed predator.

The wolf shrugs. *How lucky am I? To find you all alone, without your stupid car to protect you.*

"I don't understand," I cry. Theo's voice is coming from the direction of the wolf. It is so clear.

Didn't you hear? There is a new boss in town. And she needs something. Something that you have. She sent me to get it back. The wolf shakes his head, his tongue hanging out the side as he pants. *Faye, it is no use in trying to make sense of this all. It doesn't matter anyway. Soon, you will just be the small-town girl no one really cared about anyway.*

I picture the couple of moments Theo and I interacted. At the time, there was no aggression in his eyes. Nothing that made me assume that he could attack in this manner. *I don't think Ted Bundy wore a sign that he was a serial killer either,* I think to myself, desperately trying to think of a way out of here. "I don't have anything though!"

No, you wouldn't know about it, would you? After all, I can't get it from you if you are still alive.

I scream as he lunges toward me. I hurl myself to the side, but I'm not fast enough. Theo's teeth clamp down on my shoulder and he drags me to the ground. I kick my legs as hard as I can, struggling to wiggle myself out from underneath him. I scratch one of his eyes and he yelps, his teeth releasing my shoulder. I push against his body, but he is heavy and doesn't budge.

You know. I almost feel bad for you. You're cute Faye. His mouth hangs open in a vicious grin, *I bet you taste just as good as you look.*

I close my eyes, waiting for those teeth to tear into me. Instead, the weight lifts off my chest and my eyes snap open, seeing nothing but the sky above me. I roll up and my head swivels around, looking for Theo. I find him not far from me, getting up on his paws. His eyes dart around and we both see the same figure hovering next to me at the same time.

The newcomer stands there, his feet apart and in each hand, he holds a longer dagger. He is younger-looking, maybe early twenties? "Lupus. I knew you were a mongrel, but I did not think you would stoop so low as to become Alnilam's pet. You know the rules."

I could hear the chuckle coming from Theo, *What are*

you going to do about it, Guardian? I can hear the sneer in his voice. *All of you were cast aside by the same stars you say you protect. Who are they to give us rules? We all know Orion is as good as dead anyway.*

The guy's face turns from calm to fiercely angry in a split second, "You're going to regret those words, dog." He suddenly turns to me, "Move, girl. Unless you really want to become stuck in this guy's teeth."

It took me a second for me to stop staring and I turned, jumping to my feet, getting myself away from the scene as fast as my tired legs would. I hear Theo snarl and I can only imagine what was happening at that moment. I only get so far before a heavy force knocks into me, throwing me into the dirt. I hear a groan and the force turns out to be the stranger. He rolls off me, standing back up. I get back up, really getting tired of having my face in the dirt. Theo slowly stalks toward both of us. I notice that the guy already has a bunch of scrapes and is bleeding from a couple of spots, but I also see blood dripping from Theo.

"These damn things aren't going to be enough," he mutters under his breath. I look between the two. He turns to me, "Do you know you have it?"

"Have what?"

"That's a no," I can see his jaw tense as Theo gets closer. He slips his daggers into sheaths strapped to his back. He turns to me suddenly and extends his hand toward me, "Give me your hand."

"Excuse me?"

"Just give me your damn hand!" He shouts as Theo snaps and lunges at us. I don't have time to think and he reaches out to me. He grabs my hand and energy surges between us. I gasp and I see a flicker of surprise on the stranger's face, but he reacts fast. His other hand splays open toward Theo and an invisible force hits the wolf, exploding outward and sending him flying backward.

The stranger tightens his hold on my hand and yanks me forward as he starts running the opposite way of Theo. "What the hell was that?" I shout, my innate fear of Theo's giant teeth keeps my hand firmly in his.

"It seems as though things aren't as we thought it was," he says out loud, more to himself than to me. I can hear a howl behind us and I glance back. Theo is standing there, his teeth bared and the hair on his neck standing on end. He does not chase us though. My feet move with the stranger as we run. We don't head toward town though.

Once we run far enough, I dig my heels into the ground and yank us to a stop. The stranger, not expecting it, grunts as he has to regain his balance. I put my hands on my thighs, panting and trying to get my breathing under control. I wince as the pain in my shoulder returns and fatigue hits me hard as the adrenaline dissipates.

I stand up straight, staring at the stranger. He is standing there, his arms crossed again. I feel myself swaying slightly and that is when he opens his mouth. "We need to keep moving. You need some medical attention for your shoulder. That can't be feeling too good."

"You're right, but I am not going anywhere with you until you tell me who you are. What he was. And what the hell is going on," I put my hand on my shoulder, hoping to stem the pain a little with pressure. My hand instantly feels warm and I realize that it is still bleeding.

He sighs, obviously irritated, "I can tell you a little, but we really need to get somewhere safe. My name is Scorpio. The wolf? His name isn't really Theo. His name is Lupus, which is stupid for a dog to name himself after a cat."

I stare at him, my brain still trying to process what he is telling me. "Scorpio. Scorpio. As in, 'what is your horoscope for the day,' Scorpio?"

Annoyance crosses his face, "Don't mock the stars. We need to go, *now*."

"Oh no. No, no, no, no. I'm not going anywhere with you! I am going back home, going back to my therapist, getting this crazy night out of my head, and…and…wake up—" My world spins hard and black spots hit my vision. I stumble and the last thing I see before my vision goes dark is Scorpio running toward me.

CHAPTER SIX

*T*heo stands with his eyes closed, soaking in the quiet energy that hummed around him. He stands in a circular room, decorated in black and gold. He faces a large set of double doors that open to a large terrace. Beyond that is nothing but stars and space, the universe open to whoever gazes out of it.

"You have failed *again*, Lupus." A quiet voice, full of silk and venom, enters the room behind Theo. He spins in place, coming face to face with another. Pale, porcelain skin. Long, white hair sways around her waist. Bright blue eyes that are cold and calculating narrow ever so slightly. "Twice, Lupus. Twice you have gone for the girl at the most opportune time and you still fail to bring her to me."

Theo's eyes turn down to the floor, "Alnilam. I-"

A slender finger raises to her lips. Theo's jaw clamps shut, teeth clenching together. She turns and as she walks over to a vanity in the room, Theo glances up at her. "Now, I know that this girl seems to be giving you some problems. But what

I don't understand is how she managed to best you on two different occasions."

"You know how she did," he talks through his teeth.

Alnilam looks at him from the mirror, "Yes. Your sense of smell got the better of you. Poor cub." Theo could feel the energy in the air thicken and it felt like someone slowly putting their hands on his throat, squeezing. Alnilam did nothing, and yet, he knew that she could kill him within moments. "One more time, Lupus. One more time you will receive my blessing to return to Earth and kill that girl."

"And what of Scorpio? You told me that none of the Guardians had their powers."

"It's the girl. Orion's soul within her is responding to them once they make physical contact. It is not permanent, but it is enough that it could cause us some…complications. But don't worry. I have confidence that you will finish the job, Lupus." Theo nods his head and heads out of the doors. His form changes once again from a human into his wolf as he leaps off the terrace and into the night sky. Two figures walk through the door behind Alnilam, almost mirror images of her.

"Do you really think he will succeed?" A voice growled. It came from one of the women, taller than the one standing beside her. Same long, white hair. Same bright blue eyes, but anger swirled in them instead of calm.

"Be still, sister. Whether Lupus succeeds or not, we will have what we desire."

"Yeah, Alnitak. You need to calm down," the smallest of the three women says with a smile. Her hair is shoulder-length, her eyes are filled with excitement and chaos.

"Mintaka, mind your elders," Alnilam chides. The girl

grins but doesn't say another word. Alnilam puts her attention back to Alnitak. "Lupus will either succeed or he will be replaced. It is as simple as that, and he knows this."

"What of the Guardians? Scorpio has already made contact with Orion's soul. He will seek out the others. You know what will happen if they all unite."

Alnilam smiles cruelly, "Then we must not let that happen, should we?"

As soon as I can feel myself begin to wake up, my eyes shoot open and I bolt up, regretting it instantly as a sharp pain causes me to gasp and clutch my shoulder. I take a moment to let the pain ebb away and then look around. The walls around me were dark and wooden. I glance outside the window, but I can only see nothing but darkness and outlines of trees. Cabin in the woods? Seems like a scene from a horror movie. Only the small bed I am in, a dresser, and an end table decorate the room.

I notice that there is a bandage around my shoulder and at the same time, I have a different top on than I had before. I hold the fabric in my hands and I cannot decide if the feeling in the pit of my stomach is anger or embarrassment. The door opens to a familiar face entering the threshold. I scowl, my face fuming, "What the hell! You took my clothes off?"

Scorpio looks at me with a bored expression, "I had to dress your wound. Hard to do that with cloth in the way."

"A little *tact* would have been nice," I hiss at him.

"Next time, I'll be sure to remember that as you're bleeding to death. Now, after however long it takes for you to get

over your embarrassment, can you join me in the living area?"
He turns on his heel and leaves me without another word.

I am sure I look like a fish in water, my mouth gaping
open with a thousand terrible names I want to call him, but
none of them pass my lips. I finally close my mouth and fall
back on the bed. I can't be angry with him. Not completely. I
know that if he did not help me, I would have bled out back
there. He saved my life and I came at him with rage. Still does
not change the fact that he saw me in my most vulnerable
state.

I finally roll out of the bed. The bandage is tight and does
not move out of place, not even enough for me to look at my
shoulder. Then I remember how my other arm was after Theo
attacked me in the car. After a while, the wound had closed
completely. I look around, not seeing a mirror, so I slip out
of the room.

The door opens to a short hallway. Beyond that, I can see
what looks like a living room area, but I'm not quite ready to
face Scorpio right now. There is another door a little further
down on the right-hand side. Peeking inside, I see a bathroom
with a claw foot tub and shower attached and I smile. I shut
myself inside and find basic hygiene items in the various
cabinets.

I know Scorpio is waiting for me but I need this time for
myself. I'm still not sure whether or not to go out and talk to
him or simply slip out the window and go home. It feels like
I've traded one stranger for another, except that one has tried
to kill me and the other saved me. For now. I take my clothes
off and turn on the shower. The water pressure makes me sad,
but it will work for now. I step in and work on slowly peeling

the bandages away from my skin. I tense as the gauze sticks to my skin, but it comes off as the water rains down on it.

I finally get the bandages peeled off, noting how they are covered in blood, but not as badly as I thought they would be. Looking at my shoulder, it is what I thought it would be. It is an ugly looking wound, but nothing that seems to be life threatening. In an hour or two, it is possible it will be gone completely. *I wonder if that's related to those hallucinations I had. And the weird power surge that happened when Scorpio grabbed my hand.* I look down, flexing my fingers in and out of a fist.

I take about an hour in the shower, mostly because the entire time, I am seeing the wound on my shoulder slowly change color a little. Like it is already closing and healing as I stand there and watch. Eventually, the water starts getting cold and I resign myself to getting out, putting my clothes back on, and making myself look like a human being again. I try to untangle my hair with my hands and it doesn't work.

"Screw it," I mutter and head out into the living room where Scorpio is waiting for me. His eyes open as I stand near him, my arms crossed. "I'm sorry. I shouldn't have snapped like that. Thank you for saving me."

Scorpio shrugs and scoots over on the couch he is sitting on, motioning with his hand. I sit down, facing him. I cross my legs, wishing there was just a little bit more space in between us. It gives me a good chance to really get a good look at him though. His eyes were blue, like a dark ocean, but the color where the sun barely touches. He looks strong but tired. "Your wound is already healing?" He asks.

I nod slowly, wondering how he knew. He must have

noticed when he dressed it. "It isn't the first time it happened. The first time Th- er, Lupus attacked me, he scratched my arm. That one healed within a couple of hours. Looks like this one is going to take a little more time."

"Makes sense. I am sure by tomorrow morning that it will be fine."

"How long was I out?"

"A couple of hours. It took a while for me to get you to the safe house. You're heavier than you look." I am about to snap again before I see the amusement in his eyes. I huff and sink down into the couch again. "I have already made contact with a few of the others. We will need to start moving again at early light."

"Wait, what? Moving where? Who are the others? *What is going on?*" This guy was crazy if he thought I would willingly go anywhere with him. I may be thankful that he saved me from Theo, but he is still just a stranger.

Calm, Faye. He is not your enemy.

It is that voice again. I look around, waiting to see if the man appears. When I don't see anyone, I turn back to Scorpio, who is looking at me with narrowed eyes. A chill runs down my spine. The last thing I needed to do was start hallucinating.

"What is it?" He asks.

"I don't know. It's...it's a voice I have been hearing the last couple of days. It isn't constant, but it just appears out of nowhere."

"Like now? When your emotions start to intensify?"

"No, not always. It has been mostly random. He sometimes appears when the voice talks to me, but I'm not seeing him now." I don't know why I was telling him this. I guess crazy sympathizes with crazy.

"He?"

I shrug, looking down at my fingers. There is still some dirt under my nails and I pick at them. After the night in my house, I knew that the voice in my head belonged to the man I kept seeing. I just did not understand why I was hearing and seeing him. "It's the voice in my head. I saw someone the other night as well. I have seen him twice now, and the second time he seemed to be talking to me at the same time."

"What does he look like?"

"Why is that important?" I say guarded. This is the second person who I have told that I have been hallucinating, but Scorpio's eyes are different than Dr. Rommen's. She watched me with concern as if there was something wrong with me that she would need to fix. Scorpio is looking at me like I hold all the answers he has been looking for.

"Just tell me."

I sigh, "I don't know! He...had long golden hair. And he was tan, like he had-"

"Been kissed by the sun. Bright blue eyes; eyes that almost mirror your own. Right?"

"Yeah," I say slowly. "Who is he?"

"I will tell you, but you need to do something for me first."

I can feel myself tense. This guy could have the answers I need, but deep down, I'm scared to know. Things like this happen to people in books, movies, and other fictional stories. I have a feeling Scorpio is about to tell me that giant wolves are going to be the least of my worries from here on out. I nod my head, letting him know to continue. I'm not ready, but I think I need to know these things.

"I need you to believe what I tell you." I feel my head tilt just a bit, almost like a curious dog. I want to tell him that at this point, I don't think I have another choice. But I haven't heard the entire story yet. I wouldn't be surprised if he told me he turned into a giant scorpion. Scorpio takes my silence as a cue to continue on. "First thing you have to know. Now that they have already sent Lupus after you, there will be others."

"More giant wolves?"

"No. How much do you know about the stars?"

The temptation to flee is becoming stronger the longer I sit with this man. "I don't know what you're getting at, but I don't believe in that whole 'your month is based on where Jupiter is at the time' stuff. They are just giant balls of gas and huge chunks of rock."

"Almost. You've heard of Orion?" I nod. "The Hunter of the sky. And then there are the others, like Canis Major and Minor."

"The Big Dipper and Little Dipper? What do those have to do with anything?"

He frowns, obviously annoyed at me, "That is not even the correct name for them. Those are the humans' names for the constellations. First off, what you need to know is that the stars are not just big balls of gas. Not really. That is simply what humans have theorized in their minds because they cannot grasp the concept of their true state, which is energy in the spiritual sense. Pure energy, created by Orion."

"You've lost me. And besides, did we not come up with the

names for the rest of it as well? Orion, Scorpio, Canis Major. Humans created those names as well...didn't we?"

"Not quite. It did take a long time for Orion to give us our names, as well as himself, but it was Orion. He simply steered humans into the names for us. I'm not sure where they got Little Dipper and Big Dipper though. Anyway, humanity has created their own religions, their own theories, on how the universe was created and where you all have come from. What I am about to tell you is the true story of it all."

"You're kidding me. Is the big bang even a thing?"

Scorpio shakes his head, "Just listen, yeah?"

"Fine."

"This is the story that Orion has told us on multiple occasions. How he came to be and everything after. It started within the Milky Way. The galaxy seems to have existed before Orion, so we are not sure how that came to be. But we have been told by Orion that there could be an even higher being than him, one that created the galaxies themselves,"

"Wait, so like God?"

Scorpio shrugs, "We have no idea. It is possible that there is another being who holds that power, but even Orion does not know. The first memory is of Orion himself. He says he remembers simply being conscious at one point in time. He is not sure how long he had been there, suspended in the middle of the galaxy. Orion was a floating ball of energy, one with a mind that gained awareness of the things around him. He said that from the time he gained consciousness, it was probably about five years before he attempted to control any aspect of his life. In that time, he learned more about himself. He started from nothing, much like human infants when they are born. Except he was born with a special memory. Just one memory.

"It was one of creation. In the five years he had been floating, he did not attempt to do anything with the memory he was born with. He said the thought of using the power frightened him, honestly. This was illogical because he did not know he could feel fear and had no clue what to do with the feeling at first. Every time he thought about using the power inside him, the one he knew he had, the fear reached around him. It started in his chest and went down to his fingertips and toes. It squeezed tight and turned the universe around him colder than it already was.

"At one point, something snapped inside of him. The fear had become too much and he ended up using his powers. It was nothing big, at first, but he found a small flame inside his hand. Within that flame, all of that fear he had been experiencing simply vanished. Amazement took its place and from that moment, there was no stopping his endless need of knowing how far his power could grow. The fire became bigger and bigger over time, turning into what you know as the sun.

"The planets are part of Orion's picture of what his galaxy should look like inside, using his imagination. At first, he found himself pleased with the way it was coming around. The planets shifted around the sun in a uniform structure. He had no instructions on using his powers, so he did what he believed would be acceptable in some kind of way. It was during this time he also started to question what the others like him were like. He found out early on that he could not leave the galaxy he was placed in, but he instinctively knew that there were others out there. As he began to dream about his counterparts, he started to experience another unexpected feeling. He had worked out other emotions, but like the fear he once felt, this was something he could not have known, for he had no reason to know it before. Eventually, he realized that it was a sense of loss around him.

"It was loneliness.

"It tore through him every time he began to think of how there were other beings like him, but he would never be able to reach out and interact with them. It was like a crushing weight in his chest and he did not think that he would be able to fix this one. Until that is, he realized the small lights surrounding him. Seemingly to come from nowhere, much like himself, they floated around him. As he went to touch one, the light transferred back inside of his own body. There was a warmth as it did so. Orion never could describe this experience to us in detail, for he did not even know how to use words to do so. The warmth that came from the little lights was like an embrace, whereas when he had fear choking him it was icy cold. This was something else entirely.

"At this point, he knew that the little balls of light had come from himself, at the point in time where he was feeling the lowest. It was also at this time when he found that if he left the little balls of lights by themselves for a while, they would almost start to take on a life of their own. They never moved past getting consciousness like Orion, but it was as though they were still alive."

"That makes no sense," I interject. "How are they alive but not conscious?"

Scorpio glances to the side in thought. I expect he was

trying to figure out a way to better explain it to me. After all, it is not every day you have to tell the story of creation to one of the byproducts of it. "Think of them like plants? Plants are technically alive, correct?"

"I suppose," I say slowly.

Scorpio nods, like the answer was obvious all along. "Well, these little balls of light were like that. They were alive, but not in a way like you or me. Some of them even grew, formed their own shape, and turned into what you see now whenever the sun sets."

"So...the stars? Wait. Are you trying to tell me that stars are...alive?"

"In a sense, yes."

Woah, okay. This is way more than just a simple history lesson. Scorpio is trying to tell me the beginning of time itself. At least, for our galaxy. Not to mention how calmly he just told me that there are, in fact, aliens in space. If there are other crazy, god-like beings like Orion, how many other creatures like this roam the universe? Unless they can't leave their own galaxies like us. Man, scientists are going to be really pissed when they find out that the other side of Pluto is just a great, big, invisible wall. Good thing we haven't figured out a way to actually explore that part of space. Scorpio asked me to believe that everything he is saying is true, but the more I sit here, the more it sounds like a crazy fantasy. How am I supposed to believe a story like this? I let him continue on, nonetheless. Fantasy or not, it was a new take on how life came to be. Maybe it could end up being a great novel someday.

"For a long time, Orion was content with learning how to harness this new ability, letting the balls of energy guide themselves across the galaxy and settling in a place where they wanted. Eventually, like everyone who develops their talent, he wanted to expand and learn what else he could do. That is when he began testing the limits of his powers. By this time, the planets had been developing for a long time and he discovered that one, in particular, had changed in a peculiar way. Earth, named that way by humans, had begun to self-sustain. The atmosphere began covering the outer layer and then, the rest is just simple evolution from there."

As Scorpio says that, I snort and cough, covering a laugh. He raises a questioning brow at me and I can't help but grin, "Don't let the super religious folks know that. A lot of us humans think that God put us here on Earth."

Scorpio frowns, "Yes. I've come to realize that. But like I said, humans have come up with their own theories on how everything came to be. Orion doesn't fret over things like that."

"So he doesn't care that we are basically destroying something he created a long time ago?"

Scorpio's lips tilt up in a smile, but it is almost ominous, "Oh he cares. More than you would think. But he is an immortal being with all the time in the universe. If humans destroy the Earth, it simply returns to Orion and he can start again. Sure he will be upset for a little while, but wouldn't you be if someone destroys something you made? Always room for error I suppose." The message was clear as it was eerie. Orion would not step in to save the Earth if it came down to it. Why would he, when he can simply begin anew? The realization chilled my bones, that there was someone out there with the power to start us over from nothing. Scorpio's creepy smile disappears and he shrugs, "I don't think it is going to happen any time soon though. Orion believes that he is starting to see a change among the next generations of humans, those who care more about the environment around them. He could be wrong, but he says that Earth is going to be around for a very long time."

"Cheers to that," I mumble.

"May I continue?" He asks and I nod. "When Orion realized that Earth was becoming its own entity, growing life on its surface, he felt proud in the way a father would be proud of a child being born, if I were to compare." That hit a strong nerve in me and my stomach twisted in knots, thinking of my own father. He may have been proud when I was born, but that did not last. "It made him wonder if that was the extent of his powers, though. So he experimented with his energies, seeing just how much he could leak out at once and figuring out how to stabilize everything together. It took him a while. You want to know where black holes come from?"

"When stars die and implode on themselves?"

"Yes, but it's how they implode. Orion would use too much energy, not enough energy, and a combination of many things before he had some semblance of what he was actually doing. Finally, though, he was able to create another being from himself: a sister, Alnilam." The way Scorpio says her name, I get the feeling that there is something dangerous about this woman. I recognize the name, but cannot place where I have heard it before. "Orion felt a deep connection to Alnilam, and together, they explored the galaxy and everything in it. He showed her all of his creations and taught her everything he knew. They even discovered that she had a bit of her own powers as well, stemming from Orion's.

He gave her instruction and she was even able to create as well, bringing about two more sisters to their family. Alnitak and Mintaka were not nearly as powerful as their sister, but they too had some power in them. None of them could match the raw power that Orion had, but over time, their abilities grew. For a long time, they led a life of peace among them. They built a home, something to give each other some space in order to maintain their magic but still be near each other. Orion actually learned it from the very early tribes of humanity, but whereas humans used clay and mud, he created a castle in the sky, with his sister's help of course. This way of life, it was enough for them.

"Until at some point, it did not live up to expectations. Alnilam was the first one to realize that she was unfulfilled, living in the shadow of her brother with the limited powers she was given. She began testing her powers in secret, learning anything she could. She wanted to be able to do more than just create. She wanted to harness the energy inside her, to use it however she willed it. Eventually, she was discovered by her sisters. Alnitak took no time at all to be convinced that she too wanted more power than Orion had given them. Together, they slowly turned Mintaka against their brother. As she was the youngest, she had grown more attached to Orion, but she was also the most unpredictable one of them all. Orion had suspected that it was because Alnilam had created her at a time of weakness and fatigue, and thus did not use her powers correctly. Once Mintaka was on their side, her mind flipped like a switch.

"Orion said that it was at this time he felt something stirring within the galaxy. It was a darkness in which he could not find the source. His sisters hid their ill intent for a very long time. Orion did not want to take anything to chance and began creating beings in order to better protect this place he had worked so hard to create. Earth may one day be ruined, but that doesn't mean that he won't have us help him protect it until the end. That is where we come in. The twelve of us, created from Orion's own soul."

"His soul? How is that different than how he created his sisters?"

"Alnilam and the other two were created from their power of creation. A magic rooted deep inside Orion himself. An essence of sorts, lain around his soul that allows him to wield it freely. Because he felt so strongly about the disturbance around him, he took parts of his physical soul and created Guardians. We are essentially Orion himself, in different forms."

"You said there were twelve of you. Are you talking about the rest of the horoscope star people? Libra, Cancer, Pisce-"

"As well as the others, yes. Again, that kind of thing is strictly man-made nonsense. Although, there is some truth in the idea that those born under that sign share the same traits among themselves. More on that another time. Humans began seeing the stars form in a cohesive order every night, turning in different parts of the sky at different times of the year. What they did not know, though, is that those clusters of stars were actually beings; an extension of Orion himself. He believed that he himself would need help if he wanted to maintain the balance of the galaxy. The constellations you see in the sky are our true selves."

"So, you're not real?"

"This body is real if that is what you are getting at. It is manifested as a way for me to be on Earth without, you know, crushing a bunch of humans and burning everyone alive." The thought of a giant star with legs pounding all over Earth popped into my head. "If this body is hurt or killed in some way, then it would take a long time for me to form again. As far as Orion can tell, our energy would go back inside of him, but the piece of his soul that he took out would still linger in its place outside of his body. It has not been tested before, so we honestly cannot say.

"The twelve Guardians each had their roles. Each of us would maintain patrol over a different region in the galaxy. Some would take our place over the planets, while others would take a stand in the outer regions. We rotate every now and then so that every one of us could experience the entire galaxy. For years, we did this. We grew to have our own personality and that personality seems to have an effect on other living beings, like humans. The position of the stars had nothing to do with it, but the energy that was above at the time. Alnilam, upon hearing what he had done and what her brother had given away, became bitter and hateful. She silenced her anger and used it as fuel to find a way to break out of the galaxy she was confined in. Along with her two sisters, Alnilam searched and searched the entire galaxy until she found a way. That way came in the form of a spell. A spell that destroyed the origin of the galaxy and allowed the barriers to shatter. It would allow her to explore the reaches of the universe, wreaking whatever havoc she could muster."

"How did she manage to find the spell in the first place? *Why* is there even a spell like that? I thought everyone just waved their hands around and worked their magic that way." I say, still entranced in the story that Scorpio has been telling me.

He shakes his head, "I don't know. I am not sure even Orion knows where she acquired the knowledge. I am sure it was already there, hidden in his secret library. Even Orion discovered that along with the growth of the galaxy, new magics began growing as well. Everything starts and ends with him, but there is a lot in between. All we know is that we need to revive Orion and stop Alnilam."

My chest tightens at his words, "You say revive him. What...what happened to him?"

Scorpio's eyes turn down for a few seconds, and I nearly miss the flash of rage in them, before returning to the stoicism he has had since I met him just a couple of hours ago. "About sixteen years ago, Alnilam began the spell. Underneath our noses, the three sisters managed to finish all the ingredients of the spell. They almost enacted it and obliterated us all. Orion used the moment they began the spell to tear his own soul from his body and cast it away, hiding it somewhere safe. Somewhere here, on Earth."

His eyes look at me expectantly, though I don't understand. Then, the answer dawns on me, "No way. There is no way I have it. You would think I would know if I had something that important!"

"I believe you do have it, but not in the way you would

think. Tell me; has anything changed recently? You said you started seeing and hearing Orion a couple of days ago. Did something happen before that?"

Another realization hits me, "The diamond I found."

"The what?"

"The diamond! I found it in the crater close to town. It's been there since before I was born. I go there every now and then, but this time, I found what looked like a piece of diamond in the dirt. Ever since then, I've been having those hallucinations. That's also…when Theo started talking to me." I chew on my bottom lip. I am still having a hard time digesting everything because it seems to be like a dream. A very surreal and dangerous dream. But the proof has been given to me already, Theo being a big part of it. I don't believe there are any wolves that big in the world, especially near Hamilton.

"Interesting. It seems as though when Orion's soul fell to Earth, it took on a crystallized form. It makes sense. He wouldn't want his soul wandering the planet with his sisters on the prowl. When you found it, did you happen to bleed on it?"

"How did you know?" I glance down at my hand, not seeing the small cut any longer. I also reach up to my shoulder, feeling the skin is now smoother than it was when I first got out of bed.

"It makes sense now, why it took Alnilam so long to find his soul. It rained down to Earth and fell in diamond form. When you found it and cut yourself, you must have transferred it into yourself. It explains why Orion has suddenly started to try and make contact with you."

I frown, "But how? When I found the diamond, it looked

like it had broken in half. I tried looking for the other piece, but nothing was there."

His eyes slide to the side, thinking. I've noticed it's his tell when he is thinking. This also gave me time to study his face a little more, noting on the side of his neck a scar that seemed to hide down under the shirt he is wearing. "You can't think of a time when you could have found the other half? His soul is active and obviously the sisters have sensed this, along with the other Guardians. This would not be happening if only half of his soul was inside you."

"I'm not sure. I went there a lot, but not so much after my mom died. Before then, not only me, but her and my dad would go there a lot, even before I was born." I picture my mom and dad sitting on the crater's edge, smiling and laughing at each other. "Could it be possible that one of them found the other half?"

"It has to be it. Most likely your mother. If she found the diamond and cut herself much like you, his soul would have gone inside her body. Whether or not it went to you in the womb or when she passed, well, I guess it does not matter which one. All we know is that as soon as the other half of the soul passed to you, you lit up like a beacon. Since we Guardians are created from his soul directly, we felt his presence. Alnilam noticed it as well. She sent Lupus down to kill you and take the soul back to her."

I thought of my first meeting with Theo. "When I first met him, he seemed so normal. He was even playing football!"

"That is one of his abilities. Every one of us, whether we are a Guardian or another being, has powers within us. Lupus has the ability to mimic a being they touch. If Theo, the human, had noticed you at all, Lupus surely mimicked the kid. He would have his memories, his personality, everything."

I close my eyes, wondering if I had met the real Theo at all, or if it had been Lupus the entire time. "What do you think happened to the real Theo then?"

"I'm sure you don't need me to answer that for you."

That answer hangs over my head like a storming rain cloud. An innocent guy, one who probably had a long, fulfilling life ahead of him, is now gone. An imposter is running around in his clothes, wearing his face, while the real one is rotting in the ground somewhere. Actually, who knows what Lupus did with him. I shudder just thinking about it.

"I think I need a moment," I tell Scorpio and slide off the couch, heading into the bathroom. I shut the door behind me and just lean against it. This is too much for just one person to take in. Friday morning, I woke up with my life completely normal. I was doing so well in school, life with my dad seemed to be improving, and of course, life threw a rock in my path.

I move to look in the mirror, looking at my shoulder. It is still ugly looking, but the color is pinker than it was. The shower helped, but my eyes are red and I look tired. I feel tired. My blue eyes, something of what Scorpio said, suddenly make me uncomfortable. He said he isn't sure whether or not the part of Orion's soul in my mother came to me when I was created in her or after she died. I realize now that I was born with this. My mother had told me before that I was born with the most beautiful blue eyes. They prickle with tears and once they start, I cannot stop them. I slide to the ground, sobbing.

I sit there for a long time with my face in my pulled-up knees when I hear the click of the door and feel Scorpio sit down next to me. "I understand this may be hard for you, but we need you. We need you to help us revive Orion and bring balance back. We *must* stop Alnilam and her sisters. If they manage to enact the spell, it will be the end of us all."

"I need to go home," I mumble without looking at him.

Scorpio sighs, "We need-"

"I know you *need* me," I snap. "I know that you need my help against the freaky sisters in space. But I need to go home. I can't leave my dad the way we left. He...We got into a fight and I left. I don't know if he is at home, but I have to make sure he is okay."

Hours ago, I wanted to get as far away from my dad as possible. Now? All I wanted to do was curl up on the couch with him with his arms around me, soothing my fears as he did when I was a little girl. I have never wanted my dad as much as I did now and I had to see him.

I thought that he would start protesting again, but Scorpio merely shrugs, "Fine. But we have to move on before Alnilam sends more of her minions after you."

I nod slowly and stand up. "Where are we anyway?" You would think it was the first question I would have asked when waking up. I know we were a couple of miles from the house earlier, but he said that we had gone a couple of hours from where we were.

"A safe house. We are outside of town where hopefully Lupus won't follow us. I'm sure he ran back to Alnilam with his tail between his legs," Scorpio says with a smug smile.

I frown, "He would have killed us both if you hadn't used that power. How come you didn't use it before then?"

He looks at his hand, flexing it open and close again,

before glancing back at me, "I'm not sure. When the sisters started their scheme, we were placed in a shell-like sphere that slowly drained our energy, causing Orion to constantly have to recharge us. That, in turn, made it hard for him to use his power to fight back. After Orion released his soul here to Earth, our bodies followed him like a beacon. But we lost track of it and ended up scattered. Since then, as far as I'm concerned, we have not had access to our powers. Not until that moment..."

His voice trails off and his head tilts as he thinks. I don't say anything and he finally looks back up at me, "Give me your hand." I hesitate for a moment before reaching out and placing my hand in his. I feel that same surge of energy I felt last time. "I knew it. Since Orion's soul now resides inside you, it means that the source of our powers is as well. When we make skin-to-skin contact, our powers must transfer to us. It seems to go away once we stop making contact. I wonder if it is as simple as that though," he says, almost absently as he studies our hands.

"So, how do I give you your powers back?" I take my hand back.

"I don't know. We need to find Regulus. He is the only one who knows how to put Orion's soul back in his body. He must also know how to give us our powers back. Hopefully, with some kind of permanence."

"Regulus?"

"Ah. Leo, as you know him."

I wrinkle my nose, "How come he has a different name and you don't?"

He shrugs, "It is what he chose. Orion gave us complete

freedom to do with our names as we wanted. Anyway, let's get back into town. Hopefully, we can avoid anything disastrous for the time being."

"Do you think he is going to come back?" His eyes darkened and they told me what I needed to know. "How long do you think we have?"

He doesn't answer me right away. "I'm not sure. Honestly, I am a little surprised we have not already seen signs of him. Alnilam is not going to want to waste time in bringing you back to revive Orion and finish the ritual." He stands and helps me to my feet. We walk out of the bathroom together. "We need to be prepared for anything."

I start to feel my stomach churn and my heart thumps hard in my chest. Either way, it sounds like someone is going to win, and I am stuck in the middle of their war. I am not even one hundred percent sure that I am with the good guys, but at least Scorpio has not tried to kill me yet. Tears well up in my eyes again, "My life is never going to be the same again, is it?"

Scorpio stops walking, turning back to where I am still standing in the same spot. He walks over to me, stepping directly in front of me and putting his hands on my shoulders. His eyes are intense as they stare into mine, "No, Faye. Your life is not going to be the same. You are going to fight and live. You are going to live with the knowledge that no other human is going to have. You are going to know that someone is watching over your world, keeping you safe. You will live, grow, have a family, become old, and perhaps become part of the stars as well. Your life will not be normal again, but something better."

I frown, "But what if I don't live?"

Scorpio smirks and shakes his head, "You're a Cancer, aren't you?"

"What's that supposed to mean?" He isn't wrong, but the assumption irks me.

"Cancer tends to give people a tender nature, and they are also more emotional than most."

"I am not emotional!"

His smirk doesn't go away, "You feel your emotions stronger than most, do you not? You tend to want to take care of everyone else first, and you're not very good with confrontation. Sound familiar?"

I feel unnecessarily called out. Usually, when reading the horoscopes online, it seems to be accurate about my sign, but I do not live by it. Everyone is different, no matter when they are born. "Whatever. Can we just go?" I shrug his hands off my shoulders and push my way around him, heading out of the small cabin.

When I walk through the threshold, a blast of cold air hits my face. I notice a little sedan sitting in front of the cabin. "You have a car?" I turn and see him locking the door behind us, the short swords he had earlier strapped to his back once again.

"You don't think I've been walking everywhere?"

We get into the vehicle and Scorpio backs all the way down a gravel path until turning onto a paved road. At the same time, little droplets of water start dripping onto the windshield. As the rain pours, we ride in silence. I glance over to Scorpio, who is watching the road diligently. He has obviously spent time driving, which for some reason surprised me.

I turn and look back out the window, resting my head against the cool glass. Everything around us is still dark. I realize that I am watching for any signs of a giant wolf running around. Paranoia is hitting me hard right now.

Faye. Do not be afraid. You will be all right.

Orion? I feel tense, the knowledge that someone else was inside my body is still sitting like a weird dream. I don't think I can bring myself to be comfortable with this, but if he is feeling in a chatty mood, maybe I can use this as an opportunity. The feeling that it was more than just Scorpio and I is strong. I even look in the backseat, but there is no one there. *I don't know which is better: knowing you are real and I did not have any freaky hallucinations, or the fact that I can't just sit in a padded room for the rest of my days.*

I can almost feel a smile in his voice as he replies, *I see you are more comfortable than you were before upon hearing me.* He becomes silent for a moment. *I'm sorry, Faye. I did not think that my soul would be found by one as young as you. Or your mother.*

Is all of this truly real?

A chuckle, *Yes. It is very real. Which is why you need to believe in Scorpio and my other Guardians. They will protect you until you can find Regulus and bring my soul back to me.*

And your sisters? How are we supposed to save you with them around?

I feel rage in my chest but I know it is not coming from me. I also know that the tears in my eyes are not my own. Alnilam's betrayal burns a fire in his soul and the effect it has on me is more than I thought it could be. Our connection is more than a ball of energy inside my body. Orion's soul is intertwined with my own.

My sisters have become my burden to bear. I cannot say what will happen now, but I do know that their schemes are unforgivable. I can only hope that everyone can remain safe.

My shoulders shake as I open my eyes, feeling Orion's presence return to its slumber in me once again. I wipe my eyes and catch Scorpio glancing in my direction. "Are you all right?"

I nod. "Orion. He spoke to me."

"Your souls must be linked together inside your body in order for him to speak to you so clearly. You are going to be able to understand him. However, we have to be careful. We do not know what effect his soul being in your body will have and Alnilam will not wait forever. Eventually, she may choose to be rid of Orion's body altogether and find another way to release her and her sisters out of the galaxy." Scorpio's hands grip the steering wheel tightly. It must be really frustrating for him. I know my life has been hard, but I don't think I can compare. Orion and the other Guardians are his family, and now they are separated from each other. We lull into a silence once again and I end up falling asleep, still tired from the events from earlier.

My body suddenly lurches forward hard and I yelp as the seat belt catches. Tires screech as the car comes to a halt. I turn to yell at Scorpio but stop myself upon seeing his face. His eyes are narrowed and his jaw is clenched. I follow the direction he is looking and my eyes widen as I see the view in front of me. I throw my seat belt off and hear Scorpio call my name as I throw myself out of the car. We are standing on the side of the road up on the hill with the town in front of us.

The town is now ablaze with flames higher than the forest trees.

CHAPTER SEVEN

"No. No, no. No!" I shout and I immediately take off toward the town. I hear Scorpio curse behind me and know he is following close behind. He grabs my arm and yanks me backward to a painful halt. I wince as my arm pops, but it doesn't come out of place, but damn it hurts! The motion causes my feet to slide and I slip to the ground. Pulling my arm out of his grip. I get myself back up and start toward town again, but once again, Scorpio stops me.

"Faye!" Scorpio shouts and his hands manage to grab my shirt, pulling me against him as we tumble down to the ground.

"*Get off me!*" I scream. Scorpio manages to pin me under him and I struggle against him. "Get off! We have to get down there! We have to-"

"Faye, stop!" Scorpio's hands tighten around my wrists. I realize then how much stronger he is than me physically.

I stop fighting against him, my breath coming out ragged,

"Scorpio. We have to go down there. We have to help them. My dad...Luke..." Hundreds of thoughts looped inside my mind. All the people I grew up with were caught in the inferno and I have to find some way to help them. I have to hope that my dad decided to go out of town, whether it be out of rage from our argument or the simple need to continue to drink and pass out somewhere. Hope that Luke was able to get to Martin's house and get everyone away from town.

"We will go, but we have to be careful. This is Lupus's doing, I can feel it. If we are careless, we will be falling right into his hands. We will get your family out. I need you to stay close to me. Can you do that?"

We stared at each other for the longest time before finally I nod. I know that I cannot do it by myself, but maybe having a celestial being next to me will be enough. Scorpio lifts himself off me and pulls me up. We stare at the town engulfed in flames. I can hear the sirens of fire trucks. I flinch as I hear the sound of gunshots. I turn toward Scorpio, the question in my eyes answered by the answer in his.

Theo.

We both run toward the town, leaving the car behind. I hear the howl come from the east side of town. I run ahead of Scorpio, leading him the way to my house. I just hoped that Theo stayed wherever he was long enough we could get to my loved ones and get out of there. Everything is so hot. Cars and houses alike are burning. A car explodes near us and Scorpio grabs my arm, pulling me away and shielding me from the blast. He curses and looks around, trying to see if there is any part of town that isn't caught on fire. He finally motions to an alleyway across the street from us and when

I nod confirmation that it will take us where we need to go, he takes us across the street. I let him ahead of me. I can feel my body shake with a fear I have never felt before. Scorpio leads us through the areas the fire hasn't spread as I give him directions to my house. I feel relieved when it comes into view and I see that it is untouched by the flames. I see my father's truck in the driveway and I race ahead. I get to the door and rattle the handle, finding it locked.

"I don't have my keys!" I shout frantically. I start banging on the door with my fist, "Dad? Dad! Are you in there?" I call, hoping that he is unharmed and more importantly, not passed out drunk.

"Move," Scorpio takes a step away from the doorway and brings his leg up. I step to the side as he kicks the door open, splintering the wood frame. He shoves it open and I make my way past him into the house. It is dark and when I try to turn the lights on, nothing happens. "The fires must have taken down the transformers across town. Do you have your phone?"

I shake my head. Everything was left in my car, which is still at Martin's. But I know this house like the back of my hand. Entering the living room, I guide us past the furniture and into the threshold of the kitchen. The dining room table is off to the side and we start moving toward the back of the house, toward the hallway that leads to our rooms. As we slowly move through the house, my foot slips in something wet and I have to catch myself on the counter to brace myself. The counter is wet as well and I try to see in the dark what it could be. "Can you make any kind of light? There is something here," I turn toward Scorpio, and before I finish, a small light forms in Scorpio's hand. I glare at him. "I thought you couldn't access your power."

"We have touched several times since I used my power against Lupus when I first found you." I glare at him, the way he says it so casually causes an uncomfortable buzz in my stomach. "Since I can still use it, the power must be stored in my body until I am in need of it, but we can theorize later. We need to find-" his words cut off as his eyes land on the floor in front of me.

I follow his line of sight and my stomach lurches violently. There is blood everywhere. On the floor, on the counter, and on my hand. It leads to the other side of the kitchen and into the hallway. I have never seen so much before. Horror movies do not prepare you for seeing this kind of thing in real life. It explains the strange smell in the air as well. "Scorpio, you don't think…"

"I don't know. I have a bad feeling, though. Stay here." I don't miss the brush of his hand against my arm and the slight surge of power that transfers between the two of us as he walks away to the back of the house. I don't even hear the creaking of the wooden floor, another tribute to Scorpio's supernatural being. I wait there, holding my breath until I can't help myself and I slowly move from the spot I'm standing in, being careful to step in the cleaner parts of the floor. I walk around the counter and peer down the hallway. Just as I look around the corner, Scorpio's light disappears into my father's room. I continue to step slowly until I hear Scorpio curse, which causes my feet to freeze in place.

Without warning, Scorpio's body comes flying out of the bedroom, crashing into the wall. The glass from the window next to him shatters from the force. He rolls away, narrowly being missed by the dresser that flies at him. He rolls and comes up, backing up toward me, his long daggers in each hand.

A form walks out of the bedroom, holding something in his hand. "Guardian. I was hoping that you would show up. I see you brought me my guest of honor. I threw this party just for her, after all." I recognize the voice and now that my eyes are adjusted, I can see him. I flinch as the house next door suddenly bursts into flames, the fire illuminating the hallway and Theo. He looks just as he did the first day I met him and every day since. Except this time, his charming smile is accompanied by splattered blood all over him.

It is then I look down at what Theo is holding in his hands. I grab onto Scorpio, clutching his shirt as I see black spots in my vision and my legs threaten to collapse under me. Theo grins, showing his sharp canines, "I was hoping you would have come home sooner. Dressing those wounds I assume. You look like nothing even happened earlier. Since you were out longer than expected, your father was kind enough to keep me entertained. Don't worry. I made sure he suffered," and he heaves the object in his hand in our direction.

My father's face rolls up to stare at me, the look of shock still there. His eyes are clouded over with white, his face pale from fear. A scream rips out of my throat and Theo launches toward us at the same time, changing form as he does. Scorpio wraps an arm around me and throws us out of the way before Theo can get to us. We charge out of the hallway and I slip on blood, pulling Scorpio off balance and to the floor. Theo flies over us and lands, sliding across the floor.

"Faye! We have to go!" Scorpio grabs my arm and hauls us up. With the surge of energy running from me to him, he is able to turn around, splay out his hand, and hit Theo with an invisible force. It throws him hard into the side of the house, causing the wall to collapse around him. Scorpio keeps us moving and out of the house. A howl pierces through the air and I wince. "Where is your friend's house?" Scorpio asks me as we run down the steps and onto the road once again.

"What?" I look at him, my eyes going wide as I hear a chorus of howls around us.

"You mentioned someone else! Where are they?" We hear the pounding of footsteps in the direction we had come earlier. From the smoke, we see a pack of wolves charging in our direction. Scorpio curses, something I notice he does an awful lot, and we are suddenly heading in the opposite direction. I take a chance and look behind us, watching Theo stagger out of the house. He snarls and barks at the pack of wolves that surround him. They howl in unison and once again they run in our direction. Scorpio turns sharply down an alley and I have to put an arm out to stop myself from running into a brick wall. Debris from the buildings fall around us, but I look back to see Theo snarling as he cannot get through with his large size. He seems to bark at something around him and when he backs up, the smaller wolves charge through.

"Scorpio!" I shout and without hesitation, Scorpio grabs my hand and pushes me against the brick wall. A panic blooms in my chest and a thousand images of him throwing me to the wolves come to mind. Instead, he suddenly crushes his mouth against mine. A new sense of confusion courses through me and I briefly feel what I think is his tongue against my own and a wave of dizziness washes over me, my breath rushing out of my lungs. It is no more than two seconds and then Scorpio turns toward the hoard of wolves. He brings his hands up and closes his fists, bringing them down. At the same time, the walls between us explode outward. I gasp and shield my head, although most of the destruction is laid out in front of us. The building's structure falls on top of the wolves, crushing them underneath the rubble. I look up to see Theo through the opening of the alley, the fury in his eyes evident.

I slump against the wall and Scorpio grabs my hand once again, taking off at a run. It is harder this time because I just do not have the strength to move as we were. I feel sluggish and I have to wonder what exactly happens when Scorpio uses me to energize himself.

We reach the end of the alleyway and Scorpio scans around us, not seeing any more of the wolves at the moment. "Where are we going, Faye?"

I pant and get my bearings. The buildings next to us are the small library and the post office. Luke's house is on the other side of town. I have to squint through the clouds of smoke and point straight ahead. A siren whoops to the side of us and we turn to see an officer get out of his vehicle. It is not one I recognize, which means he must have come from the next town over. "You kids okay?" When we nod, he glances around before peering back at us, "You need to get out of here and head toward the edge of town."

"Just trying to figure out the safest way. Our brother lives a couple of blocks that way and we need to make sure he is all right," Scorpio tightens his grip on my hand, the reassurance is subtle but effective. I don't know how he managed to pull the lie out of thin air and make it sound convincing, but the officer nods.

"All right, come on. I don't know what the hell is going on, but I can at least make sure you guys are safe. We will head over to pick up your brother on the way."

We hurry to the car. Scorpio opens the back door for me and helps me inside. "We appreciate this, sir," Scorpio says as the officer opens the driver's door.

"You don't have to thank me for doing my job, son. This looks like a gas line blew, but we won't know for sure until we get this fire down. Either way, let's-"

One moment we are safe, and the next the officer's words are cut off by a large set of teeth clamping down on the man's head and squeezing. Theo skids to a stop in front of the car, mouth dripping with blood as he lets the officer's body slump to the ground. What used to be the officer's head is now a mass of blood and brain matter. I gasp and cover my mouth, watching in horror as Theo walks on and over the body, hearing the ribs crack under the pressure of the wolf's weight. Scorpio reacts quickly, slamming my door shut and sliding into the passenger front seat. Theo sprints toward us, slamming himself into the car, causing the windshield to crack and the front crumple.

"Dammit! This fleabag just doesn't know when to quit!" Scorpio quickly slides into the driver's seat of the vehicle, locking the doors around us. Theo crashes into the front of the vehicle again, completely shattering the windshield. Scorpio ducks down and away as Theo tries to claw his way through the opening, snapping his jaws. Scorpio uses that moment to put the car in drive and pushes the gas, the tires squealing as we are thrown backward. I am about to yell at Scorpio, but he seems to read my mind and he slams onto the breaks, throwing Theo off the front of the vehicle and onto the ground. Scorpio puts it back into drive and weaves around the wolf.

"Faye!" Scorpio demands my attention from Theo as I stare at him behind us. His teeth are bared and the bloodlust is overwhelming in his gaze. I manage to tear my eyes from the wolf and back to Scorpio. "We have to get out of here. Is there any chance your friend may have already left town?"

"I...I'm not sure. Luke would have gone over to his grandparents' house." Luke would have gotten his family out of danger's path quickly, but there is no telling how Martin would be when it came to the bar. "We need to make sure they get out! Head left at those traffic lights and-"

A thump on top of the car breaks off my sentence and the next thing I know, claws are ripping through the top of the roof. I sink down into the seat as the screech of metal causes Scorpio to veer the car sharply around the corner. We both know who is on top of the vehicle, and he is not going to stop until we are both dead. Or at least, as close as he can make me before bringing me to Alnilam and the rest of her psycho sisters. I look around for anything that could help us, but police cruisers are not known for keeping anything that could be considered a weapon in the back where criminals could get their hands on it.

Theo manages to tear a large hole in the top of the car, his jaws snapping, trying to get his way into the vehicle with us. I climb to the other side of the backseat, down into the floorboards. "Scorpio, do something!" I scream as a massive paw reaches through, his claw tearing the seats. The more he struggles, the bigger the hole is becoming. Scorpio glances back in the rearview mirror and then I feel the car gain speed. "*Scorpio!*"

"Hang on!" He shouts and I hear the faint click of a seatbelt. It dawns on me what he plans on doing and I scramble my way into the seat, frantically trying to put my own seatbelt on. Theo's claw reaches in and hooks onto the seatbelt, pulling it from my grasp. "Goddammit!" I reach up and grab the seatbelt, trying to wrestle it from Theo's claw. I hear Scorpio shout, but don't make out the words. I manage to get the seatbelt away and barely get it clicked in before we crash into a brick wall. I feel the seat belt catch, but the force throws me forward. I cry out as the material digs into my skin and crushes me. I get whiplash and the car jumps from hitting something, tilting to the right, and I hit my head against the window. I hear the crack of the glass and I blackout.

I hear Scorpio calling my name and I slowly blink my eyes open. I look up, my vision blurry, but I can make out Scorpio in the front seat. We are still in the police car and I start looking around. "He's not here." He says, reassuring me. I look at him, watching as he finally gives up trying to undo the seatbelt and just takes one of his blades, cutting it off of him. My head is pounding and when I go to touch the spot, my hand comes back with blood on it. *I must have hit it harder on the window than I thought.* The blood on the window confirms my suspicions and I notice Scorpio crawling out the front of the car where the windshield used to be. I undo my seatbelt and try to open my door, but it won't open. Scorpio appears at my window. "Back up to the other side. The doors are all jammed, I have to break the window."

I scoot backward and have to close my eyes against the wave of nausea that hits me. I look away and cover my face as Scorpio breaks the window. I crawl back over, careful to avoid sliding on the glass, and let Scorpio help me out of the window. I wince, "I think I have a concussion."

Scorpio carefully parts my hair where I hit my head, "You may be right. That looks like a nasty cut, but doesn't look to be bleeding too much. We need to be careful. I don't know where Lupus went after we crashed into the building, but I know the bastard can't be feeling too good. Come on." He takes my hand and we make our way over the debris and out of the building.

When we stop out of the building, I can't help the little gasp that escapes my mouth. The whole town is on fire. Buildings are collapsed, cars are wrecked in the street. And the blood. There is blood everywhere and I can see bodies littering the ground. This must have been the work of Theo and his wolves. Tears well up in my eyes and fall down my cheeks. I feel Scorpio squeeze my hand, "Your friend's house? Faye, we have to go."

"Okay…" I whisper and I start walking, guiding us in the direction of Martin's house. We hear the howls start to fade around us and as we get closer, the house comes into view. "Oh my god." We stop and watch as flames envelop the house, the roof collapsing in front of us. I notice there are not any cars in the driveway, "They aren't there. Martin's truck was here earlier. They must have taken it and gone to the next town over. They're safe."

Scorpio nods, "Good. Let's get out of here ourselves." He takes the lead and we find a black sedan left in the middle of the road. Lucky for us, the keys were still in the ignition and it started up right away. I slip into the passenger seat and Scorpio guides the car through the streets. "We need to get out of range. Lupus's sense of smell is greater than any animal alive. Hopefully, he crawled into a hole and died, but I don't think we are that lucky."

"No. We're not."

CHAPTER EIGHT

week following my father's death and the burning
of my town, I step in line next to Scorpio at the
airport. It took a couple of days of planning, but
he managed to secure a way for us to get out of the country.
He left me alone for those few days we were heading to the
airport, knowing I needed them to grieve. Everything and
everyone I had grown up with was gone. I have no idea if Luke
and Martin are all right. I am hoping that they were able to
escape the carnage that ensued. But deep down, a feeling of
dread made itself at home. If Theo went after my father, then
there are no guarantees he did not go after everyone else I
loved as well.

We drove for two days out of Iowa, heading south until
we hit Atlanta. Every time I closed my eyes, haunting images
appeared. The one that scared me the most was the moment
my father's eyes looked into mine, lifeless. Theo had said his
death was horrible, and my father's face showed that it was
not painless. Scorpio, regardless of how far we went, was

always patient with me on the ride down. He helped me when I needed ait nd said some comforting words every now and then. This was not his forte, I could tell, but it made me feel better nonetheless.

Once we hit Atlanta, we stayed in a cheap motel for a couple of more days. Alone in my room, I cried. I cried until I couldn't anymore. Scorpio would bring me food here and there, but most of it would sit without being touched. I just didn't have the stomach for it. Theo is following us, I know that. He isn't going to stop tearing my life apart until he has me in his jaws, taking me to his master. I couldn't let that happen. I believe Scorpio, everything he has told me. How could I not? The proof kept revealing itself to me at every turn, but I had been still wanting to be blind to the whole story. I keep thinking that maybe, if I had believed him from the beginning, would things have turned out the same way?

Probably.

I don't know when it happened, but eventually my tears turned into anger. I was angry at Theo for destroying everything, for coming after me. I was angry at my father for the fight we had that night. Maybe he would still be alive if I had been home. I was angry at Scorpio for not acting sooner. Mostly I was angry at myself. I shouldn't have been digging where I shouldn't have. If I had just left that place alone, I wouldn't have found the other half of Orion's heart. I wouldn't have him talking to me, have supernatural beings after me, and my life would still be normal. I know my anger would do no good without something to give it an outlet. Otherwise, I would just sit in that hotel room and rage and who would that help?

So I decided to learn more. Scorpio told me about the other Guardians, as well as Orion and his sisters. He told me about their use of magic and how each of them was different, but all could still use the basics. Every Guardian uses elemental magic, but some are stronger in areas than others. And then there were different uses of certain elements that each of them could use. "We can get to those a little bit at a time," he said.

Scorpio told me a little more about his own powers. During a certain time of year, when summer is in the midst of turning into autumn, is when his powers are the greatest. His main element is water, which is where he is the strongest. Earth is an affiliation of water, so he can use that proficiency as well, but not as well as those Guardians whose main powers lie with the Earth element.

"Is that what you did those other times? When you blasted away Theo and then with the buildings?" I asked one night, while we were sitting on the bed in my room. I leaned against the lime colored wallpaper while he sat ccross-leggedat the other end.

He nodded, "Yes. I displaced the air and then, because brick is technically made of Earthly materials, I was able to move it."

"You were able to do more the second time though, right? Is that because your powers are coming back?"

He shook his head, "I don't think so. I feel the faintest flicker of power now, but that's it. I believe it's because I found a stronger outlet for you to transfer power back to me."

"Stronger outlet. What are you talking about?" My mind goes back to the event. It was all a blur at the time; us running from Theo, going into the alley, the wolves chasing us, Scorpio pulling the walls down on top of the wolves. "I don't under-stand-" Scorpio raises a brow at me, catching me off guard, and I suddenly remember. It was such a small moment, I almost did not register it enough to remember. I feel a flush on my face and I cross my arms, "What does that have to do with your powers being stronger?"

"Well, it's possible that the more of you that touches me, the more that transfers, and the more power I get." How does he not realize what he sounds like? He seems to ignore my flaming face and continues, "When my hand touches yours, I'm guessing the oils from your hand is what worked before. In the alley, your saliva. If that's the case, then your blood is what would probably give me the most power." The color instantly drained from my face and the room felt so much smaller. Scorpio chuckles and rolls his eyes, "Don't worry, Faye. I have no intention of taking your blood. It makes sense though. It means we have to be even more careful. We get our powers directly from Orion's soul, but everything is created by Orion in some way. If your blood works for us, in greater amounts, it will work for anything else."

"So, if Theo were to get a hold of me, what could he do? Drain my blood? Be a wolf on steroids? Great. Things just keep getting better and better for me, doesn't it?"

"It could be worse."

"How?"

"You could already be in the hands of Alnilam and having Orion's soul sucked out of you, likely ending your own life along with it," he reasons and it gives me chills.

"That's true." We sit in silence for a few moments. "Have I thanked you yet for saving me, again?"

"Yes, I believe you have." We gave each other a smile. We talked a bit more until I finally had to call it quits at about 1 in the morning.

Now, after a week of resting and planning, we are standing in line to get on a plane to go to the Bahamas. Scorpio told me of a couple of the other Guardians that were waiting in the town of Duncan. Leaving the country makes me both excited and anxious. Scorpio was able to get us both passports and any other documentation we may need for traveling. I know he had mentioned that the Guardians were scattered around the world, but I was hoping he was exaggerating and that they were all in the states.

No such luck.

We make our way to the assigned seats on our tickets. I hesitate and turn to him, "Can you sit by the window?"

He gives me a quizzical head tilt, "Why?"

"Um," I glance at the line forming behind us, "Never mind," I say and slide into the chair. He puts his bag in the overhead above us and sits down next to me. I close the little screen for the window, not wanting to look outside. After about twenty minutes, someone goes over the rules and safety precautions for the flight and a few minutes later, we are moving along the runway. The movement is slow at first, but the plane stops for a second before heading down the main strip. It picks up speed and my stomach lurches as I feel the plane rise up off the ground. I grip the armrests and lean back against the seat, closing my eyes.

"Faye?" Scorpio asks, but I don't open my eyes.

"What?"

"Are you good?"

I have to swallow hard, "Yeah, I'm fine." I can feel him staring at me. "Okay, so I'm not okay. I have never been on a plane before and heights freak me out."

Scorpio snorts, trying not to laugh at me, "That makes more sense. Would you like to switch with me?"

I feel the plane tilt further upward, "I'm okay. Just...tell me when it's over." I say. The sensation of the plane reaching altitude makes my stomach drop. *It feels like I'm floating. Except I'm thirty thousand feet in the air in a mechanical trap that could fail at any second.* I can tell the plane levels out a minute later but I still can't relax. The turbulence hits and I mentally prepare myself for the plane to start falling out of the sky.

A larger hand grips mine and I open my eyes, glancing down. I look over to see Scorpio with his eyes closed as well, except he looks as though he is just sleeping. But the slight squeeze of his hand tells me he is awake. Is he trying to make me feel better? I smile and lean my head back. I decide to take a chance and look out the window. I open the little window slightly, and my eyes widen in surprise at the view. It looks so green from up here. Buildings are tiny and the clouds form to look like rivers. Now I am wishing I had my phone on me. Turbulence hits us the whole time we are in the air, jostling me around. By the time we reach the next airport, my nerves are completely shot. My only saving grace was Scorpio's ever calm presence next to me.

Once we are off the plane we head inside to get the rest of our things. Somehow, Scorpio managed to buy us quite a few things we would need on our trip. I never bothered asking him where he had the means to get all the money, as well as identification. I would rather not have another thing to feel guilty about on my conscious. Besides, it is not as though we went into the stores and robbed them. We paid for everything. Just…with possibly stolen money. We grab our luggage from the conveyor belt and head outside. "We are almost there. We will catch a cab. From there, we will get onto a smaller plane to head to Duncan."

The thought of getting on another plane made me queasy. "Where we will find, who, again?"

"Aquarius. Cancer. Capricorn. Three of the other Guardians." He glances around and waves a hand for a cab to stop. We set our things in the trunk and slide into the back seat.

"You do all of this so naturally. Are you sure you're from space?" I ask, earning a questionable glance from the driver upfront. I shoot him a smile and he turns to look back at the road, even though I am sure he is still listening to the conversation.

"We were all required to spend some time here. Orion said that if something were to ever happen where we would have to spend time on land, we should at least be able to blend in. The less confusion and chaos we spread, the better it would be to resolve issues. At least, that is what we had hoped." His eyes cast downward, both of us remembering the scene from Hamilton. The destruction of the town has both of us uneasy. It wasn't the fault of either of us, but I cannot help but think that it would have been better if Theo had just taken me the first time he attacked. Then, just maybe, my town and everyone inside would still be standing.

"I guess he thinks of everything, huh?"

"Well, he has been around for a long time."

I look out the window to look at the surrounding area. "Do you think Theo followed us here?"

Scorpio nods, "Most likely. Knowing Alnilam, he will not take the chance to go back to her until he has you with him. He already messed up twice. She will not settle for the third time. I have a feeling that when he destroyed the town, it was a desperate attempt at bringing you back. Lupus has that keen sense of smell also. I'm sure he will not be too far behind."

I feel the goosebumps rise on my arms at the thought of Theo stalking us. As we continue on the drive, I unconsciously look for any giant wolves that could be lurking in the shadows. Or a really good-looking college kid with beautiful eyes and a killer smile. He could be anywhere around us and no one would know better that he is in reality a giant wolf looking to kill us. Well, kill Scorpio. He is just taking me to have a soul ripped out of me by three psychotic sisters who want to destroy the universe and then leave the ruins. I guess that would kill me also.

"Don't worry. I don't think he will be able to pinpoint us completely. Once we find the safe house, we will create a barrier that will prevent anything from getting inside. It is going to take a while for the mutt to find his way in." Scorpio crosses his arms and even though he isn't smiling, I swear there is a smugness there. I have to keep reminding myself that before the events that took place between the Guardians and the sisters, they all lived together. That must include Theo and whatever other monster is waiting for us. What could the sisters have told them to make them betray and go against the being who created them?

"That's good. But how? I understand that there are three Guardians there, but how are they able to keep Theo out without their powers?"

"Ah, well, that is where you will come in," Scorpio shrugs. "When we get there, hopefully, we can maintain enough of our powers in order to build a solid foundation."

I frown, "How many times am I going to be used as a battery for you guys? It felt like I had run a two day marathon when you used your power last time."

Scorpio tilts his head, "When I used Earth, it did seem to take a toll on you. I don't know how this works, but I don't think your body can handle the amount of energy being consumed. I can only assume your soul is intertwined with Orion's by this point. This barrier will require a bit more than I used the other day. I'm sure Camden will be able to do more with you around anyway by himself. The barrier will not be as I would like it to be, but it should be enough."

"Camden?"

"Cancer. Like Regulus, he has chosen to use a different name than what he was given. I believe it is because he doesn't like to be associated with the name of cancer that humans have given diseases. You were born in June?"

"Close, July. How did you know?"

"We can feel the association of humans with certain Guardians. You have the same energy as Camden, so you must have been born during the time he was on Earth. This is why his power should be enough to create a decent barrier with you."

"Is that because of when I was born?"

He nods. "Cancer is the youngest of us born, so his control over his powers isn't as stable as ours. It's why those born under this time of the year tend to bring about their personalities more strongly. But, with that being said, you and Camden have a bond that you wouldn't have with the rest of us. It's possible that he will be able to get more power with you without actually taking as much energy."

"Let's hope that is true. I can barely handle one of you sapping power out of me let alone four of you," I put my chin in my hand and rest my elbow on the window. We drive another twenty minutes until we get to a small airport. Scorpio leads us through until we find a smaller plane, one of those that only fit two or three people besides the pilot. Scorpio is talking to someone, who helps us load our luggage into the small plane. "Being in a big airplane was bad enough, but now we are getting into a smaller death trap? Don't these things crash more than the big ones?"

A boisterous laugh behind me makes me jump as I see a rather large man behind me. He grins at me and pats the metal of the plane, "You don't fly very much, do ya?" I scowl. I can't say anything because I'm still working on getting my stomach out of my throat and I also don't feel like letting him know he is absolutely right. "These little buggers get more maintenance and care than commercial planes. I have never once had Matilda fail on me, and we aren't going to start today!"

"Matilda?"

He nods proudly, his hands on his hips, "That's my girl. She will never let ya down. I guarantee it!"

His mood is infectious and I find myself smiling, "All right, I believe you."

"Rusty, at your service, young lady! Now, let us get a move on. Rain is supposed to be coming in," he says as he helps me into the plane, Scorpio following suit. Rusty pulls himself into the plane and looks back at us, "Make sure you strap in tight. Those headsets next to you will allow you to talk to each other. Just push that red button if you want to talk to me. Otherwise, enjoy the ride!"

We put on our headsets and seatbelts. The little plane shakes as it starts up and I feel my stomach churn and I am starting to regret my decision to agree to this. "Are you sure we have to take this to the island? Can't we just take a boat? Or swim even?"

Scorpio gives me a sideways smile, "You know, being in the sky isn't so bad. It is a freeing feeling. I will admit, it is better outside of the plane, but it is still nice."

"As nice as being in space?"

"Oh, no. Nothing is better than being among the stars. Perhaps one day you will know what that feels like." His smile falters for a second as I see a flash of sadness in his eyes. *He must miss home*, I think to myself. I hope we can get this all settled quickly. I don't want to spend the rest of my life running to protect it. I want to go back home. I want to have a proper funeral for my father and cry for his loss without something trying to eat me. I'm sure Scorpio is wishing to be back with his family as well. The other Guardians and Orion. I'm sure they are all striving to make everything normal again.

We head down the runway, the little plane lifting into the air. I whimper a little, but once again, Scorpio takes my hand. It is the reassurance I need to get myself through this. I spend the next hour staring out the window, mostly to make sure the plane does not go down. The scenery is unlike anything I have seen though. Flying over the states is nice, but this is downright gorgeous. We spend a lot of time over the water and I swear I see a whale here and there. We see land every now and then, the islands scattered throughout the ocean. I can see towns on the islands that look as small as my town of Hamilton, maybe a little bigger depending on the island. Then there are the smaller islands that look just green from the lack of population.

I look over at Scorpio, "This is awesome. Is this what you guys see when you are up there?"

He thinks about it, "Sort of. When we get closer it's easier to spot specific places, but from our home, it's more like the pictures you see of Earth from space. The continents have large pieces of land and a lot of water surrounding them. Clouds cover the surface a lot of the time, but it is still quite the sight." He glances out the window, "Are you still scared?"

"A little," I admit, "but it is not as bad as it was in the larger plane. The scenery makes it a whole lot better."

We spend the rest of the ride in silence, the occasional remark from Rusty from upfront, giving us information oaboutthe islands we pass. Eventually, we make it to the main island and start circling around it, slowly descending until we hear the radio confirmation that Rusty can land. I can't help but close my eyes as we head downwards. I know we aren't going to crash but the fear of ending up in the bottom of the ocean keeps me rigid in my seat. Before I know it, I'm jostled by the plane touching down and my eyes snap open, noting how we are on land and nounderwaterer.

"Perfect landing again, Matilda! You folks still back there?" Rusty glances back at us with a more than proud grin. I give him a tight smile as Scorpio is already unbuckling and tearing his headset off. Rusty clambers out of his seat as well, coming around to our side of the plane. Scorpio jumps down and turns to offer his hand to me. I take it and jump down out of the plane, Rusty working on getting our bags.

A thought occurs to me as I feel the sensation of power rushing between our fingertips. I draw my hand away from him, earning a brow raise from Scorpio, but he doesn't say anything about it. He helps Rusty to get the rest of our baggage out of the plane as I stand to the side. I look down at my hand, rubbing my thumb over my palm. I feel tired, and I realize that Scorpio has been holding my hand the whole time we have traveled. All that time, getting energy from me. I'm not sure if he is doing it intentionally, but it still makes me uncomfortable thinking about it.

"Well," Rusty says, pulling me from my thoughts, "it was nice meeting you folks."

"You too, Rusty. Thank you for getting us here," I say with a smile.

He returns it with a wide grin of his own, "My pleasure, little lady. I better be off. Matilda and I have more flying to do! Feel free to book with us any time!" With a tip of his cap, he turns and walks toward the small building that serves as the airport here, heading toward a door that has a large maintenance sign above it.

We head inside ourselves, heading where fliers go, and toward a large map inside a glass box. It seems to be a map of the whole island, which is crazy because the eternity of the island seems like it could fit inside Texas. Scorpio studies for a moment before pointing to a spot far up on the northeast side of the island. "This is where we are meeting the others. It looks like it will take us a couple of hours to get there, but we should be there before it gets dark. Come on," he picks up his duffle bag and hauls it over his shoulder, heading toward the doors.

I continued to stare at the map for a moment and my eyebrows furrowed in confusion. I turn and jog, catching up to Scorpio, "You do realize that this island is small right? How is it going to take that long to get there? It is not like we are walking there." He continues moving his feet. I stop and stare at him with my mouth open. "Are you kidding me? We are seriously going to walk there after spending *hours* inside planes?" He doesn't say anything, just continues walking. I curse under my breath and hurry to catch up to him. "You, sir, are a sadist." I don't get a response from him, but the corner of his mouth twitches.

A couple of hours later, when my feet are sore and bruised, we reach a gravel path off the main road. Winding its way up a hill, I can see a lighthouse sitting at the top, accompanied by what looks like a large, brick house. Walking closer, I swear it looks like a scene that should be on a postcard. The house is two stories from what I can tell, with a large chimney coming out the top. Smoke bebillowsut of the top and I cannot explain the sudden need to curl up in front of it and fall asleep. The lighthouse itself doesn't look to be anything special. Tall, white, and the circling light is already on for everyone to see. I don't understand how it is supposed to be a safe house when there is a big light that is practically pointing at our location.

As we get closer to the house, a figure walks out. I slowly fall behind Scorpio. I don't know why I have the need to use him as a protective shield, but the way the figure has their arms crossed and is staring down at us, it makes me nervous. Scorpio stops in front of the man. They stare each other down and it gives me a moment to study the new stranger. He is built almost the same as Scorpio, but whereas Scorpio has rugged features to him, this man looks like he should be a corporate monger. His sharp features were added by the dark suit he wore, black and gray peppered hair slicked back from his forehead. He has a dark goatee and his eyes are a dull gold, almost like amber. I notice a gold stud in his right ear.

"Capricorn," Scorpio says.

"Scorpio. You're late. As usual," the gruff voice replied.

He shrugs, "Got held up. Had a giant fleabag of a wolf who wouldn't heel."

"Lupus? Have you taken care of him?"

Scorpio sighs, "No. Not completely. Last I checked, he is still alive and kicking. I'm sure he won't be far behind. We need to get a barrier up around the place as soon as possible. Faye here is affiliated with Camden. He should be enough by himself."

Upon hearing my name, Capricorn finally turns his attention to me. He studies me for a moment before his features soften. "Faye. A pleasure to finally meet you. Scorpio had sent word that he had found the vessel for Orion's soul, but failed to mention how young the vessel was. Come in, child." He shoots Scorpio a quick look, something in his eyes that makes Scorpio smile sheepishly, before we head into the house.

The house itself has a homey feel to it. There is a large, wood burning fireplace that gives the living room warmth. Turning to the left, we follow Capricorn into the living room, where two more people are waiting for us. One of them jumps to his feet, a wide smile on his face, "Scorpio! You finally made it!" He looks no older than me by a couple of years. His sandy blonde hair stops short of his eyes and as he bounds over to us, I can see little freckles across his nose. He has bright blue eyes, almost like mine, but a little darker. "I was telling Aquarius and Cap that you were going to take another whole year to find us. I'm glad you proved me wrong," his smile never leaves his face as he finally turns to me. "You must be Faye." He has the energy of a puppy.

"Leave them alone, Camden," a voice answers before I have a chance to. I look behind Camden to see where the voice came from. Another man is walking over toward us. He is tall like Capricorn, but more slender. He has long, pale blue hair that looks almost silver. It holds a stark contrast to his emerald green eyes. Perched on the end of his nose is a pair of wire, rimmed glasses. "I'm sure their journey here has been a long one." He is looking at me as he says it.

The boy, Camden, frowns, "Yeah, I guess you're right."

Capricorn leans against the wall next to them, "Faye. This is Aquarius and Camden, otherwise known as Cancer."

I blink at Camden, "Cancer. That means you were in charge of Earth when I was born."

He smiles, "That's right. I knew I felt something when

you walked in the door. A connection of sorts. That's why I can sense your feelings and I'm sorry."

"For what?"

"For whatever is causing your grief. We haven't heard the details of your trip here, but we do know that Lupus had found you. If that is the case, then bad things must have happened."

I don't know why, but I feel frustrated at his comments. How could he know what I have been through? I have to stop myself, for their curiosity is nothing to be mad about. Of course, they would want to know what happened with Theo. Plus, they are practically in the same boat as me, so instead of snapping I say, "You could say that."

"Well, if you wanna talk about it, I'm sure I could lend an ear."

"Right, thanks." I glance over at Scorpio, "Wasn't there something about a barrier you were talking about?"

"Anxious, are you?" When I scowl at him, he sighs. "Right. I guess we should get this taken care of. Lupus is sure to be on his way here."

Aquarius frowns, "Surely it would take him some time before reaching us, if he can even find our location."

"Trust me, he will know. That damn dog can find anything. He has Faye's scent and once he catches it, he will have no issues following it here."

Aquarius looks troubled and Capricorn remains silent. "So, we are going to make the barrier, me and..." It's going to be interesting trying to remember all of these names.

"Camden," Scorpio nods. "Aquarius can tell you more about that. Since you and Camden have the stronger bond out of all of us, his power will be stronger than it would be coming from us."

Aquarius nods, "Yes. I know it has been a long day, but we must ask this of you before Lupus or anyone else can find us. I can now assume that Scorpio has told you a little bit of our roles and powers?"

"Yeah, a bit. He said when you guys are in charge of Earth, you have a way of influencing those born at that time. Also, you have control of the elements?"

"Good. You have the basic understanding of how this works. There are three of us for each element. One to control. One to create. One to shape. Camden is able to control the element of water. He can take the water that is already there and command it. Scorpio here can shape the water. It means he can change its form physically and atomically. Show her," he nods to Scorpio and Camden.

Camden holds his hand out toward the window. At first, nothing happens. Then I hear a *whoosh* as a stream of water comes through the door. It flows to Camden and starts circling around his outstretched hand. He has a crooked grin on his face and I can't help myself from smiling also, "That is cool."

"Yeah? Look at what Scorpio can do," Camden moves his hand toward Scorpio, who in turn reaches his own out. The flow of water separates into three different strips of water. I watch in fascination as the water compresses into spheres and then changes into the shape of butterflies, floating around Camden's hand. The moment I blink, the water butterflies go from floating around to dropping to the floor, frozen solid.

"You can turn it into ice?" I ask, not taking my eyes off the butterflies, waiting for them to do something else.

Scorpio nods, "I can change the water into ice, mist, or even make it hot."

"What about the third power?" I turn to Aquarius. "Aren't you tied to water somehow?"

He smiles and shrugs, "You would think so with my name being as it is, wouldn't you? But no. I have little influence over water. My power is affiliated with air." As he says this, he waves his hand in front of him and a breeze flows through the house, much stronger than it had been just a second ago. "Pisces is the third holder of water." *Of course,* I think to myself, *The fish. I wonder who made these rules the way they are.* Then I remember the soul I have stashed away in my body. *You don't make any sense,* I tell Orion, not knowing whether he hears me or not. I am suddenly washed in warmth from my head to my toes, feeling the amusement in my heart, and then I know he definitely heard me.

"So what do you do with air? Do you create it or control it?"

"I can control the air around us. Creating wind or making it standstill. Libra and Gemini are the other air users. But we can get more into that at another time. For now, follow me," Aquarius heads for the front door. I turn to Scorpio, who nods and gestures to follow him. I follow Aquarius outside, Scorpio and the other two behind us. We walk around the back of the house and down a worn path to the lighthouse. I stare up at the tall building, realizing that it is much bigger than I thought it was.

"It does not serve the same purpose as you are probably thinking," a voice states beside me, causing me to jump slightly. I look to see Capricorn walking by my side, his hands twined together behind his back.

I frown at him, "What does that mean? I thought all they did was warn boats and planes that there was land here."

He nods, "That is true. The light upon the spire does notify that there is land here. For humans, that is all this place is. But for us Guardians, it signifies a communication that humans cannot see." He glances over at me. I furrow my brow and he chuckles, "Everything about this must be confusing for you."

"I'm working through it."

"Do not worry. Even though you are an important piece to getting this chaos under control, we do hope that we can restore your life to the order it once was."

"I don't really think this is something I will ever forget, Capricorn," I murmur. When all of this is over, I will never have the same life I did before. My father is dead, the last parent and guardian I had. I am too young to live on my own, so I will end up going into a foster system until I turn eighteen. I don't even know where I would go either. Hamilton is gone and I don't even know what happens to a small town like that when a catastrophe strikes.

He must hear the waver in my voice, because he stares at me for a moment before turning back to the lighthouse, "This one was specifically built by Orion and the other Guardians as a safe house. The lighthouse, when lit, tells us that someone is here, waiting. There are others scattered around the world. Orion told us that it was just a precaution for if something ever happened to us. You can imagine the laughs we had about that. We never thought that we would really be using the safe houses. Of course, we never imagined that Alnilam would betray us. If we should have learned anything from humans, it is that peace is just a form of wishful thinking."

"Yeah, we suck like that," I shrug. He doesn't say anything else as Scorpio pulls open the door to the lighthouse, letting us filter in before closing it shut.

We make our way up the spiral staircase, the groan of the metal making me nervous. I can't imagine them keeping up with the maintenance of their safe houses, especially because of what Capricorn said. They never imagined that they would have to use them in the first place. *Making sure the safe houses don't fall apart when we actually use them would be helpful. If this had happened another twenty years from now, this building would not be standing.*

Our ignorance has sheltered us from many things that are coming to light. And I am sure that there will be many more to come. Orion's response surprises me and I hesitate on the steps. Scorpio turns to me with concern and I shake my head before climbing once again. *What I started blossomed beyond what I believed was under my control. Under my watch, I admit, my ignorance was the greatest of everyone. My Guardians believed what I believed. They lived knowing, hoping, that when the time came, I would be able to handle whatever came our way. I have failed them. I have failed everyone.*

Orion's voice is bitter and I can feel his guilt as my own. "Faye? Are you all right?" Camden asks. I blink and glance up, noticing everyone staring at me. I did not even realize we had made it to the top. I feel my cheeks and wipe the wetness away.

"You were talking to him again, weren't you?" Scorpio asks softly.

I nod.

Camden exchanges a glance with Aquarius while Capricorn narrows his eyes at me, "Talking to who?"

I hesitate, not knowing if I should tell the rest of them about my interactions with Orion. I told Scorpio, so I don't see the harm in telling everyone else. They are, after all, trying to revive Orion. I don't know why, but I still can't bring myself to actually tell them.

It is Scorpio who speaks up, "Orion. She was talking to Orion."

Silence filled the room for a few moments before the other three burst out all at once. I flinch. They start demanding how long I've been talking to him, what he has been saying, and if Orion has had any new word on his mission. It is all very overwhelming. I think Orion can feel the anxiety rising in me because I hear him say my name. I can't do this right now. I turn and escape back through the door, hearing Scorpio call after me. I can sort of hear him snapping at the others, but I don't stop to listen. I hurry down the stairs, almost taking two at a time. It takes me a minute to finally hit the bottom of the stairs, where I ungracefully snag my shoe on the bottom step and fall face first into the cement. I whimper and continue to lay there, trying to figure out if my nose is broken. I push myself up, seeing the little droplets of blood on the concrete. I wipe my nose, not feeling any more pain than from the fall itself, and pull the door open. I breathe in the fresh air and decide to walk around the lighthouse. I come to a cliffside, where I can hear the water crashing against the rocks below. I make sure to not get too close to the edge. With my luck, the edge of the cliff would break off and I would end up in the icy waters below me. Instead, I sit down and fall back, looking up at the sky.

The sun is starting to fall below the horizon. Above me, swirls of purples, pinks, and other colors are painting the sky. I don't know how long I lay there before I hear footsteps coming up behind me. A body sits down next to me. "I'm sorry about all that." It is not the voice I was expecting. I sit up on my elbows and turn to see Camden sitting there. He gives me a sheepish smile. I notice one of his front teeth is chipped. *I wonder if that happened in the fall.* "We were just surprised to hear that you were talking to Orion. We knew that his soul was here on Earth, but that's it. We had no idea that we would be able to communicate with him."

"Trust me, it is not as effective as you think it is. I can't have long conversations with him in my head. I think talking to me actually wears him out, staying conscious. He is there sometimes, but most of the time, I don't even notice him." I don't bother mentioning that his feelings turn into my own. I don't know what they would think if they knew how guilt-ridden he is.

Camden shrugs, "I would say that is an improvement. We thought he would just be sitting around in there, waiting for us to put him back in his body. Who knew that he would be able to consciously communicate with you. For us, it is a little bit of a miracle." He glances out toward the sea and I follow his gaze. The sun is almost below the horizon line now, leaving just enough light for us to see around us. "To be honest, I was a little sad to hear that Orion was still around."

I turn to look at him, a bit taken back by his statement.

"Why though? I would think that everyone would be happy to hear that in some way you could still talk to him."

"Don't get me wrong. We are happy that he is still around. It's just..." he sighs and rubs the back of his neck. "Look, I'm sure Scorpio has told you some stuff about us already. I'm not as old as the rest of them are. Not even close. I am still learning things. So when the sisters decided to fight against us and capture Orion, I was completely useless. Sure, I have power, but it's nothing compared to the rest of them. The spheres they trapped us in kept us from using our powers, but I keep thinking to myself. If only there had been more I could do before that happened. Maybe then Orion wouldn't have had to cast his soul away and we would not be stuck on Earth." He glances over at me, "*Not* that there's anything wrong with Earth! I love Earth."

I rest my cheek against my pulled up knees, a smile on my face, "It's okay. I think sometimes even we humans get tired of Earth. Or, at least, the things that happen *on* Earth."

His eyes turn sad and he leans backward. "I just don't want to know how disappointed he is in me. In all of us really. We are supposed to be protectors. Not only Earth, but the entire solar system, of Orion himself. Did you know that after creating us, he was not as powerful as he once was? It's like, as soon as he was finished bringing us into existence, his powers waned. I'm pretty sure it's because we are made from his soul, and thus, basically giving us his life force. It takes a lot away once you do that. So, here we are, supposed to be protecting our Creator, and we failed."

He smiles a lot, but he sounds miserable, I think to myself. I wonder if the rest of them feel the same way. That they feel as though they have failed in their mission to protect us. It is a bit ironic, Camden explaining to me that he feels like they failed Orion, while Orion himself was just telling me the same thing. Everyone feels like they potentially caused the end of the world. I don't feel anything stirring inside me, which means Orion must be sleeping. *Orion? I don't suppose you could wake up and give a little pep talk here?* I think inwardly, trying to contact the celestial being sleeping inside my mind. I get nothing of a response. I sigh, I guess he is feeling as tired as I am.

I shiver at the chill hanging in the air without the warmth of the sun, which has finally disappeared behind the horizon. There isn't too much to see, but it's not completely dark yet. During this time of year, the sun is lasting a little longer each day. "I don't think he is disappointed in any of you," I say after a few moments. "When I heard him speak a few times about Scorpio, or any of you, there was a bloom of sadness. It was not disappointing, though. It was more of a lonely feeling. He has not come right out and said it, but I believe he misses you guys." Camden is watching me with awe in his eyes. I guess hearing that Orion is, in a way, alive and well is a relief to everyone. I decide to tell him more. "I don't only talk to him. I can also feel what he does, and vice versa. Don't get me wrong, he is pretty pissed about his sisters, but not about you guys. He loves you and that didn't change because of what happened. He trusts all of you. Which, I guess, means I should as well. Since the alternative is being stuck with a giant, murdering, wolf." I wrinkle my nose and give him a smile.

Camden laughs, "Lupus was something of a douche-bag, even before turning to the dark side." His smile turns thoughtful. "Thank you, Faye. I can't say I'm one hundred percent in belief that he isn't a little bit disappointed in us, but if you're confident about it, then that is what I will hold onto." He stands and he offers a hand to me. I reach up and let him pull me to my feet, feeling the strange sensation of power flowing between us. It feels different than when it happens with Scorpio, but I supposed that is because I have more of a connection to Camden than any of the rest of them. His eyes widened slightly, "Woah. Isn't that a rush?" He releases my hand. "Come on. I think it's time for you and me to work some magic." He says with a wink and we head back to the top of the lighthouse where the others are waiting.

CHAPTER NINE

"This is going to take a lot of energy from both of you. I hope you're ready," Capricorn states. We are standing on the balcony of the lighthouse, facing the water. Once we had gone back up, it was Aquarius who spoke up, apologizing for their outbursts. Capricorn remained stoic, but I could tell by his regretful expression that he did not expect that kind of reaction out of himself.

They are all feeling a bit lost, I chide myself. This is a lot for me to comprehend, all of the events that have taken place, as well as what is in store for me. I have to remind myself, though, that I am not the only one who feels apprehension about what has happened. They may have had some time on Earth, but without their powers and without Orion, everything in their lives have turned upside down as well.

"I'm ready if Faye is," Camden says with a head nod. They all turn to me.

"Faye," Scorpio says, "if you're not ready for this, we can wait. Lupus is going to need some time to find us."

I shake my head, "No. I'm all right. I'm ready. If there is a chance we can hide ourselves away from him, at least for a little while, then I'm not going to wait."

Scorpio nods, looking pleased. I can't tell what he is thinking, but Camden holds out his hand to me. I take his hand in mine and the rush of energy surges between us. I close my eyes, taking a few deep breaths, and open them again. It feels surreal, standing here thinking about what is about to happen. It feels like there should be a movie crew standing around us. Real magic is occurring all around me at every turn and frankly, it is quite amazing. Camden breathes in deeply and I gasp as my body starts tingling head to toe, the feeling of energy transferring from us at a rapid rate disorienting.

A shimmer starts to appear in front of us. It looks like ripples in the water, but smooth like it's in a mirror. Darkness surrounds us and the shimmer starts to shine from the light of the moon that is starting to move above us. From what I remember about all the horoscope talk, Cancer is strongest under the moon. It makes me wonder how much of that stuff is true, and how much is just silly humans trying to come up with excuses for their behaviors. Suddenly, the water below us shoots into the sky like a volcano erupting underwater. I blink away from the mist spraying us as the ocean curves up over our heads, around the surrounding area, and encases us into a dome of water. I stare upwards in wonder, the water glistening in the moonlight above our heads. I look over at Camden, whose eyes are closed in concentration. A breeze blows by and raises goosebumps on my arms. The water seems to hang in suspension and slowly starts to disappear. I stare as the stars and moon reappear above our heads like nothing happened.

A wave of nausea and exhaustion rushes over me and I slump down onto the concrete. Camden sits next to me, panting. I squint, trying to see the barrier. "What happened? Did it not work?"

Camden runs the back of his hand across his brow, wiping away the sweat collected there, and smiles, "It's still there. I used a little bit of air magic to conceal it. This will make sure that nothing will see it, whether it be human or a mangy mutt." He looks a little pale and worn out. It must have been a lot to use this much magic when it was not naturally inside his body.

"That makes sense." I have to stifle back a yawn.

Scorpio comes over and reaches down, helping me onto my feet. My body feels heavy and I have to lean against the wall in order to not fall back over. "Let's get you into bed. You guys did good work and this will buy us a little bit of time. Even if Lupus finds us, it is going to be a struggle for him to break through the barrier." Capricorn walks over and pulls Camden to his feet, who sways slightly, but rights himself up. "It has been a while since you have used that much magic, hasn't it?" Scorpio asks with a smirk.

Camden nods, a sleepy smile on his face, "It was pretty great. It is so much more intense than before. I guess it is the flow of power into me that made it different instead of it already being inside me." He glances over at me and his smile turns sheepish, "Sorry. I know that took a lot out of you."

I wave him away, yawning, "I'm all right. That was pretty amazing to see, though. I didn't know you could combine your powers that way."

The satisfaction Camden has on his face makes me laugh,

"I'm good at combining them. It is one of my strong suits. You should see the way Regulus works the elements. He may be under fire, but you would never guess he was only under one of them."

"Regulus. That's Leo, right?" I ask, glancing up at Scorpio.

He nods, grabbing my elbow and starts guiding me down the staircase and back to the house. "Regulus is the eldest of the Guardians, Orion's first of us. His powers exceed all of ours. We are hoping that perhaps he was able to retain some of his powers, at least enough to allow us to do what is necessary to place Orion's soul back into his body."

"What if he can't?"

"Then we are pretty much screwed. We can only protect you so much with our limited amount of power we get from you. What you and Camden just did took a lot and that isn't even the extent of what we can do with our power normally." We go inside the house and I can feel my feet practically dragging under me. Scorpio sighs and scoops me up into his arms. "To be honest, it would be easier if we were not scattered like we are."

Aquarius huffs, "I'm working on it. I am not used to the mundane ways of finding people."

I don't really pay attention to the rest of the conversation. The warmth radiating off Scorpio's body wraps around me. My eyelids are getting heavier and before I know it, they close completely. I drift off, wondering if this is what it was going to be like from now on. Constantly feeling exhausted because they need to use their powers to protect me. If only there was an easier way.

Scorpio notices Faye's body turn limp and he glances down, seeing her sleeping face, her mouth slightly open. He smirks before Capricorn's words bring his attention back to the group. "I've managed to locate most of the others. Aries and Sagittarius are still not responding to any of our calls and have not been seen in days. Regulus says he believes he is close to figuring out how to get back home at least, but not how to remove Orion's soul from Faye into his own body."

Camden wrinkles his nose, "Shouldn't his soul leave on his own accord? There has to be some essence still inside his body, if it is still there. You would think his soul would return once it senses that."

Aquarius shakes his head, "I don't believe it is going to be that easy, and the sisters will have thought of that. I am sure they have placed warding around Orion's body to prevent any of us getting close to him, including his own soul."

"So we need to find Regulus. Help him figure out whatever it is that's going to save everyone," Capricorn walks over and peels the curtains back, glancing out the window. He has always been the more paranoid of the Guardians. He would call it being cautious.

"Genius. Why didn't we think of that?" Camden quips, the sarcasm heavy in his voice.

Capricorn's face twists into a scowl, "What did you say?"

Scorpio rolls his eyes and takes that moment to turn on his heels and head toward the set of stairs leading up into the bedrooms of the house.

"You know, the sisters are going to come after Faye with

everything they've got. I don't know if we will actually be able to protect her. We have to be prepared for an alternative solution." Scorpio turns to see Aquarius standing at the bottom of the stairs, a torn expression on his face.

Scorpio bristles, "No, maybe not. But she is the best chance we have at beating them and returning Orion's soul to his body. So, no. We may not be able to protect her all the way until the end, but I can damn well try." Any alternative would mean the end of this young girl's life. What was the point of being a Guardian if he couldn't protect her until the end?

Aquarius smiles sadly, "I know. We all will and you know it. As long as Orion's soul is in that girl's body, we will fight for her."

Scorpio nods and turns, not responding. Reaching the top of the stairs, he walks down a hallway and eases the door open of one of the bedrooms. It looks to be unoccupied and he walks to the other side of the room, placing Faye down on the bed. She immediately turns and wraps her arms around one of the pillows on the bed. Within seconds, Scorpio starts hearing the faint snores coming from her. He smirks while throwing a blanket over her. She had a mouth on her, but there was something charming about the young human. She was taking this whole experience better than he had seen a lot of humans take on simpler problems. He doubts a lot of them know that the end of the world is waiting on their doorstep, unless they can stop it. *As long as Orion's soul is in that girl's body, we will fight for her.* Aquarius made it sound like this human is the only one they were fighting for. *The whole world is at stake if the sisters claim his soul and release themselves from this cosmos.*

Scorpio rubs his face, suddenly tired. He walks over to the window, pressing his forehead against it. Since the beginning of his lifetime, challenges have thrown themselves at him. This may be the hardest one yet. He turns and leans against the window, settling himself in the small alcove. He leans his head back, closes his eyes, and listens to the sounds of Faye's snores as he drifts off to sleep himself.

Lupus stalks forward and sniffs at the air in front of him, growling as he realizes what is in front of him. Faye's scent stops where he is standing, but he knows she is just up ahead, behind this invisible wall. He paws at the ground, making a hole a few inches deep. The barrier goes down into the Earth as well. Not knowing how far down it really goes, it would take too long for him to dig a hole under. He walks around the barrier, sniffing and pawing at it every once in a while. Eventually, he reaches the cliffside. Glancing down, he can see the waves crashing up against the side. He slowly changes back into his human form, stretching and feeling his joints become stiff from compacting his body.

"This is going to be a pain," he frowns. He swings his arms back and forth, shaking his hands, and runs to jump down into the water below. He hits the water, the current stronger than he had thought, but lets his body flow with the current of the water before kicking back up, his head breaking the surface. From there, he slowly makes his way to the cliffside. He manages to find a small outcrop to haul himself up on. Lupus puts his hand against the cliffside and gives a toothy grin. There was no barrier here, but that doesn't mean there wouldn't be a wall at the top. He takes a moment to gauge the cliffside. Rubbing the back of his neck, he sighs. "It would be much easier if Aquila was here to help me. Oh well," he cracks his neck and rolls his shoulders, "I guess this is going to make a good workout."

He grips the rock protruding from the cliffside. From there, he starts climbing. The water causes the rocks to become slippery, so he exerts a little bit of energy, his fingers becoming claws. His claws dig into the rocks, giving him a firmer grip to climb up. It takes him a little bit of time to finally reach the top, and as he peers over the edge, he makes sure that no one is outside before hauling himself up. He crouches on the edge, making sure to not draw any attention to himself and stay in the shadows. He sees movement on the bottom floor, three figures that pass through the lighted windows. Three of the Guardians, from their more masculine frames. His eyes raise upwards to the upper level, finding all the lights off. *I guess she is in one of the upper levels of the house. Easy enough,* he thinks to himself. It wouldn't be hard finding her, but the real question is how many Guardians are in the house. Are there more he is not seeing? Up on the second floor or even in the lighthouse, there could be several more in the area. Lupus scowls, not wanting to have to get through a handful of Guardians. It is hard to tell how many by just his nose because they all smell the same. They smell like Orion.

He starts to move, ducking around to the other side of the house. It was hard to hide anywhere, except in the couple of trees around the house. Luckily, there was one big enough that he could stay behind. With the darkdarknessrounding him, no one would notice anything unless he moved too much.

Looking up, he could see one of the windows, a dark shadow behind the glass. It did not look like Faye, so it had to be a fourth Guardian. Scorpio? Is Faye in that room? A growl rises in his throat. "Look who is deciding to play guardian angel." He turns away from them and jogs down to the lighthouse, making sure to keep to the shadows. They must have faith in their barrier or they are losing their touch, as no one has seen him yet. Lupus starts where the barrier begins, working his way around the dome.

Finally, he found the spot he was looking for. He walks over and puts his hand against the barrier, pushing just a bit to give some force. He did not want to do it too hard. If he is correct, then Cancer will be able to notice if there is a break in the barrier. That is, if he is paying attention. Alnilam said that Cancer is still working on honing his powers, and with them being on Earth for as long as they have been without it, it's unclear if he will notice the change at all. Lupus decides not to push his luck.

Not now.

Finding this spot is good enough. This is the weakest point. With some work, Lupus can easily make a hole big enough. He stands back, his hands on his hips, grinning like the wolf he is. He takes one last look at the house, all of the lights now off. "Sleep well. While you can." He turns away and races toward the edge of the cliff. With no hesitation, he leaps off, his body changing form as he hits the water. He paddles along until he finds a spot he can climb up outside of the barrier. Once he is back on dry land, he runs to find those who wait for his call.

Darkness. Nothing but darkness is surrounding me. I can only see my own body. Underneath my feet, it feels like I am walking on water. The cool, dampness makes me shiver, but I don't actually feel cold. "Hello?" I call out. I do not get a response. Wrapping my arms around myself, I continue walking forward. Every step causes a ripple. I don't know how long I end up walking for. It seems like hours.

"Hello!" I try again. Still, there is no response. My bottom lip quivers, but I refuse to cry. The faintest of sounds cause me to stop in my tracks. I spin around, hoping to see something in this endless void, but there is still only black. But then I hear it again. Some kind of bell, a tinkling in the distance. I take off running toward the sound. The bell sounds louder and louder with every step. Finally, something is shining a little ways off. My feet continue to carry me until I get closer, slowing as I reach the source of the light. It is indeed, a small silver bell. It is floating in the air, a blue glow surrounding it.

"Curious little thing, isn't it?" A voice speaks behind me.

Startled, I spin around to see the familiar face that has been haunting me. Orion, standing with his hands behind his back, smiles. This time though, I'm not scared of the being standing in front of me. I wrinkle my nose as we both stare at the bell, "What is it?"

Orion walks over to stand next to me. "This is the source of everything. This is what is keeping the world from falling apart and collapsing into nothing."

I look away from the bell to look up at him, "This is your soul, isn't it?" He nods his head. I look back at the bell, tilting my head slightly, "It's a little small, don't you think?"

"A bit," he chuckles. "A soul comes in many forms. For you, inside your mind, it is a calling through the darkness. Something I hope continues to help you through your journey."

"My journey…" I repeat the words. It does not sound right to me. "I don't understand how my life could have changed so drastically. Two weeks ago, I was a normal, high school girl. The most I had to worry about was my exams. Now, I have to worry about the end of the world. It is kind of a big leap."

Orion nods, "A leap indeed. But, Faye, out of everyone in this world who could have found my soul, you are the most suited for it."

"Why?"

The sound of glass shattering startles me from my dream and I sit up, glancing around. The room is empty and I realize it must have come from downstairs. Footsteps thud their way toward me and I jump off the bed, looking for the first thing I can find, which happened to be an old vase. I raise it over my head and just as the door swings open, I stumble in my attack as I see a familiar face come through the door.

"Faye, what the hell?" Scorpio scolds as I drop the vase at our feet.

"Sorry!" I exclaim.

He shakes his head, "Never mind that. We have been found."

"By who? Theo?"

As if answering my question, a howl pierces through the air around us. Scorpio walks over to the window. I join him, not seeing anything at first, but then my eyes adjust. Just outside of where the barrier is, I see shadows start to melt out of the darkness. Dark shapes huddled together, dispersing around the house. It takes me a second, but I recognize the shapes as wolves.

A lot of them.

Scorpio curses and spins on his heel, heading out of the room. I tear my eyes from the window and race to follow him. We go down the hallway and head downstairs, stepping onto the bottom floor, I notice one of the windows broken, "What happened?"

Capricorn grits his teeth, "That bastard found a way in, that's what. The barrier had a weak point in it." He kicks a rock away.

I look over and see Camden staring at the floor, his hands at his side, clenched. Aquarius comes up behind him and puts a hand on his shoulder, "It's not your fault. We knew there could be faults with the barrier." I suddenly felt bad. "But there is no time for that now," Aquarius speaks again and when I look up, he is looking at me. As if reading my thoughts, he shakes his head, "We need to figure out a way to get you out of here for now. There are too many of them and I am not sure we can take care of all of them. Lupus sure brought an army though. I can't tell how many of them are out there."

Capricorn shakes his head, "The only way out of here is over the cliffside. That current is too strong for us, let alone Faye. We stand here. Block the doors and the windows. We kill them as they come in." He turns to me, "Head upstairs. In the back, there is a room with a large wardrobe in it. There is a false door in the back. Climb through and lock the door behind you. It will keep you safe."

"But what about you guys? You don't have your powers!" I exclaim as Scorpio touches my elbow. I turn to him, "I can help. I can give you guys power right?"

He nods, "Yes, but it won't work for long. You cannot sustain all four of us, especially since you are still recuperating from helping Camden with the barrier. Trust us. We have been without our powers for some time now and we have learned to fight without them. Go," he pushes me toward the stairs.

I hesitate and then head up the stairwell and toward the back room. I hear the scraping of furniture as the others start blocking the doors and windows the best they can. I walk past the room I was in earlier and open the door to the back bedroom. I quickly find the wardrobe and open the door, revealing some clothes and shoes. It looks normal enough, until I start knocking on the back of it. A little part of me cannot help but to think of a mystery moment, where they always find the hidden room, where vital clues to solve the murder is. Too bad I'm much too involved in this mystery. It takes me a moment, but I finally find where the wooden panel opens up. I crawl through and am surprised to see another smaller room. I expected to be sitting in a small box, but there is even a bed in here.

I close the panel behind me, sliding the two locks in place. I sit on the bed, wishing there was a small window in this room. Then again, it wouldn't be much of a safe room if there was another way for the enemy to get in. It is quiet, too much for my liking. I strain to hear anything at all, but there is not even whispering. After a minute or two, I stand up, determined to go figure out what is going on. And then a loud crash vibrates through the house, causing me to almost jump out of my skin. The sudden sound of fighting ensues and I am frozen in place. My chest feels heavy and my breathing becomes heavy as fear grips me.

Knock. Knock.

I jump and spin toward the sound. Someone is knocking on the door I just came through. I wait, listening for Scorpio or one of the others to say something. We did not talk about a secret word or anything before I came up here.

Knock. Knock.

It happens again and I slowly walk over to the door. It is small, so someone would have to crawl inside the wardrobe in order to be knocking on the door. I put my ear to the door, hearing nothing.

"Is someone th-"

The door suddenly slams open. I cry out as the wood hits my head and I go reeling backwards. I trip over my own feet and fall backwards against the bed. I groan and when I see someone come through, my blood runs cold.

"I would say that I did not expect to see you so soon, but we both know that is a lie," Theo, Lupus, says as he steps out of the small hole and into the room.

I clench my fists. His tall frame is taking up the entire exit and I know there is no other way for me to get out. "I don't know what you hope to accomplish here, but your mutts can't get in." I hope.

He does not look the least bit concerned. He glances around the room and then shrugs, "I don't need them in here.

They were mostly for distraction anyway. I'm sure they will have their fill once we are gone." He takes a step toward me as I slowly stand up.

"I'm not going anywhere with you. I know what you plan on doing with me and I am not a fan." I try not to be obvious about it, but trying to find something in the small room as a weapon proves impossible. I don't think I will be able to hurt him with a pillow. "I want to keep my soul and I don't think Orion would appreciate knowing that you helped his psychotic sisters blow everything up."

"Not everything. Just this galaxy. Besides, as soon as Alnilam and her sisters blow apart this system, we are free to travel where we want. We can go anywhere. Do anything. We can be completely free."

"That's bull and you know it. The sisters don't want to help you. They only want to help themselves. As soon as they leave, you're going to be left behind to rot here with the rest of us." The reality of the words I speak hit me hard and I have to stop myself from crying, although the lump grows in my throat. I don't know any of this. I don't know if the sisters really plan on leaving all of their minions behind. They could be the other percentile of cliche evil doers that actually care about their servants.

I doubt it though.

He smirks, "Believe what you want. It makes no difference to me. My only concern at the moment is to bring you to Alnilam. Anything after that, I can figure it out myself."

My eyes sting, "Why? Why are they doing this?"

"I told you. For freedom."

He walks toward me and I have only seconds to react, so

with all of the strength I can muster, I bring my foot up. I hit home, right between his legs. He yelps in pain and doubles over. I grab his head and bring my knee up, hearing a crack and hoping I broke his nose. *I've always wanted to do that*, I think and push him, sliding past him as he staggers. I dive and crawl through the hole.

"You stupid bitch!" I hear him shout and feel him grab my ankle. I kick out with my other leg, managing to connect with his face and get out of his grip. I tumble out of the wardrobe and get to my feet. I am trying to get my breathing under control when I start hearing a sickening cracking sound. I whirl around just in time to see Lupus crawl out of the wardrobe. I gasp as his half human, half wolf form lands on the floor and slowly changes into his wolf form. He growls and snaps at me, causing me to jump back. My ribcage hits the doorknob and I hiss, throwing the door open and throwing myself out of the room as Lupus launches himself in my direction. I swear I feel the brush of his fur on my arm as he slides into the wall and I run down the hallway away from him.

I can hear Theo's paws scrape against the floor behind me and his breath on my neck. He slams against me and we both go sprawling across the floor. I work on getting my breath back into my lungs as I look around, trying to find something, anything, to use against him, but there is nothing in the hallway.

The stairs are right next to me though and before Lupus can grab me, I throw myself down them. Falling down the stairs? Not a fun experience. I hit the bottom landing hard and I roll onto my back, my whole body hurting. Hands grab my shoulders and pull me up on my feet. I scream and struggle against them, but it is hard to ignore the pain in my body.

"Faye, stop! It's me," an urgent voice says in my ear. I stop fighting and turn, looking into Camden's eyes. I notice blood on his forehead. "Come on. We have to go, while the others are keeping the wolves busy. Can you move?"

I want to say no, to tell him that I just want to lay down and stop, but I nod my head. He takes my hand and we move to the back of the house. I look back in time to see Lupus jump down onto the bottom floor. He glances around and his eyes find us. He snarls and charges. Camden reaches the back door and throws it open, the bookshelf blocking it already pushed out of the way. I don't have time to check and see if the others are all right. I think I heard Scorpio call my name, but I can't be sure. I have to hope they are all okay. We run out of the back of the house, heading down the slope toward the lighthouse. I feel sluggish and it's hard to move, but Camden has a firm hold on my hand, keeping me up right so I don't fall. I can hear Lupus running behind us and I feel him getting closer. I can only hope that the pain of my kick is slowing him down enough.

We make it to the lighthouse and race inside, Camden turning and slamming the door shut. We jump back as Lupus runs into it. "It won't hold long. Let's get to the top," Camden says to me at the same time we hear the thudding of Lupus against the door over and over again. We head up the stairs, my legs burning. The pounding of the door gets further and further away, but eventually, we hear a crash and I know that Lupus was able to get through.

We finally make it to the top and Camden turns, closing

the door behind us. He locks it, but it is a simple one and again, not going to hold the giant wolf racing after us. Camden goes over to look out toward the house while I go to one of the open windows. I turn back and lean against the glass wall, suddenly tired, and slump down. I realize then it was most likely from holding Camden's hand. He was taking power. Whether he realized it or not, I just want to lay down and sleep now. Camden walks over to me and kneels, "Faye, are you okay?"

I open my mouth to answer, but there is a loud bang against the door. "What are we going to do?" I say in a whisper, not taking my eyes off the door.

"Anything we can," he replies.

The pounding on the door stops. Camden helps me to my feet. I know it is going to take more energy from me, but I grab his hand as we watch in anticipation.

There is a click and the door slowly opens. Lupus slowly walks in the room in his human form, the grin no longer on his face. He is angry, the look in his eyes murderous. "I was planning on doing this the easy way. Come in, maybe kill a couple of these Guardians, walk away with you in hand, and head back to Alnilam nice and quiet. But ever since I've met you, you've done nothing but piss me off. All Alnilam said was to bring you back breathing. She did not say anything about bringing you in one piece."

Camden scowls, "How did you unlock the door, mutt?"

Lupus rolls his eyes, "You didn't lock it all the way, ass hat."

I glare at Camden and he throws me a quick, apologetic smile before we look back at Lupus, who slowly begins changing back into his wolf form. In seconds, he is growling at us, his teeth bared.

"Dammit," Camden curses and shoves me to the side as Theo lunges at him. Camden doesn't move, but instead, I see his hands turn colors. They go from their normal skin tone to a dark brown. He reaches out and catches Theo by his jaw, being pushed back into the glass. It cracks behind him as Theo snarls, pushing against him. "Faye, go!" Camden shouts.

"What about you?"

Camden smirks, the glass cracking behind him even more, "I'll be fine! This dog has nothing on me!"

The glass shatters behind him and he is pushed against the railing. He grunts with effort, but Lupus is too big. Camden gained power from me, but it was being used to keep his hands from being torn to shreds.

I get to my feet and run toward the exit door. My feet stop on the edge. I hear the struggle of Camden and Lupus behind me. Why am I stopping? I glance back and see Camden half bent over the railing backwards, Lupus's paws on the railing. If this kept up, Camden would end up in the sea. My hands clench. "Ah, dammit!"

I turn and my feet carry me where I need to go. Not where I want to go, but I can't leave him. I jump and slam myself against Theo. I was hoping that I would just shove him off of Camden, but the momentum causes me to lose my footing. Lupus flies over the railing and I catch a part of it with one hand. I can't hold on though and my hand slips from the railing, but Camden turns to grab me just in time.

"Hang on, Faye!" He grunts and begins pulling me up-wards. My save is short lived as a body slams against Camden and he loses his grip on my hand. I have seconds and manage to see a flash of fur, and then I am falling. A scream rips through the air before I slam into the water and am engulfed in total darkness.

CHAPTER TEN

I hit against the surface of the water, the impact causing me to gasp and inhale water. I choke as I go under and can't breathe. I struggle until I finally make my way to the surface, inhaling deeply as I gag and try to cough up the water, my lungs burning. Just as I think I am going to catch my breath, the current pulls me back under. I become disoriented and the water slams me against the rocks. I want to scream, but I hold it back so I don't inhale the water anymore. I manage to keep myself from blacking out, but I can't tell where the surface of the water is. I am positive that one, if not all, of my ribs are cracked and bruised. I try to open my eyes to see the way to the top, but everything is just dark.

Fear drives into me like a bullet. I keep kicking, but it does not seem like I am going anywhere. Every time I break the surface, the current drags me right back down. I am not taking in enough air to stay under. My chest hurts. I can feel myself crying and my struggles start to slow down. I knew the possibility of me dying at an early age increased tremendously as soon as I met Scorpio, but not this soon. *I wanted to help. I wanted to be useful. I wanted to be the one who saves the world. I don't want to die!*

I feel myself losing consciousness. As the water gets colder, my body becomes more numb. The fight wears me out until I feel myself just drift into the sea. *Drowning isn't such a bad way to go. Nothing hurts anymore. Maybe this is for the best. Orion's soul can go to someone better. Someone who can actually make a difference. It's fine. I'm fine.*

My eyes close as I drift into oblivion. The last thing I see is a blurred figure. I'm not sure if they are in the water or in my mind. At this point, I don't think it matters. I am embraced by warmth and I curl into it, letting it take me to wherever it wants.

On the rocks at the bottom of the cliff, Lupus crawls up onto the outcrop that he had managed to find earlier in the night. He coughs up water and growls, sinking his claws into the ground so he doesn't slip back into the water. *Stupid, stupid girl!* He looks behind him into the water. There was no sign of her, even after he took the time to look for her in the water before he felt his body finally giving up on him. *Alnilam is going to have my head. Better get back up top.* He turns and shifts back into his human form, leaving his hands as claws to help him climb up. It takes a little bit of effort with the rocks being slippery, but eventually, he reaches the top. He pulls himself onto solid ground. He pants, his hands on his knees, before he glances up and notices three figures standing there.

Lupus smirks, "I'm surprised to see you all still alive. I obviously did not bring enough wolves."

Scorpio steps forward. He is covered in blood and Lupus can't tell how much of it is his and how much of it belongs to the wolves. "Where is Faye?"

Lupus shrugs, "Who knows? Lost at sea. Stupid girl should have left it alone. I am sure the water has claimed her as her own by now. I guess we'll just have to see who can find her body first."

"You son of a-"

"Scorpio," Capricorn stops him, his hand on his shoulder.

Scorpio shrugs him off, "Don't try to stop me, Cap. I'm going to kill him and then go in for Faye."

"Listen to me. I don't believe Orion would let Faye die so easily. If she is able to give us our powers back, then to some extent, he should be able to exert some of his power on her as well. We have to believe that she is still alive. Leave finding her to Camden. Without our powers, we are going to need your fighting abilities up here. We take him out together."

Lupus grins. All of them look like hell and without their powers, they were not much of a threat. He still did not know how Scorpio managed to use his powers before, but every time he has seen a Guardian use them, Faye has been right next to them. Without her, he did not see it as much of a fight. "Even with the three of you, you're no match for me as you are."

"No. But I am."

Lupus jumps and spins to where the voice comes from. The Guardians all share a shocked face as well. They see Faye, dripping wet from being in the sea, but she is not standing on the ground. She is floating in the air behind them.

Lupus quickly regains his composure, "You're alive! Orion must have been smart enough to realize that he needs you alive more than dead. Good. That saves me the hassle of finding your corpse." Faye's face does not change and Lupus stares at her. He narrows his eyes, noting Faye's eyes are suddenly brighter than they were before. Recognition shoots through him and he stumbles backwards, "You're not Faye." The familiarity is more than he expected. It was too much to believe that it was simply Faye herself who made it out of the water.

Faye shakes her head, speaking in a voice that is a mix of her own and another, *"No. I'm not. And your welcome on this land has officially expired. It is time to return back to where you belong, Lupus. Maybe you can try again in another couple of millennia."* Her hand raises.

"No!" Lupus shouts and lunges at Faye, hoping to drag her back down to the water. He wouldn't go out like this. He refused to disappear, all because of a child. A light shines from Faye's hand. The Guardians shield their eyes. As the light fades, they no longer see Lupus. Only Faye. They all stare at her.

No one speaks up, until Aquarius steps forward, "Orion?" His voice is hopeful. He notices Camden come jogging up to them, breathing hard and soaking wet. He must have been searching for Faye.

Faye smiles, the warmth of it washing over the Guardians, *"It is good to see you again, my children. I feel as though it has been eons, though it has not been very long at all."* The smile fades and she looks more serious. *"I don't have much time. I can already feel the strain of using my powers waning. Tell me, have you found Regulus?"*

Aquarius shakes his head, "Not yet. I've heard wind of some of the others being in Greece, but other than that, we have not gotten word."

Faye nods her head, "*I understand.*" Her eyes start to flicker, almost as if a lightbulb is shorting out. "*I'm out of time. Find Regulus and the others. We cannot do anything against Alnilam and the others without all of you.*" The Guardians all nod, a new determination on their faces. She smiles once again, "*To speak to you all again makes me believe that not all is lost.*" Her eyes flicker one last time before they return to the normal, blue that belongs to Faye. "*Please,*" Orion's voice echoes as his own, "*Protect Faye.*"

It feels like I'm waking up out of a dream as my vision goes from black to slowly focusing on things around me. I'm standing on the ground, soaking wet. I can't remember how I managed to get back onto land. I rub my eyes and notice Scorpio, along with the others, standing there. They are all bloody and bruised. A smirk forms on my face "You guys look like hell."

Scorpio is the first one to move. He runs over to me and reaches out his arms as I fall into them. The cold of being in the ocean water catches up to me and I start to shake, the breeze blowing not helping. Scorpio wraps his arms around me, "I thought we were done with the stupid antics?" He says in my ear. He must have an idea of what happened up in the lighthouse.

I shrug, "I'm not sure that's possible." I notice the others around us as well. I look over at Camden, "I'm sorry I wasn't much help."

He grins, "Don't sweat it. Maybe next time, don't throw yourself off a lighthouse?"

I smile, "I'll be sure to remember that. But," I straighten myself and Scorpio releases his hold on me, "how did I end up back up here?"

"What is the last thing you remember?" Capricorn asks.

"Falling. I fell into the water and then nothing." Aquarius and Camden share a look. "What? What happened?"

"Nothing bad," Aquarius assures me. "But now we know that in a pinch, Orion has more influence than we originally believed. It seems as though he saved you. Us as well. He took care of Lupus."

"So he's..." My mouth goes dry.

Scorpio snorts, "I wish. Technically, we cannot die. Unless Orion absorbs any of us directly back into him, we just stay in a suspended state. I doubt even the sisters can reverse it. For now, he is simply floating somewhere in the galaxy, awaiting for Orion to come back and figure out what to do with him."

I don't know why, but a little bit of relief washes over me. Lupus has tried to kill me over and over again, but some part of me didn't wish death on him. The promise of freedom has the power to turn anyone against each other. I can do without the constant death looming over my head, but I cannot say I totally blame them. Alnilam is the one who is behind everything bad happening in my life and she is the one who needs to be taken care of.

A strong breeze blows and I shake, trying not to let my teeth chatter. "Come on," Aquarius walks over and puts a hand on the small of my back, "Let us get you back inside. There are some warmer clothes and we can start a fire." I nod, more than happy to get back into the house.

Walking back through the door, now hanging slightly off its hinges, I can see the extent of the damage. It makes me nauseous looking at it. "Maybe we should have gotten rid of those," Camden says behind me.

Bodies of wolves lay scattered around the floor. I swallow hard so I don't get sick all over the floor, "You think?"

Scorpio sighs, "You better get used to this kind of thing. We are all targets now, for every sort of attack. Come on, I'll help you upstairs. Just...close your eyes."

I scowl at him, but do as he says and close my eyes. He grabs hold of my upper arm and gently tugs at me, urging my feet to move forward. My stomach is in knots, knowing every time he makes me turn a different direction, because I know it means we are moving around another dead body.

Eventually, he brings me to a stop. "Okay. You can open your eyes. Just don't look behind you."

I blink my eyes open and see the stairs in front of me. I turn slightly to look at him, willing myself to not look any further, "What are we going to do now?"

"First and foremost, you are going to get warmed up. We don't need you to get sick on us. After that, I'm not sure. According to Aquarius, Greece is our next stop. Hopefully, that is where Regulus will be, or someone who knows where he is. Once we find Regulus, we will be able to find everyone else."

"I get that he is the oldest of all of you, but what makes you think he can help us find everyone else?"

"Because he has a link to everyone else. When Orion made him, he gave Regulus the ability to sense and feel the other Guardians to a point. We are hoping that even without his powers, that link is still there. And, when we get you there, hopefully the link will be even stronger. With his help, we can get everyone together again and save Orion."

I nod and don't say anything else as I head up the stairs. Debris lies on the ground where Lupus rampaged up here. I pick my way across to the bedroom I had first slept in after the barrier was put in. I felt tired, but I knew I would not be able to sleep. Instead, I lean against the wall, resting my head against it. It all still feels like a terrible dream, that one day I will wake up and be back in my old bed, in my old house. Hearing my dad stumble back into the house after one of his drunken nights away. Taking my tests for college and wishing I could skip high school altogether. I finally pull myself away to find the bathroom, turning on the hot water, and stepping under it once I peel off my wet clothes. It feels fantastic after being in the icy cold water of the ocean. I want to stay in this shower forever.

I'm not sure how long I'm in there for but a knock on the door tells me I am taking quite a while. "Faye, when you're done, hurry downstairs. There is something you should see." I hear Scorpio's footsteps receding, but then they stop, "Oh, and don't worry. We got rid of all the wolf bodies."

"That's comforting," I murmur, not wanting to know what they did with the wolves, but I have a distinct feeling that the fish around here are going to eat pretty well the next couple of days. I finish washing up, feeling the gross of the night run down my body and into the drain. I reluctantly turn off the water and find a towel under the sink. Wrapping it around myself, I peek out the door, making sure there wasn't a dark haired, brooding Guardian waiting around for me. Convinced I am alone, I head back to the room, where surprisingly all of my things are still there. Lucky for me, none of the wolves tore into here. I change into a simple dark blue sweater and jeans, opting to leave my shoes off for now since they are still wet. I rummage through and find my brush, dragging it through the tangles of curly hair before finally settling for good enough.

I head downstairs, where the others are standing in a circle next to the fireplace. A small radio I did not notice before is sitting on the top. I'm surprised it did not get broken in the fighting. Aquarius turns to look at me, "Have you ever been to Billings?"

"Uh, no. Is that a bank of some kind?"

Capricorn snorts. "Not quite. It is a town in Montana. According to the news, there has been an outbreak of an unusual amount of violence happening."

"And? Welcome to the United States. We aren't exactly known for our totally peaceful times."

"We know about you humans and your desire for violence," Capricorn snaps. I bristle but don't say anything, seeing Camden's apologetic shrug out of the corner of my eye. "This is more than that. People are being described as almost demonic in their destructive tendencies. It sounds like..."

"Libra." Aquarius breathes. "Do you think she is there?"

"Hard to tell. This chaos though. If something were to have happened to her, then it would most definitely be her doing. I admit, though the humans are a crazy lot, this sounds a bit uncharacteristic of them."

"Hello, human here." I say, waving my hand and catching their attention. "Libra. I think my mom was a Libra. What does she have to do with what is going on in Billings?"

This time, Scorpio is the one who speaks. "Libra is the holder of peace and chaos. Humans have complete free will over their actions. Libra is the one who makes sure that one side of their personalities don't overcome the other. Sometimes, she does not catch everyone. Thus your serial killers or tree huggers. People who are overly chaotic or happy, those have either been touched by Libra too closely or not enough. Most of the time, it is when she is furthest from Earth when those like that are born. If she somehow managed to tap into her powers while in a town full of people, and they went out of control, she could absolutely cause something like this."

"So, does this mean we aren't going to Greece?" Camden asks.

Capricorn shakes his head, "Not if it is Libra. Humans will start killing each other if this keeps going on. If it is Libra, it is our duty to stop her. Regulus can wait. We need her anyway," he looks to Aquarius. "Get us plane tickets to Billings. The sooner the better. Camden, go with him." Camden looks like he is going to protest, but a scolding glare from Capricorn snaps his jaw shut.

I watch the two of them head out the door, Camden glancing back to throw me a little wave before trotting off to catch up with Aquarius, and I look back to Capricorn, "Why are we not going with them?"

"Because we are taking a different path. Before you two

got here, we hired a couple of private planes. They have been waiting for us, and now we need to make haste and head over to the designated craft for us. We made sure we had a few set up around the island in case we needed a quick escape." Capricorn looks at Scorpio, anger suddenly in his eyes. "You were supposed to be watching over her. Why is she like this? Why did she not stay with you?"

Scorpio glares, "She did not fall with me. Unlike Regulus, I cannot sense where everyone else is. You think I didn't look for her?"

"Not hard enough."

Oh, man. I can cut the tension with a knife between the two of them. "Guys? I don't mean to get in the middle of your pissing contest, but we have to go. If Libra is in trouble, it is no time to be fighting over this, right?"

They continue to glare at each other. Finally, Capricorn spins on his heel. "Get whatever you think you may want for the trip. I'm sure some of your things were ruined, but there are extra replacement items around the house. I'm going to secure our perimeter to make sure we won't be followed by anything else. Scorpio, make yourself useful and go lock up the lighthouse."

Scorpio scowls. We make eye contact and he simply shrugs before going to the back of the house. The door leads to the path heading down to the lighthouse.

I am alone in the house as Scorpio locks up the lighthouse and Capricorn waits for us outside. Even with him watching for any more threats, the thought of being alone anymore is beginning to turn into a frightening experience. I make my way toward the stairs and back up to my room where my luggage is. I don't bother looking in the wardrobe for anything else. Lupus ruined anything that could have been in there and even though he is gone, I feel like he could jump around the corner at any second. I grab everything and head back downstairs, Scorpio already waiting for me in the living room. "Took you long enough," he says, his tall frame leaning against the fireplace.

I shrug, "Where's Capricorn?"

"He went on ahead. He is meeting us at the porairt." So much for being outside watching for danger. He chuckles as a frown forms on my face, "Don't worry. It is not as long of a walk as the last one."

"Yeah, okay." I mumble and together we head out of the house, Scorpio locking the door behind us.

Lucky for Scorpio's kneecaps, the port was only an hour or so walk from the house. A much shorter walk than last time. It is kind of sad that we were leaving already. The atmosphere of this place is relaxing and warm. Well, when there aren't giant, ravenous wolves running around trying to kill me. Maybe I can come back here one day. I'm not sure how Lupus left Hamilton, but I don't think there is much for me to go back to. At least not for a while, and I still have two years before I can legally be on my own.

"It is not going to be like this forever."

"Hm?" I ask, glancing over at Scorpio.

"That look on your face. I'm not very good at reading humans, but I can see a discouraged person. It's not going to stay like this. We are going to find the other Guardians, get

Orion's soul back into his body, and then put an end to this once and for all."

"You sound awfully confident in that statement."

He grins at me sideways. "Damn right I am."

I roll my eyes, but a small smile creeps onto my face anyway. We walk the rest of the way in silence. My thoughts continue to roam with the endless questions I have. I know they cannot all be answered, but I'm sure I could squeeze a few through. I will save them, though. I know Scorpio can answer some of them himself, but I would rather have the others around as well.

We get to the airport after a while, with Capricorn already there. He pulls Scorpio aside while the pilot introduces himself to me. He isn't as rambunctious as Rusty, but he is still nice either way. When the other two come back, Scorpio is scowling. I wonder what they talked about as we load up into the small plane and once again we are in the air, heading back to a larger airport that will take us to Montana. The ride is not as bad as last time, but my stomach still drops to the floor when we start our descent. We give our thanks to the pilot and take a cab ten minutes to the larger airport.

We get our tickets at the desk and I recognize a familiar face on our way to the waiting area for our flight. "Camden!" I call and wave my hand. Camden's head snaps up and his eyes scan the crowd until they land on me. He smiles and tugs on the arm of someone standing next to him, Aquarius, and they head toward us. We meet in the middle. "Our flight doesn't leave for another hour. Are we really stuck sitting here until then?"

Aquarius shrugs, "We have to. It is not as though we can create a magic portal to transport us to Montana."

"Can any of you actually do that with your powers?" I say, squinting my eyes at him.

"Unfortunately, not." He replies, shaking his head. "We are forced to rely on human technology to get us there. If that technology says we have to wait an hour, then there is not much we can do otherwise."

"We could check out the cafe they have over there. I overheard an old couple say its coffee is really good," Camden quips.

"Sure!" It was better than standing around. Without waiting for the other three, Camden and I head toward the cafe not far from our flight door.

When we get there, I order a large coffee with some sugar and a lot of cream, along with a blueberry muffin. Despite their earlier grumblings, the other three had followed us into the cafe. When all sitting at a table, I noticed there were a lot of eyes on us. I realize that the scene must look strange. Three grown men, another looking in his early twenties, and a young teenage girl. I sink in my seat just a tad.

Capricorn notices the movement and looks around himself. He quirks a brow at me, "Something wrong?"

"Everyone is staring," I mumble.

"So they are," he says, shrugging.

"Do you think someone will tell security?"

Capricorn sighs, "The only reason people will think we kidnapped you is if you keep looking like you're being kidnapped. Stop looking so anxious and ignore them." He continues drinking his Chai tea.

I pout and look into my cup of coffee. He is right. There was no need to draw attention, especially when we aren't doing anything wrong. I just can't help but to think that everyone staring at me is going to change into a giant animal and try to take me to their maniacal leader.

Camden smirks, "Just think of yourself as a celebrity, surrounded by your trusty bodyguards."

Scorpio snorts and I roll my eyes, "I'm not much of a celebrity."

"If everyone knew what we did, I think you would be the biggest celebrity out there."

I know he is trying to make me feel better, like Scorpio had earlier, but all I can manage is a small smile before taking a sip of my coffee. It is hard to feel anything outside of fear and uncertainty when you know your whole life is riding on being able to bring back a celestial being. It's kind of funny how people think God is the one who created everything and life on Earth. Well, I guess Orion is kind of a god depending on who you talk to.

That opens a whole new can of worms that I am not prepared to handle right now, so we are going to push those thoughts in the back of my mind and never deal with them again.

Eventually we hear the boarding call for our flight. I get a window seat, Camden next to me in the middle, Aquarius on the outside. Capricorn and Scorpio are a few rows back from us. I close the blind, not wanting to see the ground below us take off. I lean my head back and close my eyes. The trip is going to take a while. We have one stop in New York and then the rest of the way to Billings. At some point during the flight, I am able to get Camden to switch seats with me, an uncomfortable switch that included what I believe was my elbow in Aquarius's face, but we manage to get seated before the turbulence hit.

One of the flight attendants walking down the aisle from behind us stops at our seats. "Faye?" She asks and I tense. I can feel the other two lean just a little closer to me. The woman must not have noticed as she held out a phone and some headphones. "Your brother said you had forgotten these with him." She points behind us and I sit up, turning ever slightly to see Scorpio give me a little shrug before turning his attention back out the window.

"Thanks," I say with a smile as I take the phone and head-phones from the woman. She seems pleased and continues on her walk to care for the other passengers.

"Where the heck is my phone?" Camden exasperates.

I laugh and hand him one of the sides of the headphones, "If you're that bitter about it, you can share with me. I'm sure Aquarius won't mind getting some quiet."

"Not at all," he says and takes the opportunity to lean the seat back just a bit and close his eyes.

Camden narrows his eyes, "I see how it is." But he ends up taking the offered earbud and puts it in his ear. "There better be something good on here." He mumbles before settling back into his seat.

I grin. "Don't worry. I have the best playlist." I don't question when Scorpio had time to get this phone, as he has been with me almost the entire time, but I am grateful to have it. I download my music app and sign into my playlist, since it is all saved under Google anyway. The familiar tunes start to waft into my ear and I am instantly more relaxed than I was five minutes ago. We spend the rest of the flight like this.

We finally hit the airport in New York, running to the flight deck with two minutes to spare. Camden profusely apologizes because he was the one who insisted that our flight deck was on one side of the airport, but in reality, it was on the other. We get the same seating arrangement as last time, and once again, we are in the air. I decide not to change places with Camden this time and he doesn't ask to share the phone again. With both headphones in, I take a chance and glance out the window once we are in the air, lifting the small window pane.

The view is as breathtaking as last time. Everything below us is just acres and acres of green, especially once we get out of New York. Rivers of clouds pass beneath us and I think to myself that maybe I am getting used to flying. That is, until the turbulence hits hard and we bounce in the air. I quickly shut the screen and Camden chuckles beside me. I glare at him and he holds his hands up in defense. I opt for leaning my head back against the seat and closing my eyes for the rest of the flight. I'm okay with not looking out the window for a while. Music and sleep is the only thing that is going to keep my anxiety down while thirty thousand feet in the air.

While asleep, I dream of stars. Stars floating around me, lighting the darkness that surrounds us. The stars are warm, letting me know that everything is going to be okay. One star floats down in front of me. I hold my hands up so that it can rest there. The star is black, with a little bit of blue swirling inside it. There are no words, but for some reason, this star is giving me a sense of ease. Of hope. I smile.

I wake up with a jolt as the plane touches down on the runway. As the plane stops, I glance out the window, "We are here already?"

Camden shakes his head. "Not quite. We are at the Bozeman Yellowstone International Airport. We are about two hours from Billings."

"Why didn't we go straight into the city?"

"There are no direct flights into the city. Besides, from what I have been hearing from the other passengers, they aren't letting people into a certain part of the city. They are saying there was a large gas main break. My guess? Libra's powers are more out of control than we believed. They probably have the city on lock down. No one questions a gas line breaking, since it's more common than people think. And with it being at the airport, which is practically in the center of the city, they are going to be evacuating who they can and containing the rest. Libra's powers are going to be affecting those under her time of the year on Earth the most, and then the rest slowly over time. Hopefully, we can get there before that happens though."

I frown and look out the window while waiting for the people in front of us to inch their way out of their seats and down the aisle. "So what are we going to do?" We shimmy out of our own seats and I grab my suitcase from the overhang, moving forward down the aisle.

"First, we find a way to get into the city," Scorpio's voice says from behind Camden. As we shuffle out of the plane and head toward baggage claim, he continues. "I'm not sure how many entry points the city has, but we are going to have to be a little unconventional in our approach."

"Meaning?"

"We are going to have to find a different way besides the main roads. Come on. Let's see if we can find a map. Hopefully we can get into the city before it starts getting too dark."

We find a map at one of the Kiosks and decide on a route that seems like it would be the easiest to get in without too much traffic. We head outside of the airport and flag down one of the many taxis coming and going, looking for passengers. Capricorn sits up front, giving directions to the taxi driver. As well as to get more information. I stand at the door of the backseat, Scorpio sliding into the last available of the three seats.. "How the hell are we all supposed to fit back here?"

Scorpio shrugs, "You will just have to sit across us."

"What? Why do I have to?"

"Because you're the smallest. Obviously."

"I don't think so," I scowl.

"It is not that long of a drive. Would you rather one of us sit on *your* lap?"

"Will you two stop bickering and just figure it out? We have no time to lose." Capricorn barks from the front.

I roll my eyes and with a huff, finally crawl into the back-seat. I have never felt so awkward in my life. I end up crawling over and sitting with Camden. Maybe it is because we have the same sign, but I feel more comfortable with him than the rest. I could have sit with Scorpio, but I'm still bitter about his insinuation of me being small. I mean, I *am* the smallest, but for some reason it irritated me. Besides, if it wasn't for the fact that all of them are probably over a thousand years old,

Camden is closer to my age in terms of humanity. *I think this is what it would be like to have a brother,* I think. I drape my legs over the other two and we set off.

While Capricorn talks with the cab driver in the front, we sit in silence in the back. Camden starts snoring softly next to my ear and I see him with his head back against the seat, his mouth open slightly. I can't help but smile. He is the youngest of the Guardians and it shows. Aquarius also has his eyes closed, his arms crossed and his head down. Scorpio is simply staring out the window of the car. As if sensing me staring, he turns and our eyes meet. He raises a brow at me and then turns to look back out the window. I wrinkle my nose and lean my head back against the glass. The quiet conversation from Capricorn and the driver, plus the soft snores of Camden make me want to close my eyes. The sleep I've gotten on the planes should be enough, but I have a feeling I'm going to need all the rest I can get before we get into town.

I wake up to a slight tapping on my foot. Scorpio reaches up behind Aquarius to smack Camden, waking him up with a start and earning him a glare. Capricorn turns in his seat, "We are here. Come on."

As soon as we step out of the taxi, there is a strange feeling in the air. Almost like the pressure of a small animal sitting on my chest. The cab driver doesn't seem to notice it. He leaves us at a small gas station outside of town. I can see the sign for Billings though.

"You feel it, don't you?" Aquarius asks, standing next to me.

I nod. It must have been the effects of having Orion's soul

in me. "I don't understand though. How is Libra able to do this, when the rest of you don't have your powers?"

"She doesn't have her elemental powers, but Libra is the essence of Chaos and Peace itself. She isn't going to lose that."

"Is this Alnilam's doing?"

"Most likely. I'm not sure how, but this is definitely Libra's power we are feeling. Come on. Let's get going before things become too chaotic."

Capricorn explains the route to me while we start down the side of the road. Going a bit north of where the interstate goes into the city, there is a large chunk of land that is under construction. The cab driver said that they were building a new suburb there. With everything going on in the city, he said that work has come to a standstill. Most of the workers were sent home until the "gas leak" issue was resolved, leaving only a handful on site to keep track of progress. Capricorn says that it shouldn't be too much of an issue getting past them, but we needed to be ready, just in case. "You need to be prepared to let us use our powers if we need them."

"Cap-" Scorpio starts, but Capricorn cuts him off.

"I know. I don't like it either, but if something goes wrong, there is only so much we can do with our hands. We don't have our weapons with us and we don't know what state Libra is in. I know it is asking a lot, Faye, but relying on you is our best course of action in case anything goes wrong."

"I know. It's fine," I reply and Scorpio looks away. I can tell he is upset, but he must know that Capricorn is right. If I am the only source to their powers, then it is my job to make sure they get it. "The sooner we can get Libra back to normal, the sooner we can start looking for everyone else."

And so we continue on, heading toward the construction site. I swear, I am going to end up having calves of steel, because by the time the new suburbs came into view, they were burning and my feet were hurting. I start to wonder to myself how many miles I have walked in the past couple of days. Everything between Hamilton burning, to the fiasco at the lighthouse all happened so fast. We haven't had time to rest and it is starting to really wear on me. The construction site is, of course, surrounded by a large chain link fence. Scorpio holds his hand out to me. In his eyes, I can see the question in them. I'm surprised that he is asking me, instead of just having me give him power. Something about it makes my stomach tingle, makes me feel like I'm not just some battery to be used whenever they need a jump.

Okay. Well, I still feel like that, but it's nice to be asked.

We join hands and Scorpio holds his hand out flat, like he is going to chop a board in half. He brings his hand down and at the same time, links in the fence snap as if being cut.

"Wind?"

He shakes his head, "Water. I condensed its properties to make it slice through the metal. I could have used wind, but since water is my element, it is stronger when I use that."

"Cool."

We file in through the fence and slowly make our way through. There is a lot of open field, but there is also plenty of heavy machinery around to hide behind, just in case someone walks past. The cab driver was right when he said that not many people were here. A few workers here and there are walking around, but most of them were either preoccupied with conversations or had their nose in their phones.

Regardless, it seems like forever by the time we finally reach the main gate. It is open, but unfortunately, a majority of the workers who were left behind to monitor are also here. They did not look like they were moving any time soon. We make our way behind one of the small trailers being used as an office space.

"Now what?" Camden asks from next to me. There is probably two hundred feet between us and the gate. There are several workers who are standing around the gate, looking out into the city to see if they could spot any of the action.

"They seem normal enough," I cut in.

"I'm sure they are," Capricorn says. "I don't think any of them are under Libra, so her powers have not taken effect on them. That, and the proximity. Which means she could be on the other side of the contained area."

"Great. Now how do we get through?"

"Where is Scorpio?" Camden suddenly asks.

We all look around and sure enough, Scorpio is nowhere to be seen. "Where did that bastard go?" Capricorn growls.

Aquarius narrows his eyes toward the gate, "Wait, look."

We all turn toward the gate. At first, I didn't see anything, but after focusing my eyes, I noticed a shimmer next to the gate. "You guys can be invisible?" I ask.

"No, not quite." Aquarius replies, shaking his head. "What he is doing is most likely using the water in the atmosphere to create a reflective barrier around himself. He better hurry to do whatever it is he needs to though. That takes a lot of concentration and if he uses too much of his power, it will dissipate and he will be exposed."

We watch as Scorpio heads around the workers, making

sure to avoid touching any of them. I have to remember to breathe, but it is hard when unsuspecting people almost walk into him. He continues on and my eyes widen as I realize where he is going. One of the machines is sitting unoccupied, one of those big rollers. I turn to the others, "Is he serious?"

As if to answer, the machine starts up. Every head turns toward the machine, all the same confused, slack jaws on all of them. The shouts and running begin when the machine starts to roll by itself toward one of the houses being constructed. As all of them clear away from the gate, Aquarius taps on my shoulder and motions for us to move. I nod and we quickly move our way toward the opening. No one notices us as we pass through, and we are inside the city. I take a quick glance back just to make sure no one has spotted us, but the workers who were here are still busy stopping the roller and figuring out how it moved on its own. We hurry across the street and slip into an alleyway between a couple of shops.

The heavy air I noticed at the gas station intensifies as soon as we get further in and it is harder to breathe. Scorpio comes jogging up to us, "Libra doesn't seem to be as far as we believed her to be."

"You're right about that."

I jump at the new voice, spinning around and expecting to see another person standing there. I am wrong. Instead, there is the panting face of a dog standing there. She is a Shiba Inu, with all the normal colorings, except her eyes, which are bright red and the color of fire.

"Minor! You've found her then?" Aquarius kneels down as I am left standing there, gaping at the sudden appearance of yet another talking canine. How many times is this going to happen?

"Yes. Major is keeping her at bay for now, but he is not going to hold on for much longer. He has already exhausted most of his strength." Her eyes move from Aquarius to me. "Is this Orion's vessel?"

Scorpio answers before I can, which is fine because I am sure I still look like a fish out of water. "Faye, her name is Faye. And yes, she is holding Orion's soul for the time being, so don't be a bitch."

The little hairs on the back of her neck stand up as she bristles and she bears her teeth, "Watch it, Scorpio. Now come on. We don't have time to sit here and bicker. Major needs us." She turns and begins running off.

Capricorn shoots a look over at Scorpio that reminds me of when my dad would reprimand me before taking off after Minor. I look around at everyone else, "Um, is anyone going to tell me why there is a talking dog? Is *she* going to turn into a person also?"

Camden shakes his head, "No, not this time. We'll explain later, but just know that she is on our side. Come on or we are going to lose them."

The rest of us follow after the Shiba. "Are we really running after walking that whole time?" I cry.

"Come on, Faye! Running is the best form of exercise there is!" Camden calls from in front of me. I groan and continue after them.

CHAPTER ELEVEN

The further we get into town, the more dense the air seems to become. Following Minor's lead, she weaves us in and out of the shops around town. It looks like a ghost town and I can't help but wonder what happened to all the people who should have been there. I looked it up on the way here, but Billings is home to over one-hundred thousand people. Even with part of the city cut off, I would think we would still hear or see movement within the buildings. We stop behind a car when a couple of people stagger out from a shop, looking around like they are confused about where they are.

"They look drunk out of their minds," I whisper from behind the blue sedan we are watching them from.

"I'm sure the feeling is relatable," Aquarius replies. "Without knowing what Libra's powers are doing to them, we need to take caution. We don't-"

One of the affected men turned and narrowed his eyes toward where we were. I duck down back behind the vehicle, hoping he did not see my head sticking up. I managed to get a look at the man and it gives me chills. His eyes seem sunken in and his skin is pale, like some kind of sickness. Aquarius also slides down, but he turns to Minor, "Is this how they all are?"

Minor's ears twitch, "For the most part. Except for the civilians closer to Libra. They are unusually violent. I don't even know how many of them are left wandering around."

"And Libra?" Capricorn asks.

"She's held up in an antique shop. No one has been inside since it started and I'm not even sure if there are still people inside. It's getting worse. Major went in at the same time I noticed your presence. Or rather, Orion's." She glances over at me and her ears fall back slightly before turning back to Capricorn. "That wasn't too long ago, but who knows what kind of damage could have ensued during that time."

"Then let's get going. The sooner we get to Libra, the sooner we can get this settled," Scorpio injects. We wait until the two affected people walk away until we continue moving.

With Minor leading the way, Scorpio insists that I stay in the middle of the group. I can tell we are getting closer to her and at the same time, more people seem to be showing up. *They must have sensed Libra's powers in some way. Maybe they were drawn here. Either way, if they are getting violet, we have to be careful.* We have to start moving slower, ducking behind the different vehicles and into the buildings. I don't know how we manage to make our way through with how much noise I seem to be making. I am slightly jealous of how quiet the others seem to be, while my shoes slap against the pavement every time we run. We finally reach a small bait shop that is sitting across the antique shop Libra is holding up in. The power surrounding the shop is palpable and I feel the goosebumps rising on my arms.

"Okay. Faye and Camden, you stay here with Minor. The rest of us will go in and handle Libra," says Capricorn.

Camden frowns, "Why can't I go with you?"

Scorpio rolls his eyes. "One, we need someone to stay here and protect Faye-"

"I can handle myself!"

"Two, we need someone whose power aligns more with her." That shut me up. "If something goes wrong and we can't get Libra under control, you need to use your power against her."

"Fine. But if things do start going south, I'm coming in there," Camden scowls.

Scorpio nods.

"Let's go," Aquarius says and they head out of the bait shop.

Minor lays in front of the doors, her ears flat against her head. Camden locks the doors of the bait shop after the other three leave, making sure no one can come in. He then comes over next to where I am pacing and slides down behind the counter. We wait there in suspenseful silence.

"So Minor and Major, as in Canis? Orion's hunters?" I ask. I need something to distract me from the endless ways I see this going wrong inside my head.

"That's right. Personal companions to Orion himself. Major is the larger constellation, the leader and the power house. Minor is the brain of the two. The tracker and the cuddle bug," he says with a grin.

A growl comes from next to us as Minor comes over and sits next to us, "Please don't refer to either of us as a 'cuddle bug.' We are much more dignified than that."

"Is that why I walked in on you, stomach bare, with Orion rubbing your stomach and your tongue hanging out?"

Minor snorts, "I don't know what you're talking about."

I smile and manage to even laugh. They both look at me and then look at each other, giving a shrug. "Sorry. I just...you guys have a great family vibe going on."

Minor shakes her head, "Family vibe? You do know we aren't technically...a blood family, right?"

"Blood doesn't always have to mean family. I know you are technically extensions of Orion's soul, but you act like siblings. You have been together for, well, forever. You're comfortable with each other and you trust each other with your lives. That is family, if you ask me." A warmth spreads through me and I know Orion heard me. His soul is smiling and filled with love for these Guardians. He is the father over them and a father's love is something special. I used to know that feeling. Even after my mother died and things declined with my own father, I could tell there was something deep down. He still worked to take care of me, made sure my schooling was paid for, and that I was well. He just did not care as much for taking care of himself without my mother around.

"They have been gone for a long time. I think I should go help them," Camden says, standing up.

"It has literally been ten minutes. I don't think-"

The antique shop door explodes outward, along with half the wall of the building. I put my hands over my head as the glass of the bait shop shatters. Camden is over me in an instant and we stand there until the glass stops raining down around us. A loud groan comes from the front of the shop and we see Scorpio laying in the entrance of the bait shop.

"Scorpio!" I run over to him as he peels himself out of the glass and sits up, his hand on his head. "What happened?" Camden and Minor come over as well.

"Libra. It is as if she is sleep walking. It was like she couldn't hear us when we tried talking to her. Her powers are going out of control." He stands and we all look toward the hole in the antique shop.

The hairs on the back of my neck stand as a woman walks out of the shop. She is tall and slim, with smooth pale skin. The air seems to swirl around her, causing her hair to sway. I notice it is actually two colors, one side a darker purple and the other side a light pink. She is stunning, except for the fact that her eyes are completely white. I take a step back.

"Libra. You need to snap out of it!" Aquarius stumbles out behind her. He put a hand on her shoulder. At the same time, I gasp as it feels like someone knocks the wind out of me and Aquarius is shot backwards down the street. He skids to a painful stop, sprawled on the pavement. I can see his chest moving up and down as he slowly sits back up, the side of his head bleeding.

Scorpio glances at me with a worried look and then back to Libra, who is now staring at me. "She knows. She senses Orion's soul. Faye, you need to go. You need to run. Now!"

Before any of us can move, an invisible force hits all of us. Scorpio and I go flying backwards and I hit the counter top, falling to the ground on the other side. Out of the corner of my eye, Camden and Minor are sent sliding across the ground on the other side of the shop. I hear glass crunching and Libra comes into view. She looks down at us and reaches out her hand. I lean away from her, but a bark catches her attention and a blurred figure knocks into her. Hands pull me up and Scorpio drags me around the counter and outside of the bait shop. Back inside, I can see another dog, standing their ground and growling at Libra.

The canine glances back at us, "Get her out of here, now!"

Scorpio nods and grabs my hand. "We can't just leave them," I shout, digging my heels against the pavement.

"We have to! Libra knows Orion is here and her basic instinct is taking over. I don't know what she might do if she gets her hands on you, but we don't need her siphoning any power without her back under control." He turns and looks back to the shop. "She must have gotten Capricorn. Dammit."

He starts to pull me to follow him, but I look back as I hear a yelp. The canine that stopped Libra from grabbing me is thrown into the antique shop and out of sight, while Libra exits the bait shop and turns toward us. Scorpio curses again and holds up his hand. The Earth trembles beneath us as a wall of dirt suddenly shoots up, blocking Libra's path. I realize that Scorpio has been holding my hand since we left the shop, but the power he seems to be taking from me isn't as noticeable as before. Does that mean I am getting used to exchanging their power?

"That isn't going to hold her for long. We have to get you far enough away where she won't sense Orion."

"And then what? It doesn't look like she is going to stop!" As if she heard me, the wall is blasted apart. We shield ourselves against the raining dirt and see Libra walking toward us once again.

"We will figure it out!"

A pair of arms come up behind Libra, linking under hers and pulling her back. I notice the blue hair of Aquarius as he holds her there, "Scorpio! Hurry!"

I watch as Libra struggles against Aquarius, fury etched into her beautiful features. She opens her mouth and an awful wailing leaves her. The sound is much louder than a normal person's cries and I have to cover my ears against the noise. As Aquarius tries to keep Libra at bay, I notice movement beside us. "Uh, Scorpio." I tug on his hand to get his attention.

"Oh, no." He sees what I do. People start coming out from the other shops and around the corners. We are suddenly surrounded by what seems to be a hundred people, and I sink against Scorpio. He puts me behind him, looking around and trying to find a way through all of them. "This isn't good. It doesn't look as though they have any consciousness of them."

"They look possessed," I can't squeeze myself any closer to Scorpio as the people around us get closer. "Where are your freaky daggers when we need them?"

The first of the civilians lunges at us. He is a middle aged man who doesn't look like he regularly gets into fights, but he was wielding a large wrench awfully confident as he brings it down toward us. Scorpio pushes me backward and ducks down to the left. The wrench swings past him and Scorpio brings his fist up into the man's stomach. It doesn't knock him out, but the man doubles over in pain. Scorpio then takes his hand and brings it down flat against the man's neck. The man's eyes roll into the back of his head as he falls onto the pavement, not moving.

I am going to have to have him teach me that.

Two others converge onto Scorpio at once, a man with what looks like a plastic pipe tube and a woman with a taser. Scorpio catches the pipe as it is brought down toward him and he brings his foot up, kicking the woman away. He yanks the pipe down, throwing the man forward and brings his knee up into the man's chest. The man falls forward and Scorpio kneels down, punching him in the face. I call out to Scorpio, but the woman reaches him first and brings the taser into Scorpio's side. He shouts in surprise and grits his teeth as the volts of electricity go through his body. He manages to turn around and he chops the lady's hand, making her drop it.

Scorpio punches the woman in her stomach, making her slump over like the other two. He reaches down and picks up the taser, throwing it my way, "They aren't any stronger than they would be normally! We need to try and get out of the crowd." He turns to take care of more people coming toward us.

I yelp as someone grabs my shoulder and pulls me to the ground. I don't see the face of whoever grabbed me, I just threw my hand up and turned on the taser. I hear a cry and see a woman slump to the ground. She doesn't look much older than me. I get to my feet and dance back away from more hands. I find myself alone, surrounded by stranger's faces. With the taser in front of me, I try not to cry as they get closer to me.

A blast of air blows by me and into a couple of people standing in front of me. I quickly turn around to see Capricorn standing there. A bruise was already forming around one of his eyes, his lip and eyebrow were busted open, and he held himself around his chest, most likely from bruised or broken ribs. "Go!" He shouts as one of the civilians tackle him and they struggle against each other. I want to go back and help, but I would only be getting in their way. I have no fighting experience, no magic, and this taser will only do so much.

I hear a scream and watch in horror as Libra has Aquarius on his knees, his arm wrenched back behind him. It's too much of an awkward angle to be right and as she reaches her hand down toward him, I grip the taser in my hand. "Hey!" I shout. Libra's head snaps up and her colorless eyes meet mine. "You want me? Come and get me!" I turn on my heels and run, managing to slip past the people trying to grab or hit me. I am sure I hear one of the guys call after me, but I don't stick around to figure out who it is. I don't get very far before I am blasted off my feet by wind and land face first into the pavement. I groan and glance behind me. Libra is heading my direction and moving quickly. The crowd doesn't even seem to take note of her as she weaves through them. I get back on my feet and keep running.

I have no idea where I am going, but it looks like anyone who would have been wandering around here is back with the others. I feel bad for leaving them, but I know Scorpio is going to be even more pissed for what I am doing now. Which, to be honest, is a pretty stupid idea. I have no weapon and no idea where I am even going. I turn the corner to head down an alleyway and head straight into a dead end. I frantically look around for another way, but the one door I saw is back toward the entrance. The same entrance that Libra is now standing in. I turn and look up, seeing how high the wall goes up. It's not terribly tall, but it is not something I can jump to. Luckily, I notice a couple of boxes and crates lying around me. I quickly start to pile them on top of each other and with a quick crossing of my fingers, I climb up.

The pile I have created wavers, but it holds just long enough for me to grab the top of the wall. I haul myself up, grateful that I managed to keep some semblance of upper arm strength. I reach the top of the wall just in time for Libra to now be standing where I was. She looks up at me, her white eyes narrowed. Can she really see me? I don't want to stick around and ask. I throw my legs over the other side, but something strange happens. All the sudden, the air around me seems to disappear. I try to take deep breaths, but nothing is entering my lungs. Losing my footing, I tumble over the edge of the wall, landing painfully on the other side. A scream tries to escape my throat as I land on my wrist, probably breaking it, but I can't make a sound.

Gasping and fighting off the darkness that creeps along the edge of my vision, Libra lands next to me on her feet. She reaches down and drags me up by the front of my tank top. I grit my teeth as my feet leave the ground. Libra closes her eyes and breathes in deeply, sensing Orion's power this close to her. I don't give her the time to take it though. Bringing around the taser I managed to hold onto after I fell, I push it against her shoulder and turn it on. Libra cries out as she drops me and I gasp as air refills my lungs. It almost hurts, but as long as I can breathe, that is all that matters. Libra growls and reaches for me again, but I move at the same time toward her, throwing the taser into her thigh. Her screams gurgle through the pain and I take her monetary incapacitation to get back to my feet and continue running.

Reaching the entrance of the alleyway, I glance back to watch her already coming back for me. Damn. This is one tough woman. I turn right down the deserted street and I run. And run. I keep running, even after my lungs burn and my legs ache. Sensation of presence flows through me and I know that Orion is there with me.

You need to go back, Faye.

Excuse me? I can't go back to her! She's trying to kill me!

No, not kill. The voice is silent for a moment. *She is lost, just like the others. The chaos inside her is controlling her. We have to bring balance back to her mind or she will be lost to us.*

I turn a corner and suddenly run into a wall, a wall that seems to reach out and catch me as I start to fall backwards. I bring the taser up to my new foe. "Faye, it's me!"

I actually take a second to look and see Scorpio. He is breathing heavy and he is covered in dirt and blood. I am afraid to know how much of it is his. Or isn't. "Scorpio. Orion says we have to try and get Libra balanced again."

Scorpio looks behind me and grabs my hand, our feet moving down the street. "All right. I'll bite. How exactly do we do that?"

Orion? I ask internally.

Push my power into her.

Isn't that the complete opposite of what we are trying to do?

I don't think she is after the power. I believe she is seeking my soul, acting on pure instinct to be with it once again. If you force my power back into her, it should overwhelm one side of her being and force the balance once again.

175

You sure that is going to work?

There is a pause. *Not really.*

Orion's voice causes me to stumble. Scorpio tugs me upwards and I dig my feet into the ground. I pull him back, "Wait! We have to go back to her."

"Are you kidding me?" Scorpio growls and uses his strength against me to continue me forward.

"Scorpio, stop! Orion says we have to go back!"

This makes him hesitate in his steps and he turns back to me. Glancing over my shoulder and then back to me, "What do you mean? What did he say?"

"That I need to get close to her. I need to give her power."

"Isn't that the *exact* reason we are getting you away from her?" My thoughts exactly, but Orion is the celestial being who created everything, so even though his answer was hesitant, it is the only thing we have to go on.

"I need to give her direct power from Orion. He said it's the only way to reverse the amount of chaos taking over her."

"I don't think that will be much of an issue," Scorpio murmurs and I turn. Scorpio yanks me back behind him after coming face to face with Libra. "Come on, Lib. I know you can hear me. Do you think Orion would approve of you letting this happen?"

Hearing Orion's name seems to trigger something in Libra's mind and she pauses. No one moves a muscle. I am afraid to even breathe. Scorpio slides his foot backwards, trying to create some distance between us. This brings Libra back and her hand rises in the air and she closes her hand. Suddenly, the air leaves my lungs and I can't breathe at all. Scorpio gags and stumbles to his knees. Libra continues to pull the air away from us and there are black spots in my vision. Panic begins to set in as my chest begins to hurt. My lungs scream for air that just is not there. This is the second time this has happened to me and I am not a fan.

There is a voice calling to me far away. I don't understand what they are saying, but I know the intention behind it. I grit my teeth and with the last bit of strength I have, I make my foot move forward. And then the other one. Libra shows no emotion as she closes her fist. By this time, Scorpio is lying on the ground and I don't see him move. My legs finally give out on me and I fall, but I manage to grab Libra's hand, dragging her down with me.

I can feel Libra trying to pull away from me, but I tighten my grip on her. I close my eyes and find Orion's soul inside me. After this last month of having it inside me, I now know what to look for. I dig deep and bring it to the surface, picturing the bright blue energy in my mind's eye, pushing it into Libra. A scream rips through the air and I'm not sure if it is her or me. The pain of pushing power into someone who does not want it hurts. It hurts so much that I almost stop, but I keep pushing the power into her and eventually I can feel the air return. I take in big gulps of air and my eyes snap open. Libra is sitting across from me, her chest heaving heavily, facing the ground.

Finally, her chest slows and her breathing becomes slow. Her eyes open and she blinks, as if waking up from a long, deep sleep. Looking up, our eyes meet. Hers are a bright, soft purple. She looks around and then she comes back to me. Her eyes water and spill over onto her cheeks. "Orion?"

I smile weakly, my hand dropping from hers cradling the

other one that still hurts like hell. "Close. I'm Faye. Nice to meet you."

A sob escapes her lips, "What have I done?"

"A whole lot, Lib," Scorpio groans as he slowly sits up. I shoot him a smile, grateful that he is still okay. He gives me a nod before turning back to Libra. "Your power went out of control. We still don't know how, but we believe the sisters had something to do with it."

Libra sighs and shakes her head, "It wasn't the sisters. This," she sweeps her hand behind her, "is my fault. I..." Her lip trembles.

"It's *not* your fault. If anything, I should have been around. The fall was hard on everyone, but I am the one who was supposed to take care of you. Alnilam may have caused our powers to leave, but we failed as Guardians." He stands and walks over to us. He helps Libra to her feet and then reaches for me. My feet are unsteady, but Scorpio keeps a hand against my back to keep me upright, "This is on all of us. We are going to find Regulus and figure this out."

Libra wipes her eyes and nose, nodding. My curiosity piqued at Scorpio's words, but I will have to ask him about it later. I'm too tired now. Giving away that much power, even with my body getting used to it, still wore me out. "We have to get to the others. Figure out if they are okay." I am worried about Aquarius and his arm.

Libra's attention focuses on me. "You're the holder of Orion's soul, aren't you?"

"That's me. Pack mule for all magical powers for celestial beings." Her face flushes and her eyes turn downward. Suddenly feeling bad, I reach out with my good hand to grasp hers. She jolts a little from the exchange of power between us and she looks at me again. "I'm kidding. Yes, Orion is with me. He is the one who told me how to help you."

This alights her eyes and she squeezes my hand, "Truly? He speaks with you?"

I nod. "He does. When he can, that is. He sleeps most of the time, I think, but every now and then he shows up. Luckily, it is usually when I need him the most."

Relief causes her body to visibly relax. "Thank goodness. We weren't sure what happened to him when we fell. Some of us feared he was gone or lost for good. I'm embarrassed to say that I am one of those. I just...don't know what to do without him. Alnilam turned out to be stronger than we had ever thought she could be."

"Faye! Scorpio!" A voice calls out and we look to see the others making their way over. Capricorn has Camden's arm over his shoulder, but he is waving with the other one. It was my turn to be relieved.

Aquarius is the first to reach us, grasping Libra's hands. "Are you all right?" The worry is apparent in his eyes.

"I am. Thanks to everyone. I'm so sorry, Aqua."

"You're back now. That is all that matters." Aquarius pulls her into a tight hug. She smiles and then as if the relief is too much, she goes slack in Aquarius's arms. He reaches down and picks her up in his arms. He glances around to the rest of us, "Let's get out of here. It is going to take a little bit for the effects of Libra's powers to wear off, but we do not want to be here once that happens. We will head back toward the construction site and hopefully we can go back out the same way we came."

"Wait. I thought she broke your arm?" I ask in surprise.

He shrugs, "I have always healed quickly. Plus, at some point when we exchanged power, I had kept it for a time I believed we would need it. It is still sore, but the break is healed."

We start walking, but Scorpio grabs my arm and keeps me back. "Let me see your hand." I've learned by now not to question the man when he asks something, so I show him my hand and wiggle my fingers. He rolls his eyes, "The other one. I know a broken wrist when I see one."

"You mean this? Psh, nothing I haven't dealt with before." I hold out my wrist and he gingerly runs his thumb over the bruised and swollen skin. I wince as he does.

"With Orion's soul healing you, it shouldn't take too long for this to recover. Possibly a little longer than normal with how much power you gave Libra."

"Yeah. I think somehow, he is dulling the pain. It doesn't hurt as much as it did before." It's true. When it first broke, the pain was agonizing, but I couldn't worry about it at the time. Not with Libra after me. Once that was all over, I noticed that the pain wasn't as bad as before. I've heard of pain getting worse once adrenaline wears off, but I guess this is what happens when you have basically a god inside your body.

"We will take care of it. Let's catch up with the others."

We head back toward the outside of town. It is a bit easier to get out than it was to get in, the few people we did see were in some sort of daze. Camden tells me on the way that at some point while fending off the townspeople, they just all dropped out of nowhere, unconscious. They were all alive, but the toll of Libra's power did a number on them. We continued on the move through the construction site and out of the city until we reached the gas station where we had first started.

"Wait out here. I'll go get us some water," Capricorn says. Camden goes inside with him, leaving the rest of us sitting outside. Aquarius slides down the side of the building with Libra still in his arms. Minor lays over next to him. I sit on the curb and Scorpio leans against the wall near the corner, keeping his eye out.

The dog from earlier that I hadn't recognized before comes over to me. Canis Major, or Major, as the others had called him. He is another one of Orion's companions and known as being one of the hunters of the sky. It is the first time I am getting a good look at him. He is a large dog, looking like a cross of a German Shepherd and a wolf. His eyes are bright, copper with golden flecks in them. He is a beautiful dog and he looks at me. "Your name. It's Faye, isn't it?"

I nod, "That's me. Orion's vessel and personal chauffeur."

Major huffs and shakes his coat, sitting down. "Your role is not so little of importance as to call yourself that. It is an important responsibility and from what I heard, you are taking it seriously."

"As well as I can, I think."

He tilts his head, "Do you not think that you are doing well?"

"Considering everything that has happened? Being attacked by giant wolves and a whole town trying to kill me isn't exactly my idea of doing well."

"The events taking place are not your fault. Alnilam would have sent her minions after anyone who had the unfortunate task of housing Orion's soul. You just happen to be that unfortunate person. It is not an easy role and things are going to be dicey from here on out. For one as young as you, you are doing well. How old are you, Faye?"

"Sixteen. I will be seventeen this year." I won't be home to celebrate it. Every year, my father managed to be home for my birthdays. Sometimes he wouldn't be exactly sober, but being there had meant a lot. Luke and his family would invite us over to the bar and we would usually have a small party there. My sixteenth birthday had been celebrated with a lot of glow sticks, neon lights, and a whole lot of paint we ended up having to clean up the next day.

Major nods, "Do you believe that most children your age could handle what has happened as well as you have?"

I think about it and shrug, "I'm not sure." I suppose I have been through enough in my life that it has simply made my adaptation to crazy situations easier. "Probably not," I decide.

"There you have it. If it was someone else, Lupus most certainly would have gotten Orion's soul by now because not many your age can fight like you can. Physically you could use some improvement, but your heart is strong, Faye."

If it wasn't for the fact that I am still trying to get over having an actual heart to heart with a talking dog, I would have definitely cried. "Thanks. I appreciate that." We sit in silence for a few moments before I try to change the subject, "So what kind of powers do you and Minor have?"

"Us? Oh, we don't have any powers."

This surprised me. "Really? Nothing?"

He seems to shrug and shakes his head, sliding to the ground to lay down, "Really. Sure, we have a little bit more going for us than the average dog, but otherwise we are pretty normal."

"As normal as supernatural beings that live in space can be."

"That is very true." There is amusement in his voice. He reminds me of Martin. His voice is kind but wise. The thought of the older gentleman causes my chest to tighten. I hope that they are all right. The thought of trying to contact them has not even crossed my mind since Theo attacked my town. Now the only thing I want is to talk to them, to see if Luke is all right. He is the closest thing I have to a brother and I'm not even going to entertain the thought of him being gone. I can't. My heart is still trying to accept the fact that my father is gone.

We continue to talk a little bit more about his times with Orion and how he had created Major and Minor as companions more than anything. Humans label them as Orion's hunters. A possible truth to that, but Minor hates the thought of being labeled by humans. "She's not very fond of us, is she?"

"Hm. There is a certain dislike, but there is no hate. She grew weary of watching how much chaos seemed to control humans. Libra can only control so much of what happens down here, but Minor always believed her to have a little less control than we thought. The interesting part of free will, I guess."

"Could that be true? That she doesn't have that good of control?"

"So some say. I believe her control is enough. It's just... creatures who are given free will tend to want more than they have. Especially since humans are so advanced, more than anything else on Earth. If Libra were to be on Earth through-out the entire year, every year, then I believe that there would be complete control on Earth. That kind of control would come with a price though, not only for Libra, but everyone else as well."

"Libra being here all the time would make everyone ba-sically the same, right? So, we would end up being zombies, without the appetite for brains."

"More or less. Minor is a great companion. She loves Orion very much, possibly more than any of us. And like us, she is taking Orion's fall particularly hard. So do not take her sour attitude to heart. She means well."

I smile and glance back at the smaller Shiba, lying her head against Libra's thigh. Her ears are relaxed, but twitching every now and then when she hears a sound. I can't imagine what she must be feeling. All of them have been working hard to bring everyone back together in order to bring back Orion and stop the sisters.

"Cabs are here," Scorpio calls and pushes himself off the wall. He goes over and offers a hand to Aquarius, helping him up with Libra still in his arms. Two cabs pull up. Aquarius places Libra in the back of one and slides in next to her. Minor gets in with them, Capricorn getting in the front. I slide in the backseat of the other one. Camden and Major join me, with the canine sitting in between us. Scorpio takes the front seat of the second cab and we head out. The further we get away from Billings, the more distance we can put between the incident. Camden tells me that there is no way they could figure out it was Libra who caused everything, but I have to remind him of the power of technology. If we are lucky, then the cameras either got wiped out or just couldn't catch Libra. I have a feeling we would be seeing about a dozen armored vehicles and men in white lab coats ready to take her away.

"Where are we heading?" I scoot up and ask Scorpio after a little bit

He doesn't turn around, but I notice the little hairs on the back of his neck raise. I guess he didn't expect me to get so close. I lean back a little as he answers, "Laurel. There is no point in heading all the way back to Bozeman. We will get a couple of hotel rooms. We will give Libra some time to recover. Hopefully, once she is back on her feet, we can get some air tickets."

"To Greece?" I ask excitedly.

"That's the plan," Scorpio replies and even though I don't see his face, I can hear the smile.

I lean back against my seat and grin. The one silver lining in all of this is being able to travel all over. The Duncan Islands were an amazing experience. I could do without the killer wolves though. Greece is one of those places I would see on the internet or on a stranger's social media accounts. It is always a place I can imagine myself loving, but having no way of getting there. I look over and see Camden staring out the window. His eyebrows are drawn together, creating a worried crease. I reach over and pat his hand.

Camden jumps and glances at me with a quickly fading, startled expression. "Yeah?"

"What do you mean, yeah? Are you okay? This is the quietest you have been since I've met you."

"Oh. Yeah I'm good. Just tired from getting my ass handed to me. Did you see how many people there were?"

He shrugs and turns his attention back out the window. I purse my lips but don't push. I haven't known Camden long enough to know if there was something wrong or not, but there was something nagging at me. I'll ask Scorpio later and see if he will talk to him. I am not sure how we share the same sign, the same personality traits. He is outgoing and seems pretty friendly toward people. Me on the other hand, tend to be more reserved, although I consider myself to be pretty friendly. I guess it's not an exact science. Everyone is different in their own way.

We ride the rest of the way to Laurel in silence. Major eventually finds his way down on the seat, with his head in my lap and his bottom pushing Camden against the door. He does not seem to mind, in fact, seems to hardly notice at all. My hand idly strokes the canine's fur as I watch the landscape pass us by.

My mind wanders, going back over everything from the last week or so. Has it really been that short of time? The beginning of the past events brings me back to the story Scorpio told me about Orion and his sisters. How does one come to hate someone so much, they would go so far as to destroy everything? Orion brought his sisters to life. Given them a home. Give them to each other, so that they would not be lonely. Do they really require so much more than what he has already offered? *I guess celestial beings and humans are not so much different after all. Anything that can think for itself, always wants more. When will it ever be enough?* Then I remember how much I took for granted before my mother died, and then even after that, before my father died. I was always wishing for more, whether it be a way out of my high school, a way out of my father's house, or just senseless things in general. Now? I would go back to all of it in a heartbeat if I could.

I brush the stray tear that falls away from my cheek as we pull into a hotel behind the other cab. Capricorn heads inside to get us set up for the night while the rest of us unpack our things from the trunks and haul it inside. Capricorn comes back to us, holding out key cards. He gives me a set, "I figure you would appreciate a room of your own. Camden, you're with Scorpio. Aquarius will be with Libra and I."

"Thanks," I say and take the key cards from him. I can't help but notice the attendants at the front desk were all staring at us with a mix of confusion and concern. I can't blame them though. We all look pretty rough, but Capricorn must have already addressed it, otherwise the rent a cop by the desk surely would have said something already. I gathered my luggage and we all headed toward the elevator. Luckily, we all managed to get rooms next to each other. I slip the key into the slot and open the door to a standard room with a queen size bed. There is a mini fridge and a microwave, along with a television on a dresser. The smell of cleaner tells me the cleaning people have been along. I drop my suitcase onto the floor next to the dresser and fall backwards onto the bed. I sigh as I sink down into it.

There is a knock on the door and I sigh. It doesn't look like I will get any time alone after all. I trudge over to the door and open it to see Scorpio standing there. "You got a second?"

"Sure," I move to let him in. I go back and sit on the edge of the bed while he opts for leaning against the dresser. "What's up?"

"How are you feeling?"

The question catches me off guard a bit and it takes me a moment to answer. "Um, fine? How are *you* feeling?"

"I'm serious, Faye." I wonder if I will ever get used to the feeling I get when he says my name. I've heard it a million times during my lifetime. "You have been through a lot. More than I think most humans go through in their lifetime. I've seen humans go crazy over such frivolous things as not being able to buy a pair of shoes." I snort, trying not to laugh. His face looks serious, but out of all the examples he could have used, he went with shoes.

I shrug and look down at my hands. The tiny scar is still there from when I cut myself on the crystal shard that originally held Orion's soul. It never occurred to me that while my other injuries are healing fast, this one is always there. Even the pain in my wrist is gone and the angry purple bruise has lightened significantly. I press my thumb against the scar and look at Scorpio. He arches an eyebrow, waiting for me to answer him. "What is your connection with Orion?"

This time, it seems, I am the one catching him off guard. "What?"

"It is something I have been meaning to ask you for a while now. For some reason, when I am giving Camden power, it is a feeling of soft energy flowing from me to him. With you? It is like an electrical current. I can feel...something when it happens between us."

"Maybe it is our undeniable bond?" He asks with a grin. I roll my eyes and he shrugs, "Perhaps it's different between the twelve of us. Have you tried with any of the others?"

"I don't think so. With Libra, it felt like something warm

passing between us. I haven't touched Capricorn or Aquarius long enough to know if it's the same."

"See? I wouldn't worry about it. I'm sure you will feel the same if you exchange power into Regulus or Sags."

"Sags?"

"Sagittarius. His name is too long so we gave him a nickname."

I laugh, "I'm sure he loves that."

"He ought to. I gave it to him myself." We sit there with stupid smiles on our faces, well, I'm sure mine is the only stupid one, before his fades back into his usual, stoic self, "Are you sure you're all right?"

I sigh, "Honestly? I don't know. I'm just tired."

"That's understandable." He moves away from the dresser and comes to kneel down in front of me. "Know this, Faye. Whatever you are going through and whatever trouble you may find yourself in, I will be there for you. We all will. It is not just because Orion's soul is inside you, either. You are a fiercely brave girl who is standing up to face danger like no other. I think we can all admire that." And cue the little stomach flutter. Scorpio stands, "Get some sleep. You deserve it. My room is right next door. The others are across the hall."

He turns to leave. I stand and watch him go, Scorpio giving me one last nod of his head before the door clicks shut. My head is still feeling light from his words. After a second, I go to the door and open it, sticking my head out. Certain that no one was standing there waiting to ambush me, I slink back into my room. I walk over and fall face down into the bed. I roll over. I know I told Scorpio that I was feeling tired, but sleep is not going to come easy. I slept in the cab on the way over here, so now I feel a second wind hitting me. I sit up and decide that first and foremost, I need a shower. I head into the bathroom, pleasantly surprised by a decent sized tub and there is even a robe hanging in the small closet.

"How in the hell are they affording all of this?" I wonder aloud. I don't ponder too long as I turn the shower on and step inside. I know it wasn't too long ago since I took one, but I feel like showers are a luxury I need to enjoy while I can. Who knows when something will happen and I find myself without one.

I don't stay under the water too long, just enough to get whatever dirt and other debris left in my hair after the incident with Libra. I dry off, put on the robe and walk over to the window. We are on the third floor of the hotel, so I can get a pretty good view of everything. Everything looks so normal. Like the end of the world is not looming on innocent people's doorsteps. I wonder what my parents would say if they knew what was happening. What I was doing. A thought occurs to me and I turn my attention inward. *Orion?* I ask, but I do not feel the surge of the familiar presence. I will have to ask him next time I feel him around. If everything that dies goes back with him eventually…does that mean my parents as well? It's a somber thought. I go through my luggage and find some clothes, opting for a simple black t-shirt and jeans.

I grab a key card and push it into my back pocket and head out of the hotel room. At the same time, Camden also comes out of the room he is sharing with Scorpio, scowling. He sees me and a smile replaces the scowl, "Hey Faye. You heading out?"

"Maybe." I shrug. It did not occur to me to go anywhere

other than the lobby of the hotel. The thought of running into more giant wolves had my skin crawling. But... "Do you want to get out of here? There was an outlet mall a couple of blocks from the hotel. Maybe do a little window shopping." The need to get out and do something normal overwhelmed the fear of being attacked. Besides, with Camden with me, I should be okay.

"Why window shop?" He asks, wrinkling his nose and shoving his hands in his pockets. He is wearing black cargo pants and a long sleeved, army green shirt. It's crazy how someone so normal looking could be someone so powerful.

I laugh, "Because it is what normal people do. Come on. I cannot stay cooped up in this hotel and you look like you could stand some time away from Scorpio."

"You're not wrong about that. The guy can't stop moving. He's driving me nuts." His smile turns mischievous. "I bet he will be pissed knowing we left without telling him."

"See? Let's go, before the parental units make us stay in our room."

CHAPTER TWELVE

The walk is a short one. The sun is beginning to set and the air is cool, but not so much that I need a jacket. I love the transition between winter and spring, how the warmer days feel inexplicably uplifting. We reach the edge of the parking lot, which is still pretty full for this time of day. I'm glad we still have a few hours before they close. The outlet is structured in a square, the majority of the walking being done outside. I have visited similar outlets like this and I enjoy the idea of walking in the fresh air after being inside a stuffy store.

"How is Capricorn paying for all of this?" I ask out of the blue one we hit the first store. It is one of those small business stores, where everything is basically hand made. We politely acknowledge the store employee and I don't miss her subtle attempt of checking out Camden. Looking at him again, I guess I can't blame her. "I know the cab rides must have been expensive. Not to mention the hotel rooms. You guys didn't rob banks or anything when you fell, did you?"

Camden's smile is rather smug as he reaches into his own pocket and pulls out a wallet. He slides a black card out of the sleeve and waves it in front of me, "We have learned a few things here and there. Especially how much humans rely on these."

"Oh, so you didn't rob banks. You're just using phony credit cards," I hiss quietly. I glance around to make sure no one heard me before turning back to Camden.

He lifts one shoulder in a shrug and shoves the card and wallet back in his pocket, "How else are we supposed to get around? It's not like we have social security numbers or jobs to pay for any of this. We had to adapt. We don't plan on being around long enough to integrate *that* far into society."

It made sense. For some reason, I expected them to just be able to have money, like any other supernatural creature I've seen on television. Ever notice how they all seem to have money, even though no one knows they exist? Perhaps they did things the same way these Guardians did. I don't know, but I'm glad we aren't sleeping in the woods because we are too broke to afford a bed for the night.

"Well since you are the one with the funds, I guess this just turned into a shopping excursion instead. I think I saw a Starbucks around the corner. Let's grab some coffee and then we can shop for real." Camden grins and we head into the Starbucks at the start of the outlet mall. I grab an iced coffee and Camden gets one of the chocolate Frappuccino's. I tell him that it's a dessert and not a coffee, but he shrugs me off.

"You're the one who wanted to get coffee so late in the afternoon." He retorts, proceeding to scoop whipped cream out of the cup with his straw.

"Yeah, well." I stop before telling him what I really feel, that I did not want to be alone in the room with my thoughts. On the outside, I look well-adjusted to everything going on. Inside, I'm sure even Orion is being wrecked and rolled by the turmoil in my heart. Unlike other teenagers who get to spend their days in class, with friends and enjoying their days, I am stuck in a hotel room with a bunch of strangers. My town was ruined, my father is dead, and I have been attacked numerous times. I am sure if I were to tell Dr. Rommen of my adventure, she would have me admitted for sure.

Camden seems to sense my distress and gently elbows me, pointing at one of the stores, "Let's go in there." It is an antique store and I smile, knowing it is his way of trying to make me feel better. There are always hidden treasures in antique stores. It amuses me that someone who looks like Camden would willingly choose to go into an antique store. When we reach the door, I hesitate. Last time I was around a store like this, a celestial-made being was trying to possibly kill me. "Don't worry. Nothing to hurt us here." Camden reassures me and holds the door open for me.

We head inside and the cashier greets us with an unenthused hello. They close in an hour, but that gives Camden and I plenty of time to browse around. There is a lot of the usual stuff. Old farm aesthetic items, old kitchenware, kid toys, and plenty of other items. Eventually we have our fill of finding the little oddities of the shop and we decide to head out before the workers come find us and herd us out of the shop. On the way out, something catches my eye and I stop. Camden stops next to me, a quizzical look on his face.

I walk over to one of the shelves and pick up a little heart shaped crystal. It is almost the exact same as the half of the crystal I had found in the crater. The one that first gave me Orion's soul. The one that started all of this.

"Are you okay?" Camden asks.

I blink and notice my cheeks are wet. I quickly wipe my face and place the crystal back on the shelf, "Yeah. I'm good. Sorry, let's go. I think the cashier is getting ready to get the broom and chase us out." As if on cue, the cashier pokes their head around the corner, a glare on their face.

We make our way out of the antique store and stop by a toy store. We spend a good amount of time playing with the various toys they had out on display. At one point, I find a pair of plastic ninja swords. I pick them up and turn to Camden, "Didn't Scorpio lose his during our fight with Lupus?"

"Unconfirmed. But I'm sure he wouldn't mind the upgrade." We laugh and decide to purchase the toys, along with a couple of games I think the others would enjoy. Camden tells me that none of them have really had much time getting into pop culture of the modern era. They spent most of their time learning how to get money, traveling, communication, and the other convenient things that are needed to try and save the world. "Not that we didn't have some time to get into the crowd, but it just didn't seem like the most appropriate thing to do."

Ouch.

"Oh. Yeah, I guess that makes sense." Now I'm bummed. "I guess you guys have better things to do than spend time playing silly human games."

"Woah, hey." He grabs my arm and stops me from walking

any further. "I didn't mean it like that. It's just that...well, you know."

His flustered face is enough to make me smile again, "It's fine. I know what you meant. Trust me, I know how important this is to everyone. With Libra getting back on her feet, we need some time to rest though. I figured it wouldn't hurt to do normal things for a while until we are back on our world saving quest."

"Universe."

"What?"

"Universe saving quest. We are saving everyone, kid."

"Damn right we are."

We browse the store more, trying on the funny masks around and finding more trinkets to bring back the others. By the time we walk out of the store, my arms are wrapped around my stomach because it hurts from laughing so much. We spend the rest of the time that the outlets are open going in and out of the various clothing stores. I show Camden my version of window shopping, which includes finding the most ridiculous outfits and trying them on. We find full suits with comic words and other cartoonish characters on them. We keep finding the craziest outfits and try them on, posing and laughing in front of the mirrors they have.

Eventually, one of the store clerks came over to let us know that they are closing in ten minutes and to make our way to the front with our purchases. Still giggling like children, we manage to find our way out of the store. The sun is pretty much set under the horizon at this point, the only sources of light coming from the street lights that are on.

We start walking back to the hotel, but we don't get very

far before my stomach growls loudly. Camden laughs and I flush. "I just realized I have not eaten in...forever. Oh my god, I'm starving! Let's get some food. Wait, do you guys eat food?"

Camden rolls his eyes, "You watch too many movies. There was a pizza place we passed on our way here. It's getting late and we can continue our window shopping excursion tomorrow. I think we are going to be in town for a couple of days, so we have plenty of time."

"Sounds good to me. I want to see how Libra is doing anyway."

"Same. Using that much power must have taken a toll on her. I'm hoping that when you released your power into her, it helped what was depleted." We find the pizza place Camden mentioned and we head inside, ordering a few pizzas and sit outside on the bench to wait for them. "How are you doing in all this?" He asks me.

"You know. I wish everyone would stop asking me that."

"Well, to be fair, we are more affiliated with each other than the others. I have been sensing distress from you since we first met. You don't show it very much though."

I sigh and rub my face, leaning back against the bench. "I don't know what you guys want me to say. Am I okay? No, not really. A couple of weeks ago I was just a normal girl trying to get through school. Next thing I know, I'm being attacked by wolves, my body is inhabiting a celestial being's soul, my father dies, and I have had more close calls with death then anyone should have to go through." I have to consciously release my fists because my nails are biting into the skin on my palms. I look to Camden, "So I'm not doing all right. I'm having a hard time dealing with all of this, but what am I supposed to do? Lay on the bed and cry? I don't see how much good that is going to do for any of us. You guys need me and I need you. We won't get anywhere if I mope around all the time. So every once in a while I will take my cries when I can, but otherwise, I will continue on. So stop asking me if I'm all right. The answer is no. But I'll deal."

We stare at each other for a while, our contact breaking when one of the employees for the pizza parlor comes out with our order. We each take a couple and we start heading back to the hotel. It is silent and I start to feel bad. Did I snap too much at him? Glancing over at Camden, I can see him walking in concentration. I go to say something to him when his gaze snaps up toward the sky. He stops walking and glances around.

"What is it?"

He stares a little bit longer before shaking his head, "It's nothing. I think I saw a bird or something. It caught me off guard."

I laugh, "And to think I am the one stressing. You're freaking out over birds."

The smile he gives me does not reach his eyes, "Birds can be trouble too, you know."

We reach the hotel and wait for the elevator to hit the ground floor so we can go up. When it finally comes, Camden waits until I get on and then follows me in. We hit the three button and head on up. "Faye," he begins and I slide my eyes in his direction. "I apologize about everything that's been happening to you. If we could change it, we would do this on our own."

"Yes, but there is no changing the past. Trust me, I would

have a long time ago if that was the case. I would have warned my mother that she was going to get sick. I would have told my father that he needed to work hard to not relapse back into drinking. But I'm not mad at you guys. You have done your best in fixing things. I appreciate your apology, but it is not needed. It's not your fault. It's not any of your guys' fault."

He doesn't look convinced, but nods anyway. The ding indicates that we reach our floor and we head over to the room where Aquarius, Libra, and Capricorn are staying. Aquarius opens the door when we knock, "Perfect. We were wondering where you guys went."

"Is that them?" I hear an angry shout.

Aquarius smiles a bit sheepish, "Come in. Just remember, he means well."

"Well, maybe some food will help," I say and he shrugs. I walk in past him and all of them are either sitting or standing in the room. My eyes land on Libra, who is sitting on the bed next to Capricorn. She looks tired, but much better than she had earlier. "We have brought sustenance. I know you guys don't really need to eat, but pizza makes everything better."

"Where did you go?" Scorpio growls.

We set the boxes down and I turn to him, "I wanted to check out the town. Camden says we are going to be here for a few days and I am not staying stuck in that room."

"What if something had happened to you?"

"But it didn't. I had a bodyguard the whole time."

"That doesn't mean anything. Even with one of us with you, there is danger, especially with someone as inexperienced as Camden."

"Hey!" He interjects.

"Scorpio, you're overreacting! I understand that there are dangers-"

"*You don't understand anything!*" He shouts.

"Scorpio," Capricorn warns, but Scorpio ignores him.

"Lupus was just the first of the creatures who live among us and he is not nearly as deadly. The next time Alnilam sends someone after you, we may not be as lucky as we were. So stop being so damn childish and stupid, and *stay put.*"

The room is silent. I am fuming. Glaring at one another, I don't say anything. What's the point? Instead, I grab one of the boxes of pizza and storm out of the room. I put my card into its slot, walk into the room and kick the door shut behind me. I'm glad none of the others have a key card to my room. Or did they? I don't know. Just in case, I lock the door and slide the clasp on the top so that even if they do have a key card, they can't get in. I was going to get some alone time, dammit.

I throw the pizza box onto the bed and fall down next to it. I absently reach inside and grab a slice. My hand and mouth move automatically, but my mind is elsewhere. Stupid Scorpio. I wish he could treat me a little bit more like Camden does. This afternoon has been the best time I have had since receiving Orion's soul and he can't expect me to sit around and wait for the enemies. Being human meant doing human things, whether he likes it or not.

I roll over and sit up against the bed frame, deciding to see what is on tv for a while, eating the pizza on hand. My stomach growls in appreciation for the food. I turn on a random movie that seems interesting and the rest of the night is pretty quiet from then on. No one knocks on my door and

I don't go looking for anyone. Eventually I shove the pizza box off my bed and onto the table in the room. I turn off the lights, opting to leave the one from the bathroom on. It's not as though I was afraid of the dark, I just want to be able to see if something comes lurking in the night. I crawl under the covers, the thick comforter warming me and I quickly fall into a deep slumber.

I dream again of magic and soft, warm lights. Orion doesn't talk to me in my dreams and when I wake up the next morning, I lay in my bed wondering why. You would think it would be easier to talk to me while unconscious, when I'm busy inside my own mind. *Orion?*

Nothing.

I should probably get out of bed. Just as I am contemplating doing that or just sleeping in, there is a knock on my door. I sigh and throw the comforter off of me and slide out of bed. I pad my way over to the door and throw it open expecting to see Scorpio standing there with another lecture for me. Instead, Aquarius is there with Major by his side. "Good morning. Did I wake you?"

"No, not really. What's up?"

"We are heading down to grab breakfast. Are you hungry?"

I know I shouldn't be after all the pizza I ate, but I could still go for some coffee. "Give me a few minutes to change and I'll meet you guys down there."

"Sounds good."

"Do you mind if I wait here with you?" Major asks.

I should be annoyed by the prospect of a babysitter, but I genuinely like the idea of Major's company. "Not at all. Come in." I look back to Aquarius, "See you soon?" He nods and I close the door. I turn and lean back against it, Major sitting there with his tail slowly wagging back and forth. "They stuck you with babysitting duty, huh?"

Major sneezes and he shakes his fur, "Not quite. I offered my services."

I laugh and shake my head. "Feel free to use the bed. I'm going to change and we can head downstairs with the others." He does just that as I grab clothes out of my suitcase and go into the bathroom. When I look into the mirror, I can see heavy bags under my eyes and I swear my cheeks have sunken in a little. I guess that's what happens when you're constantly on the run. I splash water on my face to try and bring it back to life as much as possible before changing into a green tank top and leggings. I brush my hair and throw it in a ponytail and make my way out of the bathroom. Major's head perks up when I come out. "Come on. Let's go meet the others."

Major jumps down off the bed and does a little stretch before following me out the door. We walk down the hall until we get to the elevator and we take it down to the first floor. As we get to the cafeteria, I see the others gathered at a table, talking amongst themselves. Major heads over to them while I grab some coffee and a handful of sugar and creams. I pull a chair up and sit between Libra and Camden, slowly peeling open the creamers.

"I'm just saying. We should wait here another couple of days. Just until everyone is back on their feet and fully recovered." Aquarius said with exasperation.

"It's going to take a couple of days just to get to Greece and find the others anyway. We can use that time to recover. It's better to keep moving rather than stay in one place.

Alnilam has been keen on our locations until now. You can bet it won't take her long to figure out what happened in Billings and trace us back here." Scorpio countered, sipping his own coffee.

"If this is about me, I'm fine. Really. We should hurry and find the others, find Regulus." Libra interjects. I'm beginning to think I should have just stayed in my room.

"I'm surprised you're not the first one jumping at the chance of seeing Regulus, Aquarius"

Aquarius's face turns a slightly pinker shade. "He will understand if we are held up."

I look between the two of them and then over at Camden. He chuckles and leans over toward me, "Regulus and our Aquarius here are what you humans call an 'item,'" he says with air quotes.

"Ah. Gotcha." I stare at Aquarius and wonder what kind of person Regulus is. "Why wouldn't you want to go see him?"

Aquarius sighs and runs his hand through his hair. "Regulus probably understands this situation better than any of us, and some time to rest isn't going to interfere with our travels. Besides, we don't even know if he is one of the ones in Greece. I would rather take the time to get us there safely without any more incidents. We rest up, make sure we are completely back on our feet, and then we head to Greece. I think we can spare a couple of days."

"I agree." I speak up.

"Why? So you can go running around town to get hurt, kidnapped, and possibly killed?" Scorpio snaps.

"Dude," Camden throws his hands up, offended.

"I'm not a child, Scorpio." He raises an eyebrow at me and

I feel my hands tighten around the coffee cup. "Just because I'm a minor doesn't mean I'm stupid. Not only did I have Camden with me, we only went a few blocks away! I'm sure if anything had happened, you guys would know."

"That's not the point-"

"What is the point then?" I shout, earning some concerned glances from the patrons around us. I flush and lower my tone. "You seem pretty set on keeping me confined in tiny rooms for the remainder of whatever the hell this is. I'm not some animal you can keep caged."

"I'm sorry. You seem to be forgetting that you are in *danger*. There are powerful beings wanting to rip your soul out of your chest and you want to go shopping. So yes, if I have to keep you locked inside a tiny room, a tiny room you will stay in."

"You can't do that!"

"Watch me."

"All right, that's enough you two!" Capricorn slams his hands on the table. I didn't realize we had stood up until I look at him, still sitting and looking pissed. "Here is what we are going to do. I agree with Aquarius on waiting until we are completely recovered." He holds his hand up as Scorpio opens his mouth to speak again. "Get your head out of your ass, Scorpio. Look at the two of them," he motions to Libra and I. "They are exhausted, even after a night of sleep. We are going to stay another night or two." He turns to me, "While roaming is not suggested, you are not a hostage with us, Faye. But I will strongly recommend that you are with one of us at all times. Not only for safety, but for peace of mind as well."

"Fine." I sit back down and sit back against the chair, sipping my coffee.

Capricorn turns to Scorpio, who falls back into his chair. "Fine. We'll stay."

I try not to smile into my cup. Scorpio may act like a badass who can fight off giant wolves, but I am starting to figure out who has more of a say in things between everyone. Regulus is obviously the leader of them all, Orion's second hand man. It seems as though Capricorn is pretty high on that pole as well.

"So," Camden starts. "I think we should all do something around town since we are staying a little bit longer." Scorpio glares at him and Camden grins, "You can stay in the hotel room if you want, grouchy. Faye and I don't need a babysitter."

Scorpio wipes his mouth and throws the napkin down, "Do what you will. I'm heading back to the room."

I watch as he leaves the small cafeteria. I'm not sure why, but I feel a little guilty about him being so angry. I don't want to be trapped in a room, waiting for someone else to come and try to take me away. I want to experience some type of normalcy. I sigh, "I'm going to head back up also."

"I'll come get you when I find something for us to do, okay?" Camden says.

"Sounds good." I make my way through the hotel and find the elevators. I get in and push the little 3 button. I move aside as a family gets in with me. I stand in the corner and we start going up. There are two little girls standing there, hand in hand, talking to their parents about something that had to do with the pool and a bird. Their parents are enthusiastically entertaining their stories with head nods and agreements. The little girls are both blonde haired and don't look any older than four or five.

I smile and lean my head back against the elevator. The family reminds me of when I was younger, back when both my mom and dad were still alive. I don't remember much, but we were happy. I was happy. I bet I used to do the same thing, talk their ears off. I think it's the joy of being able to talk that makes little kids want to do it constantly. The door opens on the second floor and they head off, back to enjoying their vacation, blissfully unaware of the danger they are really in. The door closes and once again the elevator starts back up again.

I get off on the third floor and walk along the maroon patterned floor until I come back to my room. I slide the keycard in and once inside, I close the door behind me, and sigh. Now what? I walk over to the window and pull open the curtains, looking out at the city. Laurel was another small-town, bigger than Hamilton but still small. There were a lot of stores placed right next to each other and train tracks. I can't imagine there being much to do in a place like this, but of course, there are always hidden gems in places you would least expect.

I close the curtains back up and hear a thump coming from the room next door. I stand there for a second before hearing another one. *What is Scorpio up to over there?* I grab my key card and head out of my room, walking five feet to the next door over. I listen with my ear against the door, trying to figure out what could be going on when the door suddenly opens. I yelp and jump back, startled at Scorpio's sudden appearance.

"What are you doing?" He asks, brow raised.

"I thought I heard…something." I manage. I can't help

but notice his lack of shirt and quickly look back up at his face. "What are you doing over here?"

He shrugs, "I'd rather work out up here than down in the gym. Can't use my blades in a public setting."

"Wait, I thought you lost those. When did you get new ones?"

He smirks and steps back, beckoning me into the room. I walk past him and when I get into the room, I notice the plastic toy swords that Camden and I found last night on the bed. "These bad boys happen to have been a gift. I'm sure they will do plenty of damage against any enemy that may come after us."

I roll my eyes. "I bet. But seriously, why are you doing all this in here? There is a perfectly good gym downstairs. You may as well use that since you're paying for it. With stolen money, might I add."

"Ah, Camden told you about that, huh?"

"Yeah." I plop down on the edge of the bed. "So when do I get mine?"

Scorpio snorts, "What makes you think you get one?"

"Well, I figure since you all have one, shouldn't I? Little orphan Annie will need some way to pay for crap when she's all alone again."

Scorpio sighs and runs his hand through his hair. "Faye-"

"No, it's okay." I stand up. "I think I can figure out a way to manage." I walk past him and stop when I reach for the door handle of his room. I spin around. "Can you teach me?"

"What?"

"Can you teach me how to fight?"

"Um, I don't think you're ready for that."

I cross my arms, "Why not? Don't you think I should learn how to defend myself against the big nasties that are going to be coming after us?"

"That's what you have us for," he says, leaning against the dresser.

"Scorpio. Let's be realistic for a second. You and I both know that you guys are not always going to be around. I need something to defend myself with. If you're not going to give me a weapon, then teach me to use these." I put my hands up in fists.

Scorpio pushes off the wall and comes over to stand in front of me. He puts a hand up, palm facing me. "All right. Let's see what you got. Hit me."

"You serious?" He nods. "All right." I flex my fingers and bring my hands up and punch his hand.

"Come on, Faye. Is that the best you can do?" I frown and punch his hand again. He grins, "You know. I don't think this will even hurt a toddler." I punch again. "Nope. Nothing. I hope you don't expect Alnilam to be afraid of a little-" I cut him off as I punch him in the face. He doesn't reel back like I thought he would and it hurt way more than when I was just punching his hands. I cradle my hand and Scorpio wrinkles his nose. "Okay. You win, Faye. I'll teach you to fight, but don't go looking for one, you hear me?"

I grin. "So when does our first lesson start?"

The door opens and Camden walks in, pancake sticking out of his mouth. He looks between the two of us and raises his eyebrows. "Am I interrupting something?" He asks, taking the pancake out of his mouth.

"No!" Scorpio and I shout in unison.

Camden laughs, "My bad." He comes in and jumps on his bed. "I was checking things out around here and there isn't much to do. I think we should order in, rent some B-rated movies, and then check out this hotel's pool."

"What happened to wanting to run around town and being the miscreants you are?" Scorpio asks.

"If I am going to run around causing chaos, it is not going to be in some small-town. I want it to be somewhere big like L.A or New York. I want to make sure my face will be on a billboard before we leave."

I laugh. "Slow down, buddy. How about we stick your face on a billboard to save the world?"

Camden claps, "Even better!" He jumps back up. "I'm going to check out the rest of the hotel. You guys coming?" We both decline and Camden slips out of the room.

I look at Scorpio, "So?"

"So, what?" I throw my hands up and punch the air a couple of times. "Ah. Well, come on. Let's see if there is a place we can practice. Might as well do it now before any of the others come after us." He grabs a t-shirt off the floor and slips it back over his head, swiping the card key off the table and we head out. We step into the elevator and head down to the first floor.

"When are you going to tell me about that?" I ask as we head down.

"Are you ever going to just come out and tell me what you want? Or are you going to start all of our conversations with a question?"

"Touché." We step out of the elevator when it dings and the doors open and walk down the halls. We reach the gym and notice that it has a large area where people could use the various free tools. We face each other on the floor. "Your scar. I noticed it before when we first met, but I didn't know it was so big. What happened?"

Scorpio puts his hands on his hips and tilts his head ever so slightly, "It's personal."

"That's it? It's personal? Come on. We're friends now."

"Oh? Is that what we are?" I give him a 'are you serious right now?' look and he laughs. It's rich and throaty and I find myself grinning with him. "I guess we are. I want you to remember that after this is over."

"Why's that?"

"Because training with me is not a fun time. You ready?"

I nod and the worst three hours of my life ensue after that.

Scorpio taught me a lot of defensive moves. He taught me how to get out of different holds someone might use against me and how to immobilize after enough to get away. He was right. This is not fun. When I am laying on the floor, sweating and probably bruised everywhere, he leans over me with a smirk on his face. "Well? Do you feel like you can take on the world?"

I take a swing at him and he easily dances out of the way. I take a deep breath and sit up, "Not at all. But if anyone tries to take my purse in the middle of the park at night, I think I'll be ready." I take the hand he offers me and I stand on shaky legs.

"You two look like you worked hard," a voice comes from behind us. We turn around to see Libra standing there with Aquarius. Libra was in a pair of track shorts and a black tank top. "Lib wanted to come down and get some of her energy back up. You guys done down here?"

"I am. I need to sit in a tub full of ice." I put my hands on my back and stretch, hearing popping in places I don't think should pop.

"Scorpio doesn't really know how to take it easy on the ladies," Libra says with a smile. She looks much better than she did last night. She has color back to her cheeks and the bags under her eyes are gone.

"Hey now, she asked for it. I simply obliged a request." Scorpio says, crossing his arms.

"I did not request to get my ass kicked."

"In asking me to train you, yes, you did."

I roll my eyes. "I'm heading to my room. I need a shower. I'll see you guys later." I squeeze past them and walk down the hallway. The smell of chlorine gets stronger as I pass the pool and I stop to look through the glass doors leading to it. No one is swimming and not surprising as I don't really see too many people in the hotel anyway. I move away from the doors and head back up to my room.

Once there, I fall back on my bed with a huff. I am exhausted and it is only noon. I do feel better though and now I feel like I won't be completely useless during another confrontation. I know I can run, but running only gets you so far. Today sucked, but I am going to convince Scorpio to train me more. I may not have magical powers, but I will certainly know how to poke some eyes. I manage to drag myself out of bed and get into the shower. Hotel showers always hit differently and I'm not sure why. I finish and get out, I scoot onto the bed and turn on the tv. I decide that if Scorpio is going to train me, I am going to spend the rest of the time either sleeping or spending time out with Camden. Even after what happened to Hamilton, I couldn't relax. I knew Lupus had been out there, looking for us, and every time I closed my eyes I would see my father's face. I still see it, but it isn't as impacting as it was. I'm not sure if that's a good thing or a bad thing.

Eventually I get bored of what's on tv and turn it off, tossing the remote onto the nightstand next to me. Okay so maybe not sleeping the whole time. I didn't know waiting for impending doom could make me so restless. I decide to go next door and bother Camden. Maybe I can convince him to head back to the outlets or one of the parks around here. I go next door and raise my hand to knock on the door when I hear Camden's voice. Normally I wouldn't think anything of it, but he is talking fast and he sounds upset. I put my ear to the door, trying to listen to the words, but it's too muffled. *I can't hear anyone else in there,* I think. There are pauses, but I don't hear another person. Could they just be talking quietly?

I rap on the door and Camden's words stop. I hear his footsteps and seconds later the door opens. Camden looks like he always does, with a smile on his face, but there is a look in his eyes, almost like he is looking too happy. "Hey Faye. What's up?"

"Well. Scorpio beat me black and blue earlier and I need a change in company."

"He did *what?*" Camden's smile fades real quick.

I laugh, "Not like that. He was teaching me some defensive moves. I figure if I know how to fight a little, I won't be as useless when the big bad guys come around."

He looks relieved and leans against the door frame,

crossing his arms. "Well, you chose the right change in company. What are you thinking?"

"I wanted to go back to the outlets to find a swimsuit, then I was thinking we could spend some time in the pool." The last time I had been swimming was during last summer. I decided to drive over to the college and use the Olympic size swimming pool they have there. It was the first and last time I got to use it. About two weeks later, they banned from all non-college students from using the pool due to a sexual harassment incident involving a college student and high school student. Even though I did technically take one class there, they considered me a non-college student because of my minor status. Better to be safe than sorry. Thus my short-lived free swimming experience. Any time I wanted to go after that, I had to pay to swim.

"Sounds great. Lead the way." He shuts the door behind him, but when I glimpsed through the crack, I could have sworn I saw something big in the room. *Must be a shadow,* I think. A shadow…with feathers? I shake my head. I must be going crazy.

We head down to the lobby and make our way back to the outlets. It is much busier than it was before, but we managed to find a clothing store that was putting out their swimwear for the summer season. I browse through the different selections while Camden heads over to the men's to find something for himself. I settle for a two piece, with a black top that has a gold hoop in the middle and black bottoms that have a skirt over it. Camden finds a pair that is black also, but has blue ocean waves. We check out and head back to the hotel.

On the way back to our rooms, I glance over at Camden,

who looks deep in thought. "What was in your room?" I ask. Scorpio was right. I do start all of my conversations with questions.

He seems to snap out of whatever process he had going on in his head, "What?"

"I thought I saw something, like a big bird."

Camden laughs, "I don't think there was a big bird in my room. Maybe you saw Scorpio. He came back for a little bit to shower."

"I'm surprised he didn't stop us from leaving." I hide my skepticism.

"I'm also surprised he didn't just come to the door naked." He grins suggestively, "Or is that what you were hoping for?" He wiggles his eyebrows.

"Ew, no!" I squeak out. I feel my face flame and as the doors open, I rush out of the elevator as fast as possible. Camden laughs behind me and I reach my room, slamming the door shut behind me. "Stupid." I mutter as I throw the bag with my swimsuit in it on the bed. I sit down next to it, Camden's words still circling around in my brain. Of course I don't want to see Scorpio naked. He's a million years older than me! Not that he looks a million years older than me. He looks about the same age as Luke, if not a couple of years older. Besides, I've already seen him without his shirt on and it's not that big of a deal. My face gets hotter as I remember it, though.

Yeah, right.

I groan and rub my face with my hands. Thinking of guys without their shirt on is the last thing I need to be imagining. I hurry and change into my newly obtained swimsuit. It fits as well as I hoped it would and I grab one of the white towels in the bathroom, wrap it around myself, and head next door with my keycard in hand. Before I even knock on the door, Camden steps out of the room. He has his towel over his shoulder.

"You ready?" he asked.

"You betcha."

The door behind us opens. Libra and the other three step out as well. Libra has a pink one piece on that has a diamond pattern where her navel is. "I heard there was going to be some swimming. Mind if I join?"

Her smile is contagious. "Of course. The more the merrier." I look around at the guys, none of whom has any swimming wear on. "What? Too good to swim with us in a human pool?"

Scorpio scoffs but it's Aquarius who answers, "It's not that. We just think it's better to keep an eye on things outside of the water."

It is the lamest excuse I have ever heard, but I shrug. "Whatever you say. Come on." We head down to the pool, where it is still empty. I throw my towel on one of the chairs and stand on the edge. I stick my toe in it and grin, "They have it warm! No cold water!"

"Perfect!" Camden says behind me and before I can get away, he scoops me up and jumps into the pool with me. We hit the water and we sink to the bottom. I kick my feet and gasp as I break the surface. I wipe my eyes and look around to see Camden coming up to tread water next to me. "You know what we need? Pool noodles. How come they don't just have them automatically stocked?"

"That would require spending money on things that little kids for some reason feel the need to eat. We would need to buy our own if we wanted to have anything like that." I lay on my back and float, kicking my feet ever so slightly.

"Also, you aren't five years old," Capricorn throws out.

"Screw you, Cap." Camden retaliates and starts swimming around the pool.

Libra sits on the edge of the pool, swinging her feet back forth in the water. I swim over to where she is and grab the edge of the pool. She smiles down at me. "How are you feeling?" I ask her.

"Better, much better actually." Her smile turns down a little, almost sad. "Did I ever thank you, by the way?"

"Nah. It's okay."

"I know you think so, but Faye, something like that happening...well, it shouldn't have happened. I should have had better control over my powers."

"It's okay, Libra. This fall must have been hard for all of you." I haul myself up over the side of the pool and sit next to her. "Speaking of powers; I thought all of you lost yours during the fall. I know yours are a bit different from the others, so does that mean you had some awareness of it down here?"

She shakes her head, "It's not like that. Our elemental magic is something that is inside us. It is still separate from our bodies. But it's different for me. One time, I asked Orion what these powers were and why he had given them to me. He told me that he needed someone to help him maintain balance, someone who was made with a level head. He could have asked some of the other Guardians, but he also said that

I was born with a natural ability to bring harmony around me. Balance is what life needed and he believed I was the best one for it."

"So, he created you this way? To bring balance to everything." I think about that. How would I feel if the entire planet relied on me to bring balance all around me? I think it would drive me crazy. I don't think I would be able to have that kind of responsibility on my shoulders. "You're amazing, Libra."

She chuckles, "Thanks. I used to think so also."

"So, if you're the embodiment of balance, you still had those powers. What made them go so out of control?"

"You ask too many questions, Faye." Scorpio says, coming over to sit next to us. His pant legs are rolled up and he sticks his feet in the water.

"Don't pretend like you don't want to know the same thing." Capricorn calls him out and both him and Aquarius come over to sit around us. Camden swims over and suddenly we are all staring at Libra.

She sighs, "I don't think it was a singular thing. During the fall, Scorpio and I were separated. I ended up somewhere in Canada. From there, it was just going through trying to find everyone and figuring things out down here. When I ended up in Billings, I just...got tired. I had a run in with some angry people in town and eventually it just became too much. At one point I was there and the next I'm staring face to face with Faye, a sleuth of destruction behind me."

"It wasn't your fault, Lib. The fall was hard on all of us," Camden pats her knee.

"How long have you guys been down here anyway? Long

enough to figure out how to scam credit cards into your name."

"About a year now?" Capricorn says. "I believe it will be a year to date in about a month."

"Oh." I say.

"Oh?"

"About a year ago — I did not think anything of it at the time — I was watching the news with my dad. There was a story about how there was a meteor fall that happened that night. It was a small one; only thirteen meteors were seen around the world."

"That's an awfully accurate number. How did they spot all thirteen from around the world?"

"I don't think it would normally be something they would keep track of, butI remember listening to the meteorologist saying something about how they seemed to fall with an unusual color around them. I guess I understand why. That was when the fall happened." How strange. At the time, it was the most traumatic event for these guys. For me? It was just another Friday night at home. Who knew we would be connected before we even knew each other.

"I guess I already got my fifteen minutes of fame and didn't even know it. Damn." Camden splashes the water.

There was a collective eye roll. "Glad we got it over with now. There are worse ways to get it." Scorpio says. "And we don't need you to be running around acting like a fool to get yourself on television. Anonymity is key, here."

I stand up and stretch my arms over my head. "Yeah. Because we have done such a good job at that. Besides, why not have a little fun!" I shove Scorpio into the water, clothes and all.

Scorpio breaks the surface and glares at me. "Not cool, Faye. Not. Cool."

I shrug. "Loosen up, old man." The others are laughing at him and I grin. "Don't think you guys are out of the fire either!" As if reading my mind, Camden grabs the arms of Capricorn and Aquarius and pulls them into the water. Libra laughs and jumps into the water after them. We spent the next couple of hours in the water, everyone actually having fun. Even the ever stoic Capricorn seemed to have fun.

Eventually we all got out of the pool and headed back up to our rooms. I couldn't stop giggling when the boys had to trudge upstairs, holding their clothes in their hands, walking through the hotel with just their boxers on. We all separate into our rooms to change into some dry clothes. I take a few minutes to wash my hair and get the chlorine out before changing into a long shirt and shorts. Between the training with Scorpio and all the swimming we did, I feel my eyes get heavy. I lie down on the bed and decide a quick nap couldn't hurt.

I am woken up by a knock on my door. I sigh, and roll out of bed, not wanting to get up but I know if it is Scorpio behind the door, he will kick it down if I don't answer. When I look through the peephole, I see Libra standing there and I unlock the doors.

When I open the door, she smiles, "Sorry, did I wake you up?"

"What? No, not at all," and my body betrays me by making me yawn.

"I did. I can come back-"

"No! It's fine. Come on in." I step to the side so she can walk into my room and I shut the door behind us. I crawl back onto the bed and Libra sits on the other end, crossing her legs. "What's up? Get tired of spending all the time with the boys?"

She chuckles, "Something like that. I guess I wanted to come and see how you were doing." I frown and open my mouth, but she speaks again before I can. "I know. Camden told me that you gave him quite an earful when he asked you. I just...I guess I can't help but wonder how someone can go through all this and not turn around, screaming for home. I have studied humans for a long time and it is almost the same way when things get scary. You're unusually brave, especially for someone your age."

"Thanks, I guess?" I lean back against the wall. "It's not like I had much of a choice. Sure, at first I thought I could just talk to my therapist, take some pills for a while, and things would get back to normal when I first started hallucinating. Or, seeing Orion. After the first time Lupus attacked me, it started to feel more real, but still felt like things could be normal for me. That changed when Scorpio showed up. Don't get me wrong. I'm grateful to him for saving me when he did, otherwise I would be puppy chow by now. Sometimes I think that if he didn't show up though, maybe all of this could have ended sooner for me." I look up, trying not to cry. "I know it's selfish of me to think, but if Lupus had gotten a hold of me already, I may be dead by now. Then I wouldn't have to live with knowing, with seeing, what has happened to everyone I love. I wouldn't have had to see my city burn. I wouldn't have had to see my dad's decapitated head."

Libra reaches over and takes my hands. I look at her and see the sympathy in her eyes, "I'm so sorry Faye. I can't imagine what you have been through. The fall was hard on us, but at least we still have each other. You've lost everyone and that is something that I would give anything to change for you." This woman is going to make me lose it. I blink back tears as much as I can. "But you have no idea how thankful we are to have you. You are a strong, willful, young lady. The guys may not be very good at showing their appreciation, but they all feel the same way. I'm sure Orion is happy that you are the one who received his soul to hang onto."

"I hope so. I don't feel like I've done much good since this whole thing has happened."

"You've done more than you realize, I'm sure. Scorpio at least thinks you've been super helpful."

That surprised me. It must have shown on my face because Libra laughs. "I didn't think he cared much for me."

"I get that. For a long time, we all thought Scorpio hated us."

"Hate you guys? How is that possible? I mean, I know him and Capricorn seem to go at it, but aren't you all basically siblings?"

She smiles, "That may be true, but you have to also remember. Born from Orion, we are also made with free will, much like humans. The only difference between me and you is the fact that I can do some extra tricks here and there."

"I don't think being the one who controls chaos and peace throughout the world can be considered anything close to someone like me. I'm a mouse compared to you guys, especially you, Libra. But I get the free will thing. That still doesn't explain why you thought Scorpio hated everyone."

Libra sighs, "He has changed a lot over the years, but there was a time where Scorpio got lost in trying to do the right thing." I frown. I wonder if it had anything to do with the scar on his body. "He is one of the best Guardians out of all of us. He just carries the burden of what is happening heavier on his shoulders more than he needs to."

"I can see that." Scorpio has taken his duty in protecting me seriously. "What would happen if one of you guys disappeared?"

"Hm. I guess we would just go back to our original state, which would be part of Orion's soul."

"Would he be able to bring you back?"

"Sure," she shrugs. "But I don't think he would be able to bring us back into what we are now."

"What do you mean?"

"Well. When we are first born, we start out as sort of a blank slate. We have our powers and understand our purpose, but we don't have our own identities. We develop those over time to become who we are now. If we are reborn, I don't think we would become the people we are now. We would have the same powers, the same purpose, but we wouldn't have the same identity."

It's a sobering thought. If after spending so much time with each other, how would it feel if that same person was suddenly someone else? "Which is why you need me."

"Which is why we need you," she repeats my words with a sad smile. "But, as daunting as all of this is, there is no doubt in my mind that we will be able to save Orion."

There is a knock on the door that startles both of us. I shrug at her and I slide off the bed to look through the peephole. There is no one there. "Rude," I mumble to myself. I go to open the door, but Libra is behind me in an instant, grabbing my hand and pulling me away. "Libra, what the-"

She puts a finger to her mouth. Mine instantly closes and my eyebrows furrow in question. Libra herself goes over and looks in the peephole. I don't think she sees anything and she grabs my hand again, pulling me to the other side of the bed. "I don't think that was one of our boys. I have a bad feeling about this, Faye."

There is another knock on the door. Neither of us move from the spot we are in. Silence stretched between us. Suddenly, the windows behind us shatter. I scream and Libra throws her arm over me, both of us dropping to the floor. Libra's arms are no longer around me as something lifts her up and throws her against the door. Something heavy hits my back, pinning me to the ground. The wind is knocked out of me and I struggle to breathe.

Libra gets to her feet and I can hear pounding from the other side of the door as the others try to get in. Libra manages to get the door open and Scorpio bursts into the room. His eyes go from me on the floor, to whatever was pinning me down.

"Faye. Are you okay?" He asks. I swallow hard and nod. His eyes never leave mine as he slowly walks toward me. Pain shoots through me in multiple spots. It feels like knives digging into my sides. I can't take it anymore and I slowly turn to see what is above me.

I whimper as I see what looks to be an eagle over me.

Except this is not your average sized raptor. I have never seen something so big. It reminds me of the pterodactyls in Jurassic Park and I tense up, causing its talons to dig into me more. I gasp in pain and glance back at Scorpio. "You better get me out of this," I cry. Scorpio nods and I did not notice before, but his hand was behind his back and is now slowly coming out. One of his blades is in his hand and he slides his foot forward.

The eagle emits a terrifyingly loud screech and beats its wings. The wind pushes Scorpio back and I feel myself being lifted off the ground. Scorpio curses and launches himself at us. I reach my hand out to him as he reaches back for me. Our fingertips brush before I am free falling through the air and then soaring upwards away from the hotel.

CHAPTER THIRTEEN

*S*corpio watches as Faye disappears into the clouds. He doesn't notice the cut in his hand from the glass remaining on the window until the pain laces through his hand. He curses again and turns to head out of the room. Capricorn grabs his upper arm, "Where are you going?"

"Where do you think I'm going?" Scorpio growls and pulls his arm out of Capricorn's grip.

"Do you even know which direction she went? Where they are going? Aquila did not show up here on her own accord." Scorpio stops walking and turns back to him. "It's like Lupus, don't you think? The sisters must have the others under them. I don't know what Alnilam is offering them, but it must be enough to betray Orion. Aquila might be taking Faye back to one of the sisters."

"She can't survive in our home, so it has to be somewhere here on Earth," Aquarius adds.

Scorpio rubs his face and sighs, "Right." He glances around at the damage. "Let's get out of here before the cops show up. Last thing we need is to explain to them why the window is missing."

Canis Major and Minor come up to them. "We have a problem," Minor says.

"What's wrong?"

"Camden is missing as well."

Everyone glances around, just now noticing the younger of the Guardians are gone. "Damn. Did they take him too?"

"I don't know why they would, but I guess the more hostages, the better," Capricorn shakes his head. Scorpio glances at the room. He had gone back to his room he shared with Camden after Libra left to talk to Faye. Camden had stayed with the others, so he isn't sure what happened after that. He did not even notice whether he came to the room when they heard the crash from next door. *Dammit. They are always one step ahead of us.* He is sure that the sisters had found them from the incident with Libra.

"Let's get out of here, like Scorpio suggested, and get a good distance for now," Aquarius motions for them to head to the fire escape stairs. He glances at the two canines. "Do you guys think you would be able to pick up their scent? If we find one, we find the other one."

Major and Minor look at each other, "We should be able to find them. Meet us downstairs and out back. It will give us time to get what we need from their scents."

Scorpio and the others head toward the stairs, just in time to hear the elevator ding. Footsteps pounded on the floor as they made their way down and out the back of the building. They head down the road and sit behind one of the nearby gas stations until they see the smaller forms of Major and Minor coming toward them. "Well?" Scorpio demands.

Minor bristles but Major is the one who speaks up, "We picked up on her scent. They are moving north. But we need to go now. Her scent is already fading. Aquila is moving fast."

"So we need something fast as well. Is there anything around we can use while still allowing you to track her scent?" Libra asks.

Glass shattering next to them causes everyone to turn, seeing Scorpio reaching in the driver's window of a black convertible, "No problem. Get in, before the owners come out."

"Stealing is not exactly going to score you brownie points, you know," Libra murmurs, but like the others, she quickly slides into the vehicle as Scorpio undoes the panel under the steering wheel. He pulls out the wires and within moments, the vehicle comes to life and idles quietly.

Scorpio puts the vehicle in drive and they speed off without anyone coming out of the hotel after them. Major climbs to sit between Scorpio and Capricorn in the front, while Minor sits between Libra and Aquarius in the back.

"What is the plan here? We know that Aquila is now working for the sisters, but we don't know if all three of them are here or only one. What if the others are around also?" Aquarius asks, sitting forward a bit.

Capricorn shakes his head, "Alnilam won't leave home. Someone needs to be there to watch over Orion's body. She isn't going to chance his soul returning without them being there to complete the spell."

"So that leaves at least two of them who could be here," Scorpio says, taking an exit at Major's direction.

Capricorn nods, his brows furrowed. They continue driving north, Major and Minor directing them as they follow Faye's scent. Capricorn glances over, seeing Scorpio's eyes never leaving the road, his knuckles white on the steering wheel. "We will get them back."

Scorpio shakes his head, "Camden I'm not as worried about. He can handle his own. It's Faye I'm concerned about. Did you not see her face as Aquila flew off with her? She may act tough and have a mouth on her, but she is still just a kid."

"She is tough, though. We have to believe that she can hold her own until we get there."

"They have to take Orion's soul out of her before being able to use it. It'll kill her, Cap."

Capricorn is quiet for a moment. "Then you better drive faster."

As soon as the eagle flies out of the hotel room, I cling onto its claw for dear life. If there is anything I am afraid of, its heights. My stomach drops when we dive downwards and then shoot back up. I can't even scream, I'm so scared. The eagle takes me higher, until I feel the dampness of the clouds and then we are above them. If it wasn't for the fact that I was in the clutches of a giant bird, this would have been a beautiful sight.

Instead, I am hanging on and hoping that the plan isn't to drop me from thirty thousand feet in the air. I am sure that the only reason the sisters want me is to kill me in order to get to Orion's soul. I'm not sure what the process for that is though and an endless amount of scenarios play through my mind. I can only hope that Scorpio and the others find me.

The flight seems like it lasts forever and yet I can feel us descend not too long after we started. Being so far up is terrifying, but the thought of the destination is even more so. I have to close my eyes against the water in the clouds, but once we are clear of them, a large lake appears under us. The eagle circles around the lake a couple of times, getting lower until it finally shoots downwards toward a cabin sitting on the lakeside. I close my eyes, hoping this bird knew what it was doing. Sure enough, before we hit the ground, I feel the whiplash of it bringing its wings open, catching the wind and then gently setting onto the ground, but not before dropping me into the dirt.

I groan and roll onto my back, glaring up at the eagle, "I bet your brain is as small as your-"

"Aquila, my love." A voice soft as silk coos behind me. The words catch in my throat as I immediately freeze up. "I had hoped you would not keep me waiting much longer."

The eagle chirps a couple of times and then in a single stroke, beats its large wings and flies back into the air. *Not much one for conversation, that one.* I sit up and slowly get to my feet, turning around to see the face that matches the voice. *So this must be one of Orion's sisters.* She is a beautiful woman with long, white hair and dark eyes. Her skin is porcelain, but her body looks strong.

"You must be Faye. Do come in, my dear," a smile turns up the corners of her lips as she turns and heads into the cabin. I stand up and breathe in through my teeth as the pain in my sides flare up where Aquila had dug her claws in my side.

I hesitate, but follow her inside. I glance up one more time before crossing the threshold. In the clouds, I can barely see the outline of the eagle, Aquila, circling above us. Watching for anyone coming our way, I guess. It disappears over the clouds and I walk inside the cabin.

It is bare, like a hunter's cabin that only gets used a couple of weeks out of the year. *A perfect spot for murder,* I think bitterly. The front door leads into a living space, a sofa against the wall to the right of the door. A wooden coffee table sits in front of it, with an end table on the other side of the sofa. A loveseat sits directly across from me, in front of two large window doors that lead to a back porch. To the left of me is the small kitchen with a table almost in the middle of the cabin, more to the left side. The back left corner has a door which I assume leads to a bedroom. Small and in the middle of nowhere.

Great.

The sister walks over to the loveseat and sits down in it, crossing her ankles and putting her hands in her lap, like a damn proper lady. She gestures to the sofa with a smile, "Please come in and make yourself comfortable."

I stand at the door, crossing my arms and not making an effort to move, "I don't think so."

Her smile never fades. "Aquila can see a tiny mouse in the desert and has the speed of a bullet train. Even if you start running now, she can catch you and bring you back easily. And this time, she won't be as kind." The threat in her voice makes the hairs on the back of my neck stand up. I weigh my options. I make my way over to the couch and sit as far away from her as possible, not daring to relax lest she decides to pounce on me. "You have nothing to fear from me, darling. I mean you no harm."

I snort, "I highly doubt that. You and your deranged sisters are trying to destroy the world. The whole freaking universe. I have every right to fear you."

Her cheek twitches ever so slightly, but it's the only reaction I get from her. "I see you have been talking to the Guardians. What would Orion think if he heard of them talking about his own sisters in such a way?"

They must not know I am able to speak to Orion. Scorpio and the others didn't think I did either.

"I don't know what they have been telling you, but I assure you, we are not here to destroy anything."

"That's the biggest load of crap. I know you are trying to get to Orion's soul in order to blow open the solar system." Her smile turns sad. The look she is giving me is so innocent looking, it's hard to keep my bravado going. "And I know you need to kill me in order to get to his soul." My voice falters, the thought of dying jumping to the front of my mind like a nightmare comes to life.

She shakes her head. She uncrosses her legs and stands. I jump to my feet, but she simply turns away from me, looking out the glass door behind her. All I can see of her face is the reflection in the glass. "Please, Faye. Hear me out. I know it may seem like you know the whole truth, but you do not."

"Oh, yeah? Enlighten me," I say sarcastically. It is at this point I wish Orion was around. His presence scared me at first, but now it is a constant comfort whenever situations like this happen.

"It is true that we require Orion's soul, but we do not

wish to destroy everything. Look at this place. It's beautiful and beauty is to be protected, don't you agree?" When I don't answer, she continues. "Orion created us at the beginning of time for this system. The stars and planets you know now did not exist. For a long time, it was just us. We were happy, my sisters and I. Orion treated us like real blood, not just another piece of dirt he had created. At first, we were not quite sure what to do with our lives. All we knew was Orion and the space around us. But he taught us things: how to create things in our own way, to use our powers within us, to have fun, laugh, dance, and love. For a long time, it really felt like peace.

"That changed once Orion started to create more. He said we could be happier with more, even though we were content with the way things were. Over time, the Guardians came into being, once the planets were made. Like his sisters, he created them with pieces of his soul, not just with his powers. They were like children to him, as he told me one time. Alnilam, my eldest sister, did not like them very much and Molnitak, being the youngest, always did what Alnilam did. She, too, decided she did not like the Guardians. I decided I would give them a chance. They were kind to me, so I was kind to them. My sisters warmed up to them eventually. It became peaceful once again, but there was always a tension between everyone. The only one who really accepted us and thought of us as a friend, was Scorpio."

I find myself drawn to her words, wanting to know more. What did Scorpio have to do with anything? I remember the conversation I had with Libra in the hotel room. Something happened between Scorpio and the rest.

"He and I connected in a way neither of the Guardians

or sisters did. We would talk constantly and we became very close." She smiles fondly and I can feel my skin crawl. "Eventually, we began speaking about the universe outside of our system. Orion never told any of us much of what was outside, I'm not even sure if he knew. My sister caught wind of our conversations. We all started talking about one day seeing outside of our system, exploring the universe. It was our dream." Her smile fades and she turns to me. "Orion learned of what we were speaking of and quickly dismissed our voices. He told us that there was no way out of our system. He told us to never speak of leaving again and that our places were here. It was...heartbreaking.

"Alnilam did not take kindly to his words. It was at this point that her hatred for him began to grow little by little. Malnitak and I were concerned for our sister. She convinced us that Orion was not the older brother we thought he was, that instead he was a warden for our prison. It was at this point where Earth had started to grow tremendously. Alnilam convinced Scorpio to help us, to help us try to get Orion to change his mind. Little did I know what she had in store for him. That she was going to have Scorpio kill Orion." The words send chills down my spine and my stomach jumps into my throat. This must have been what Libra was talking about.

A wave of regret washes over me and I know in that moment that the words she speaks are true, because Orion's guilt turns my legs to jelly. I manage to stay on my feet though. *Scorpio tried to kill you? Why didn't you tell me?*

He doesn't respond. She continues on. "The attempt on Orion's life failed, of course. Scorpio was punished. Orion sent him to be the watchful eye over Libra, forever chained to her."

She lies. Orion's voice echoes through my mind.

Really? Because I am sure him trying to kill you was just something you guys laughed off.

Of course not. I can hear the sigh in his voice. *Scorpio was not punished in the way she says he was. Faye, you need to be careful. Alnitak is the most deceptive of all the sisters. Her words hold truth in them, but she is spinning them to turn me into the enemy.*

I believe him, but I can't let her know that he just talked to me. I do wish he would tell me what happened to Scorpio. The guy tried to kill the one who brought him life. Is he only doing this because he is chained to Libra? Alnitak, the sister speaking to me now, sounds like she really cares for Scorpio. Does he still feel the same?

Alnitak seems to notice the internal struggle I am having. "Faye, all we wish is to be free. We were not meant to be kept inside a cage. Don't you see? We could have an endless universe to explore. Alnilam knows the way. And," she smiles once again, "she knows how to do it without ending life. Don't you see? We can all have our happy ending."

I want to retort, to say that her and her sisters were evil and that they just wanted to destroy everything. But...did they?

Faye. Orion's voice warns, but I ignore it.

"Is it true? Can she do it without killing everyone?"

Alnitak's smile grows, "Of course, love."

Faye, don't listen to her!

It's too late. I'm already considering the possibility. If the sisters are strong enough, couldn't they do as Alnitak says? Orion's words of deception run around in my head. Alnitak walks over to me. "Faye. We cannot do this without you. I swear to you. We are not here for malice and fear. We just wish to be free." She holds out her hand to me.

I hesitate, vaguely hearing Orion's voice in the back of my mind. The compulsion to take her hand takes over, putting my own in hers. There is a sting and I flinch. It takes me a second to realize that my hand was now bleeding ever so slightly.

I look back up to Alnitak as a wicked smile appears, "Perfect."

I gasp as suddenly the exchange of power takes over, more rapid than I have ever felt before. I fall to my knees as my legs give out from under me and Orion's voice fades.

A shrill screech from outside causes both of us to look over as the giant eagle comes crashing through the cabin. Alnitak screams in frustration as we break apart. I am knocked backwards and roll to a stop against the wall. It takes me a second to get my bearings and look up, just in time to see someone come into my line of vision.

"Faye! Are you all right?" Aquarius kneels down in front of me, getting me into a sitting position.

"I think so. Are the others here?" I ask, not seeing them.

He nods. "Everyone is here. Except Camden. Have you seen him?" I shake my head and notice another figure comes running into the house. Scorpio stands over Aquarius, blades in his hands.

Alnitak's story of Scorpio makes me jump as he kneels down and reaches over to take my hand. He tilts his head, but doesn't press, "We can't wait to look around for him. We have to get you out of here. Who is here with you?"

"Just me, love." Alnitak replies. Scorpio and Aquarius both spin around to face her. Alnitak stands there, Aquila behind her. "It is nice to see you again, Scorpio. Aquarius."

"What did you do to her?" Aquarius asks, putting his hands out protectively as to shield me from her.

Alnitak laughs, "Nothing. I have done nothing to the girl but speak the truth, about everything." She looks pointedly at Scorpio and he glares at her. "This whole life is a lie. Our freedom is within our grasps. Don't you realize by now? Orion is manipulating you into thinking this is free will. He is wrong and we will show you."

She steps aside and Aquila opens her wings, screeching before launching herself at us. A form connects with the eagle before she could get to us and all I see is fur as Aquila is sent sprawling outside the glass doors, shattering the glass everywhere. Minor comes running through the house, "You guys take care of Alnitak. We have bird brain!" And she is out the back door to assist Major.

Alnitak shakes her head sadly, "I do not wish to hurt any of you. We are like siblings."

"Siblings don't try to kill each other and obliterate the universe," Scorpio growls.

"As I recall, you once shared the dream of freedom, Scorpio. What ever happened to us?"

"I was young and naive. Alnilam took advantage and you know it."

"There is still time to join us. Bring the girl, and you can have a place next to us as we reclaim the freedom denied to us." She holds out her hand.

Scorpio watches her for a moment before shaking his head, "Never again, Alnitak."

Alnitak's hand drops and she frowns, her dark eyes narrowing, "Then you leave me no choice."

Her hands raise, Scorpio and Aquarius rising off the ground. She splays her hands out to either side, sending them both flying in opposite directions. Scorpio is sent through the broken glass doors and Aquarius is thrown so hard against the side of the cabin, the wood splinters and he flies through and outside. Alnitak looks back to me as I get myself to my feet, "Now. Where were we?"

I run out of the cabin, trying to get away from Alnitak. The floorboard of the porch explodes under my feet and I end up flying down the steps and onto the ground. I scramble to my feet as an arrow shoot past my head. I look up to see Capricorn standing there, a bow in his hand. "You almost hit me!" I yell as I run to him.

"I have perfect aim. Trust me, I wouldn't have hit you." He says, reaching out to me as I almost trip over to him. He steadies me and then looks behind me, "Is it just her?"

"Yeah, as far as I know. Her and Aquila. If anyone else is here, they haven't shown themselves."

"Camden?" I shake my head. He nods and then turns his attention behind me. I skirt around him as Alnitak comes out of the cabin. I notice Aquarius, who is laying in a heap onto the porch. "Don't worry. If he had died, he would have disappeared by now." He whispers to me and then louder to Alnitak, "You're either brave or stupid coming here by yourself."

She puts her hands to her chest, "I'm the voice of reason, Capricorn. My sisters would have killed that girl on the spot and I am trying to resolve this peacefully."

"Yeah, looks really peaceful," he replies, glancing over at Aquarius.

"I cannot help those who are getting in my way. You are all making a mistake."

"The only mistake was not killing you when I had the chance." He reaches behind him and takes out another arrow from the quiver strapped to his back. He nocs the arrow and draws the line back. "Leave, Alnitak. Go running back home to Alnilam. I will not ask you a second time."

"Tsk. So resentful." She brings her hands up and we feel a rumbling underneath us.

"Faye, move!" Capricorn turns and pushes me backwards as the ground under him breaks free and flies into him. Capricorn rolls to a stop a few feet away from me. He gets to his feet and lets loose another arrow. Alnitak brings her hands up and a flurry of wind knocks the arrow off course.

Scorpio comes running out of the cabin, jumping off the porch to bring one of his blades down on Alnitak. Earth rises up to meet him instead, knocking him away. He lands on his feet, sliding a bit before running at her again, while Capricorn shoots another arrow at her.

A hand grabs my arm and I jump. "Faye, it's me! Come on! We are only in the way here." Libra drags me on my feet and we are running. All around us, all I see is desert and all I hear are the sounds of fighting behind me. By the time we stop, I am breathing heavily. And it hurts. The cold stings my lungs as I try to catch my breath, my hands on my knees. A loud explosion makes me jump and I look over. The cabin is in the distance now and I can't tell which figure is who. "They will be okay."

"She took power from me, Libra. A lot. More than anyone has yet."

The worried glance from me to the cabin makes me want to cry. "Alnitak has magic outside what we have. We just have to hope that Capricorn and the others can win."

"And if they can't?"

She bites her lip. She must be thinking the same thing I am. We need more of the Guardians.

"Libra, is it true?"

"Is what true?"

"Did...did Scorpio try to kill Orion?"

She looks at me with shock in her eyes. "Is that what she told you?" I nod. She sighs and rubs her face. "Faye, I really don't think now is the time-"

"Tell me, Libra." I grab her wrist.

She must see the desperate need for the truth in my eyes. "It is true. Look, I don't know what she told you, but you have to understand. This was an exceptionally long time ago. Back before some of us were even created. Scorpio...well, he knows what he did in the past, but it's different now."

"How can you be sure? How do you know he hasn't just been planning this all along with the sisters? Alnitak said-"

"No, Faye." She snaps, turning toward me. "You don't understand. Alnitak and her sisters are liars and will do anything to get what they want. Yes, Scorpio messed up in the past.

But he is not the same person now. You either believe that, or you will get us killed with your mistrust and misjudgment."

The conviction and the anger in her voice causes me to shut my mouth real quick. I don't think I have ever felt so small in my life. Libra's face softens. She goes to say something to me, but her words are cut off. A massive wave jumps from the lake, the water roaring as it slams into us. Libra reaches out for me, but we end up going separate ways. I am lifted off the ground and back down, looking just in time to see the water suck Libra back into the lake with it.

"There. That should be the last of the interruptions," Alnitak walks toward me.

"Bring her back! You'll drown her!" I cry, seeing bubbles surface from below.

Alnitak glances at the lake and back to me, "She will not die. I'm sure they have told you by now. None of us actually die. We simply go back to where we came from, back into Orion. Don't be sad, child. Soon, you will be back with Orion as well." She reaches down and grabs my throat, lifting me off the ground. I gag as I try to get breath back into my lungs, but her grip is too tight. I can feel her stealing even more energy from me. "I'm taking Orion's soul back to Alnilam. I am going to be the one to free us all. Don't you see? Your end is a means to a wonderful new beginning for us. But for that to happen, you must meet your end."

I see spots in my vision and I start to feel myself lose consciousness. Before that happens though, Alnitak shouts in pain and drops me. I gasp, gulping in air. Something shines in the dark and I look over to see one of Scorpio's blades sticking out of the ground next to me. Strong hands grab me and pull me to my feet. "Faye! Look at me!" Scorpio's hand grabs my chin and forces me to look at him. If it wasn't for him holding me up, I would be back on the ground. "Faye. Faye, listen to me. I need your help. I can't defeat her on my own. I need Orion. A direct source to him."

It takes me a second to realize what he means. My eyes go wide and I know he sees the fear in them. "No. No! Not like that." I sob out the words. I can't take any more of this, my body already feeling heavy from the amount of power Alnitak took from me.

"There isn't another way. We don't have time." He brings the other blade he had up and he brings it over my hand, letting it hover there. His eyes never leave mine. "Do you trust me?"

Tears slip down my cheeks and I close my eyes, "Just do it." Pain sears across my palm and I bite my tongue to not cry out. When I open my eyes, Scorpio places his own cut hand over mine and instantly, I feel that powerful surge of energy spark between us. He lets out a small gasp. It feels like lightning is coursing between us, but it only lasts for a few moments before I collapse onto the ground and everything goes black.

Energy crackles around Scorpio as he glances down over at Faye. Her complexion went from a sun-kissed tan to a sickly pale. He wanted to go to her, but Alnitak's laugh turns his attention away from the teenage girl. "Scorpio, my love. I do believe that girl is on death's door. Are you sure you're not willing to help us? Just a little more and that soul could be ours."

She was right. He took too much from Faye and now she was suffering. Dammit. He would have to end this quickly and give it back to her. If he could. The rush of power he received was unlike anything he had ever felt before. Was it because he was born with his powers and that was what it felt like to have it return again? Or...could it be that Faye's own soul is becoming one with Orion? Did he take some of hers as well?

Blades of wind fly at him, interrupting his thoughts. He brought his hands up and earth shielded them. When it crumbles back down, he glares at Alnitak, "Last chance. Go back to Alnilam or die here."

Wind swirls around Alnitak as she smirks, "I'm not leaving without that soul."

"Then you leave me no choice."

Alnitak chuckles, "You were always one of the strong ones, Scorpio. But that girl holds tremendous power inside her. Are we sure she is simply a vessel holding Orion's soul?"

Before Scorpio can question what she meant, a purple haze swirls around her and it shoots out toward him. Scorpio jumps out of the way and rolls, coming up to a stop near Faye. Glancing at her, Scorpio can't tell if she is breathing or not. He has no time to check, so he has to get rid of Alnitak to save her. He reaches for the blade he had thrown before and stands, charging toward Alnitak. He slices through the air at her and wind shoots out at her. She brings her hands up and the wind dissipates around her.

The lake rumbles behind them and Libra's head breaks

the surface. She rises up, the water parting at her feet and her hand comes up, closing into a fist as she nears Alnitak. The white-haired woman gasps, no air getting into her lungs. The air is slowly being taken away from the space around her. She falls to one knee as color flushes her cheeks.

"Libra!" Scorpio calls to the woman.

Purple lightning crackles around Alnitak and explodes outward, an invisible force hitting Libra. Alnitak gasps as air rushes back into her lungs and she turns to Libra, her hand reaching outward. Another force plucks Libra into the air, and then slams her back onto the ground. Scorpio brings his hands up and a large form of water comes from the lake, taking the shape of a tiger. Scorpio and the tiger of water rush at Alnitak, attacking her at once. Alnitak turns to them and she brings both her hands up, an invisible barrier forming that stops the force of water, but she is pushed back. Scorpio hits the barrier and digs his blades into it, slowly pushing his way through.

"Scorpio, you have so much wasted potential."

"Alnitak, you *are* a wasted potential. Alnilam will sacrifice everyone to get what she wants. You don't think you're included in that?"

"No, my love. She may have come from Orion, but she does not share his beliefs. She sees more than he ever could." She grits her teeth as Scorpio pushes further through the barrier. "She will save us!"

Scorpio cries out in effort and he finally breaks through the barrier. His blades slice through and impale themselves through Alnitak. She gasps and Scorpio pants as he feels the power slowly fade away. It's not completely gone, but he used it a lot. Alnitak looks down at her chest and she falls to her knees, blood trickling out the side of her mouth. She looks back up at Scorpio and she smiles, "I guess I get to be the first to reunite with our beloved creator. Tell me, Scorpio. What will you do when there is nothing left to fight for?"

Scorpio doesn't get the chance to answer as Alnitak's body starts to glow golden. She closes her eyes, her body slowly separating into small balls of light and those lights slowly float over to Faye's body and enter. She glows for a moment before the light fades.

I hear voices call out my name, but I can't bring myself to open my eyes. My whole body hurts and all I want to do is sleep. I feel a strange sensation in my chest and suddenly feel Orion's presence.

Alnitak's essence is reuniting with our soul.

Our?

There is much we need to talk about, Faye. Our souls are uniting.

Why?

I don't hear him for a moment and then he responds, *It is a long story. Something I heard once before and that I did not believe. Rest. We will speak more later.*

I can feel his presence slip back away.

Faye. "Find Aries." It's the last thing I hear before I lose myself into unconsciousness once again.

EPILOGUE

*S*corpio paces back and forth inside the dimly lit hospital room. Aquarius and Libra are sitting on the small bench seat. Minor is lying at Libra's feet and Major is on the end of the bed. It is quiet except for the steady beeping of the machine in the room. Capricorn walks into the room and Scorpio stops pacing, "Anything?"

Capricorn shakes his head. "There is still no word from Camden and no signs of Aries. He is still missing. Are you sure that is the name she said?"

"Yes, dammit. For the hundredth time. She said 'Find Aries.' I think it may have been a message from Orion himself. We need Aries to save her."

"There has to be something we can do for her," Libra joins in. Scorpio can see her eyes well up with tears, but she doesn't cry. She feels responsible for what has happened, since she was the one with Faye before Alnitak got to them. But he knew it was really his fault. He took too much power from her and there was no way to give it back.

"We have to find Aries, and fast. Scorpio, you and Aquarius are coming with me. I have an idea of where to start looking for him. Minor, I'm going to need you as well." Capricorn walks over and puts a hand on Major's head, rubbing it a bit, "You and Libra stay here with Faye. She is still going to need some kind of protection."

Major nods his head and Libra looks to the three of them, "We will take care of her, but hurry, please."

Capricorn nods. Scorpio walks over to the bed, looking down at the brown-haired girl who had more guts than a lot of humans. He brushes the hair from her eyes, "Hang on a while longer Faye." Her skin was hot to the touch, and he knew there was not much time. He turns to the other three, who are waiting by the door. "It's time for the Guardians to come back together."

END

ABOUT THE AUTHOR

Jessica is a full-time student at Southern New Hampshire University obtaining her BA degree. She is married and the mother of a son. She lives in Arkansas with her family, currently working on creating a small business with her husband.

Also Available from
J. Kenkade Publishing

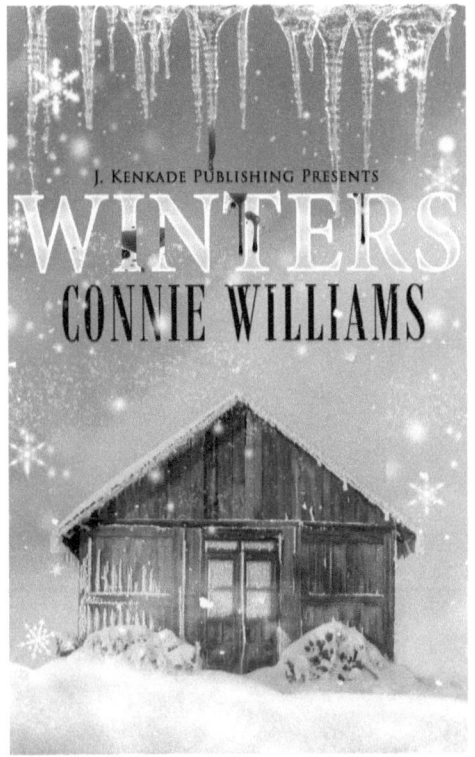

ISBN: 978-1-955186-23-0
Purchase at www.amazon.com

Winters is a captivating and passionate Christian suspense novel about a powerful, spiritual family who is anointed and ordained by God Almighty. You will feel love, pain, heartaches, compassion, grace, mercy, suffering, and God's spirit, all in one story. Find out why Winters is about the coldest season of the year in more ways than one. Come and live in the minds and hearts of Stella, Abe, Mr. Perkins, The Langley family, Hattie, Benjamin, and Minnie. So much more awaits you in this powerful Christian suspense novel. Both fiction and nonfiction, Winters will give you a chill like never before.

Also Available from
J. Kenkade Publishing

ISBN 978-1-944486-87-7
Purchase at www.amazon.com or www.barnesandnoble.com

All who hear tales of Madam MaRooska's world-renowned yet exclusive specialty resort at Bellingfast Estates clamor to be granted attendance every year. One of the most compelling events in this two-week excursion is an elaborate masquerade ball in which guests can disappear into the personas of any historical figures they wish. However, Constance Stallings knows firsthand just how quickly this game of illusions can turn nefarious. Born into wealth and privilege but determined to make a name for herself as an author, she embarks on a second trip to Bellingfast with her family in the hopes of finishing her novel, The Angel Doll, and perhaps even uncovering the tragic mystery that looms over her last encounter with the seemingly cursed estate.

Also Available from
J. Kenkade Publishing

ISBN: 978-1-955186-20-9
Purchase at www.amazon.com

The goddess of water, Reina rules her country with an iron fist, enforcing her view of peace with great ruthlessness. She was not always so cruel; however, at one point, she ruled her people justly, with her friend Clara by her side. When a nation of humans decided to not heed to the authority of the gods, a war broke out. It was man vs god, a true David vs Goliath situation. In the heat of battle, Reina bore witness to her friend's last moments, sending her into a dark spiral. This twisted version of herself that we see today is what came of her after the war, a reclusive leader that rarely shows herself to her people. What do the threads of fate hold for Reina? Will she reopen her country and spare her people from their agony? Or will her nation stay in a state of limbo forever?

www.ingramcontent.com/pod-product-compliance
Lightning Source LLC
Chambersburg PA
CBHW031712170626
46808CB00005B/1715